Finding the BASSLINE

Tambo Jones

For Michele

Because, everything.
Hugs!

Berk

I can't believe I'm at the grocery store buying condoms for my granddad.

But here they are, on the list: *Hamburger, macaroni, can of tomatoes, condoms, bag of Italian cheese, 2 liter of Coke, baguette*, all in my granddad's ragged scrawl.

Condoms. For a seventy-two-year-old retired plumber who knows how to spell baguette.

I declined a perfectly good blues gig in Memphis to end up standing in a small-town-Iowa grocery store between the bunion pads and the tampons—Tampax on sale! Sweet!—while trying to figure out what kind of condom my granddad wants.

Sigh.

Ribbed? Lubed?

Shit, his imaginary girlfriends are surely postmenopausal. Better toss some Astroglide in the basket... Trojan? Magnum? Durex? Lamb...

Whoa. Condoms come in cans? Whoda thunk?

Enough already. Dream big. You're getting the blue can, Granddad. Super Sensitive Twelve Pack. That should last you a couple of years.

I chuck that sucker in the basket alongside the asshole-glide, their clatter muffled against the end of the baguette and my *Specially Priced!* tampons.

Back to the list. Okay, the store hasn't changed much in the decade or so since I stocked the shelves, so tomatoes would be—

"Berkeley Williams? That can't be you."

Crap

I try not to sigh as I turn around, chipper smile in place, to see a short, squooshy woman about my age with stick-straight, straw-colored hair and too-tight jeans. She's wrangling two slimy-nosed kids, one in only a t-shirt and a diaper, the other barefoot and bored, all three speckled with today's March drizzle. The bigger kid's coughing.

I take a step back to add a little distance between me and rugrat plague. "Lori Gilbert?" I say. The pair of blue hearts tattooed by her left eye is a dead giveaway, even without the scar from the split-lip I'd given her our senior year. She'd added the tattoos right before the state basketball finals our senior year and her parents had responded by kicking her out of the house. Didn't stop her, or her idiot besties, from being absolute bitches to me until the day I left for college.

She beams. "It's Sandersen now."

I nod and manage to hold the smile. Bucky Sandersen. The slime who'd grabbed me and felt me up in the band storage room in tenth grade. They were perfect for each other. "You married Bucky? Wow!"

She blushes. "Yeah. Walter. Be five years this coming Christmas."

"Congrats."

She looks me up and down, and I hold my ground. I do yoga most mornings and Zumba when my schedule permits, so I missed most of the 'nearly thirty' squoosh. So what if my black leggings and moto boots have a little fresh paint on them?

So what if I'd sworn I'd never come back to this cruddy town in the first place?

She must have found whatever she was looking for because she raises her gaze to mine again and holds it. Hard. I'm a good five, maybe six inches taller than her, a good fifty pounds lighter, and never slept with the slime that's Walter 'Bucky' Sandersen, yet her gaze hardens as she stares at me. Maybe it's the rainbow highlights in my hair?

Nah. Everyone loves my hair.

"I'm guessing you're not married?" she says, those little blue hearts tilting along with her left eyebrow raise. I bet Bucky finds it fetching. Aww, her hearts tilt! Huggles!

Seeing as how I've spent the past decade building my career as a studio musician, my answer is a simple, "Nope. No time for that." I shift my basket of bread, vagina plugs, and geriatric sex supplies on my forearm in preparation for exiting this riveting convo.

"Dyke?"

As if that's still an insult? Seriously?

"Nope, thanks for the offer, but I like dick," I admit, fishing my phone out of my pocket. "I *was* maid of honor at my best friend's sister's lesbian wedding last summer, though, if that counts. We all did yoga during the ceremony. It was awesome! Wanna see the pics?"

"Good God, no!" Blue-hearted Lori sucks in a gasp of air and snaps a step backward, knocking her diapered kid on his butt. He squalls, and, when she lurches around to snatch him off the floor, I scoot the hell outta there and toward the canned goods.

"Tomatoes, tomatoes," I mumble, dodging a couple of old women digging for hidden treasure in the day-old brownies and cinnamon rolls. Two cans of fire-roasted-Italian-chopped 'maters in the basket, grab that box of penne on the way by, just need some hamb—

Lori. Again. Stomping toward me carrying one kid and dragging the other behind as if her sole reason for existence is to make me miserable. But I'm not a discarded kid anymore and she no longer has any power over me or my life.

I close my eyes for a moment to take a cleansing breath. In through the nose, out through the mouth. Soothe the chakras. Breathe. I imagine the smell of lemon and lilac.

"You were supposed to stay gone," I hear her snarl in a vicious whisper. "So help me, you'd better not stir shit up again."

I open my eyes and smile. Calm. Towering over her. I use my voice best saved for asshat vocalists and their blood-sucking managers when they want to screw with my bassline. "Fuck off."

I leave her standing there and resume my shopping.

Namaste, bitch.

༺༻

It's pouring rain when I get back to granddad's with lunch makings, but there's a silver Camry parked behind his Ram.

I'd hoped for leftovers tomorrow. Ah well.

I grab the two bags then scoot past the Camry on my way to the house.

Front door's locked. Weird.

My phone buzzes in my butt pocket as I walk around to the kitchen door. It's my neurotic drummer-and-biz partner, Dave.

It's always Dave.

Some days I wish I hadn't introduced him to Lia, my college roomie-bestie, that he hadn't married her, had two kids with her, and became so permanently entwined in my life, but we've made a lot of money together. He drives me crazy, but, damn, we can find a bassline.

"Yo," I say as I open the door and step up into the kitchen, leaning over to peer into the living room. There's no sign of Granddad or the Camry's driver.

"Berk, you gotta come back," Dave pleads in my ear. "They've called me twice. Twice! If we can get to Detroit by tomorrow, we can still make the two-K. Maybe more, he says."

Gram liked a bright white kitchen, and her favorite color was apple green. Other than a black Keurig on the counter, a new-ish cushioned rug in front of the sink, and a cardboard box of her never-used china half-packed on the table, it looks the same as the day she'd died. Nearly two years gone. Damn.

Eyes stinging, I set the bags on the counter. "I can't. I told you I have to help Granddad—"

"It's two-thousand bucks, Berk. Plus expenses. If we don't do it, they'll call Carl and Joe."

I sigh. Loudly. "We played six sessions this past month," I remind him as I start unbagging the chow. "We usually do three, maybe four if we're lucky. We can skip one job—"

"Their original vocalist tanked and they got Imelda."

Aw, hell. It's always a fun, quick session when we're working with Imelda. I turn around, ass against the counter, and stare at the ceiling I painted yesterday afternoon. Bright, white, and perfect. Gram would have approved. "Imelda? Damn it."

"Yeah. No shit. And it's two-K for a goddamn thirty-second car commercial. *With Imelda.*"

"Dave..."

"It'll be two fucking hours. Tops."

Yeah, with almost twenty hours of round-trip driving. "I *can't.* I promised Granddad I'd be here to help pack up and prep the house. He's seventy-two, alone, and he *needs* me. There's no one else to help. Plus I *really* need to visit Kelsey while I'm in town this time."

"Berk, she's a vegetable."

I finish putting away groceries. "Doesn't make her any less my friend. Joe can take my slot this time."

"Joe's an ass."

"But he can play a decent bassline." I push off from the counter and go rooting for the pasta pot. Gram always kept it in the lower cabinet, left of the stove...

"Berk..."

Found it! "Remember when Jeremy came? You deserted me for almost a whole month," I say on my way to the sink. "I got stuck playing with shitty bar bands to make rent."

"That was three years ago and he was a preemie!"

"Yep. He needed you. Lia needed you. And my granddad needs *me* to help him pack the house and move to a retirement center. It's just me and him. We don't have anyone else."

Dave sighs while the pot fills and I hear Jeremy in the background asking for *Pete the Cat.*

"It'll be just a week, maybe two," I assure Dave. "Once I get Granddad moved, we'll find some other project to do with Imelda."

He sighs again. "You're right."

Usually am. "It's just a few days. Enjoy the time off. I'll talk to you later, okay?"

"Yeah. Okay," he mumbles. "Catch ya later."

The call clicks off and I set the phone aside before taking the pot to the stove. On my way across the kitchen, I hear moaning.

Granddad?

I plunk the pot on the stove and rush to the living room where Granddad's old cat, Bill, is licking his ass on the couch. Another moan, for sure from Granddad's office. All I can think is, Goddamn it, Granddad, I told you not to paint the crown molding without me here to hold the ladder. If you've fallen...

He's crying out.

Oh, God.

Be okay. Be okay.

The office door's open a crack, so I shove it wide, expecting to see Granddad semiconscious or broken on the floor. Nope, he's in his office chair, the same chair he used to spin me in when I was a kid. The chair he paid payroll from. Paid bills from. Wrote letters to the editor from.

He's leaning back, moaning, mouth open, eyes closed, while an old woman wearing only a pink pair of granny panties is sitting cross-legged on a cushion between his feet and gobbling, no, *devouring* his knob, his balls in her hands.

I will never look at that chair the same again.

"Holy shit, Granddad!"

The woman lurches back, wide-eyed and startled, and her left hand still grips his balls while her right wipes at the corner of her mouth.

Eew.

Granddad's body goes limp and, gasping, he rolls his head to blink at me. I realize he's freshly shaved and I can smell his cologne. Old Spice. I love that smell. *Used* to love that smell.

"I didn't expect you back so quickly."

I feel my mouth moving as I struggle for words, which I don't have.

That's a first.

The woman wipes at her mouth again and removes her other hand from my granddad's balls. "Um, hello. I'm Ellen. You must be Amanda."

"Berkeley," I choke out, unable to move, unable to flee this horror. "It's my middle name. No one calls me Amanda."

"Berk," Granddad says, finally having the decency to cover his junk with a magazine. Juggs. Holy fucking hell, it's Juggs! "Did you get everything on my list?"

"I... I..." Fuck, he means the condoms!

My voice sounds weak, like I'm ten again, and the lock on my feet breaks. I skitter, backward, toward the door. "Yes?"

"Oh, good!" Ellen says.

Granddad simply smiles at me. "Would you fetch them, please?"

I throw Ellen a glare then scurry to the kitchen. The can of condoms isn't so funny now, nor is the Astroglide. Despite normally not caring about such things, I pick them up as if they're sticky and carry them to the office. Ellen has a blouse on and is attempting to put on her slacks. Granddad's in his briefs—still raring to go, one more thing I did not need to see—and has his jeans in his hands. I drop both items on his desk, turn around, and walk right out the front door into the rain.

⁂

The day is cold. Damp. Dreary. Typical March in Northeast Iowa. I drive around sodden residential streets for a while as I try to scour the previous interaction from my brain.

The Camry's still in Granddad's drive the second time I cruise around the block, so I widen my loop. Three blocks long, she's still there. Five. Add two blocks in width, then zigzag back. The Camry's still there, and the house is dark. So I drive through our three-block-long downtown, slow enough to stop at every light. I wonder if I should call Dave and tell him I'll do the session after all, but I left my phone by the sink and I'm not going back there as long as deep throat Ellen is around.

There's not a lot of driving to be done in Fayerville, Iowa, and even less to do on a drizzly midday while my granddad's being gobble-fucked by Ellen of the saggy—

Nope. Stop thinking about that.

Stop it, Berk!

There isn't crap on the radio except auto-tune pop and tin-canned country. I could grab a burger at Hardee's up ahead on the highway, but, with my luck, Lori still works the cash register like she did in high school. There's no reason to burn all of my gas, so where can I land for a while?

About a quarter mile past Hardee's, I see the neon sign of a bar glimmering from the gloom. Tony's Tap, a community landmark since the '60s. It used to be at the edge of town, but shops and houses have sprouted along either side of the highway, separating traffic from the sprawl of empty fields behind them.

Most of the buildings are new, but Tony's looks exactly as I remember. The owner liked kids, so there were always gumballs out of the nickel machine for little ones, Coke on the rocks for good report cards, and non-alcoholic cocktails for teens having a night out with friends.

Most of the kids in town partied at Tony's when they turned twenty-one. Hell, he groomed us to be good customers. I was dorm surfing in Cedar Falls when I turned twenty-one, so I'm almost seven years past due. Time to remedy that crap.

I pull up and park between a Buick and a rusty pickup with a faded Bernie bumper sticker, and there's a river of mud running from the rain-soaked field behind the bar. Tony's front wall is the same blonde brick I remember, the same red wooden door behind a metal screen, the same sprawl of Christmas lights in the window and, probably, the same couple of guys pickling their livers at the table just beyond. But there's a sign taped to the glass, backlit and blinking with holiday cheer.

Notice of Demolition. City of Fayerville.

Well, shit. I sit in my Mazda for a few minutes and decide the two customers and the OPEN sign on the door are as good as a welcome mat. So what if it's only ten past noon. It's time for a beer.

The screen door sticks, but the wooden door opens easily and the dim warmth within embraces me and feels like home. I played bass in countless bars like this in college. Rock. Country. Punk. Metal. Any paying gig I could drag my sorry-ass car to. Eight years later, I drive a sweet SUV and can be choosier about my gigs, but I still love the smell and feel of a neighborhood bar.

I walk through the place, past the pair of farmers by the window playing cards, a couple of middle-aged women divvying up coupons between their glasses of beer, and three working-class guys drinking alone. I don't fit in but no one really looks up at me except a solitary fella about my age pounding back liquor and lime. I almost think I recognize him, but he drops his gaze the moment I meet it as if my mere entrance intimidates him.

So what if I'm a young chick rocking a sweater dress over leggings and biker boots? We're all here to drink our lunch. It's a great equalizer.

I pull up a stool to sit alone at the bar and look around. It's been updated within the past couple of years and is pretty swank with newer furniture, highlights of last night's Spurs/Cavs game on a big screen to my right, a CD

Jukebox and a pinball machine blinking away to my left, and a bowl of popcorn is within easy reach.

I grab a handful and munch, smiling. It's fresh, not bagged.

The bartender is a thirty-something black gal with that easy, familiar smile bartenders have. "Hey, hon. Don't think I've seen you in here before."

"Probably not," I admit. "Last time I was in here, I was still in high school."

"You're not the only one to say that." She smiles and chuckles. "Welcome back to Tony's, and we're glad you're here. I'm Gretchen."

"Berk." I offer my hand and she shakes it. She's got a firm grip.

"Great to meetcha, Berk. What can I get ya?"

There's a sign for Old Brown Dog Ale to one side of the bar, Sam Adams on the other. They stock decent beer. "I'll take a Dog," I say, reaching for a Sam Adams coaster from the pile.

Gretchen sighs, her smile wavering. "We're out. Sorry."

Well, shit. Two weeks in this Neanderthal town will feel like an eternity if I can't get a beer once in a while.

"Sam, then," I say, flipping up my coaster to show her Sam Adams' comforting face.

This time her smile collapses. "That's all gone too."

I lean back. "So you don't carry bottle beer?"

"Max *usually* stocks Sam and Dog, but the city's demolishing the building and he's trying to run the stock out."

"Max?" I ask, far more nervous than I want to admit. I can think of only one Max in this whole town.

"Yeah, Max Jutland—"

Max's name slams me in the gut and I don't really hear Gretchen talking, not because I'm worried Max'll get all pissy with me like Lori did earlier, but because he was my childhood bestie's brother and I had an *insane* crush on him in high school. I shove those bittersweet memories back in their box and make myself listen because Gretchen's still talking.

"—from Tony three, maybe four years ago. Good guy. Closing this bar's a goddamn shame if you ask me."

"Yeah, it is a shame. This is a great bar." I want to ask a million questions about Max, but last I knew he'd gotten married, so he's off limits. Plus I'm here to erase the vision of GobbleGate out of my head, not catch up with an old crush. Right?

Right?

Shit.

"Okay. What *do* you have on tap?" I ask, thinking I've missed Max yet again, which is apparently the story of my life.

"Coke, Sprite, seltzer, and Miller Light."

"Um, no." I'm not drinking Miller. Not today. I lean forward and see what she's got in the well. Not much of interest there either, but several decent liquors are lined against the far wall. I need to be able to drive back to Granddad's after my brain scour and it's not gonna happen with a Jack and Coke. "Any bottled beer?"

Her smile returns, but it's shaky. "Actually, yeah. We still have a craft lager and an ale in the cooler. There *might* be some Templeton Red."

"Curly finished it yesterday," one of the men behind me says.

"Then it's the lager or the ale." Gretchen nods once, her smile surer.

I grin back and unzip my jacket, thankful to be out of the rain. "I'll take the lager."

Calypso Street Lager is nicely smooth. I pace myself and my otherwise empty stomach by blowing quarters in the pinball machine and playing Kenny Wayne Shepherd's *Live On* on the juke. I learned to play guitar because of that album. Because of Kenny. And this is the first bar I've seen with it in the juke.

My first ball's a big scorer and I feel better already. Two of the single guys have left, as has one of the women. The guy I thought I recognized is still staring ahead, glowering at nothing in particular as he conquers his lime cocktail, while the other woman has moved to sit with the two old guys playing cards. They're discussing Sherry's surgery.

No idea who Sherry is, but she's in bad shape.

Gretchen's been gathering her tips and dirty glasses but she pauses on her way back to the bar to stop right behind me and watch me play.

"See that blue bumper in the upper right?" she says. "There's a switch on the back side of it. Get a couple of bounces back there while it's lit, and your multiplier goes up." Then she continues on with her bus pan.

"Thanks!" I reply, letting the ball coast down my flipper to shoot it to that corner. While it's banging around up top, I take a swig of the lager, finishing it off.

She wasn't kidding about the multiplier, so I plug in more quarters and sing along with *Every Time It Rains*.

I wish Max was here. I like his bar.

Max

Max dropped mail and popcorn on his desk then walked down the short hall to the bar. "I miss anything exciting?"

He rounded the corner to see Gretchen making Karen another sea breeze. "Just a typical Wednesday, other than some new gal who came in for beer and pinball," Gretchen said. "Hope she comes back. She left a great tip."

Dwight trotted to the bar with his empty glass. "Tall, blonde hotsy. Really brightened up the place."

I can use a little brightening, Max thought. He pulled a half-gallon bottle of Old Crow from beneath the bar and refilled Dwight's bourbon. "Hopefully she'll come back before we close next weekend."

"Yeah, I hope so, too. Certainly made my afternoon," Dwight said, winking, as Max handed the drink back to him.

Gretchen slid a lime slice onto the edge of Karen's glass. "Had a weird name, though. Berk. Never heard that one before."

"Berk!?" Max stopped Gretchen before she could deliver Karen's drink. "*Berk* was in here? You're sure?"

"That's the name she gave me," Gretchen said, her brow furrowing. "Paid me ten bucks for a bottle of Calypso and said to keep the change. I definitely remember the names of good tippers." She glanced sideways at Dwight and winked. "And no-tippers like Dwight."

"Yeah, yeah, all the ladies shut me down when I wanna give 'em just a tip." Dwight laughed and hustled back to his cribbage game in the window.

Max, though, remained focused on Gretchen. "About my height, about my age, blonde and blue..."

"Yeah, skinny gal with neon highlights and a punk biker style."

Max took a step back. "Holy shit. Did she say why she's in town?"

"Nah. We just bantered about beer and I told her about the right bumper multiplier. So you know this gal? She trouble or something?"

"Used to know her. And, no, she's not trouble. She was my sister's best friend and my..." His cellphone chirped and he shrugged before checking the text from his mother about meeting her at the hospice. "If she comes back, tell her she can start a tab. I know she's good for it."

"Sure thing. You heading out again?"

"Yeah, Mom needs help with something." Response finished, he clicked his screen off then stuffed the phone in his pocket. "Also, if Berk does come back, see if she can stick around then *call me*, okay? No matter what I'm doing, *call*."

Berk

Okay. I can't put this off any longer, I decide while driving back to Granddad's in sloppy drizzle. We're both adults, and he's been a widower, what, nineteen months or something now. So what if he has a lady friend, so what if—

Shit. She's still there.

Piss. Piss. *Piss!*

I pause in front of the house, engine idling while tapping my fingers on the steering wheel. I do not want to go in there, but I also don't want to be a chicken-shit-coward because my granddad's getting some action. And I need my phone.

"Chuck it in the fuck-it bucket," I mutter under my breath as I slam the Mazda in park. Keys clenched in my hand, I step out to the rain before I lose my nerve.

I don't bother checking the front door, I stomp right to the kitchen to find The Gray Gobbler drinking coffee at my gram's kitchen table. She's fully dressed in her blouse and slacks, her hair perfect, makeup impeccable, expression neutral.

Granddad is nowhere to be seen, but I think I hear the shower upstairs.

"Sit your ass down," she says

"No." Turning my back on her, I pick up my phone from near the sink—two messages from Dave, no surprise there—and stuff it into my pocket. That's better.

Bill's in the corner and he glances at me while crunching his kitty-kibbles. Never one for drama, he flicks his tail and resumes eating, but his ears lean toward us, listening.

When I turn back to Ellen, she's set the cup down and has clasped her hands on the table. This time her gaze is hard. "Three things. First, I was married to a Marine Major for forty-three years and I've faced down entire companies of pissy young people. Second, out of all the men his age who aren't spoken for, Ted has one of only three working dicks in the county. Frank has Alzheimer's and Jeremiah... well, he smells bad and leaves a lady wanting, if you catch my drift. Jerry's dick's a big one too," she says, shaking her head. "Thick and uncut. Such a waste. Your grandfather, though, is an attentive lay. Your grandmother trained him well. Lastly, thank you for the Astroglide." She pauses to smile. "It helped things nicely."

I can't stand there anymore, so I start pacing. I feel trapped. Caged. Disgusted.

A sob clambers up my throat but I choke it down again. *Oh, Gram!*

"That's fine," Ellen says. "You don't need to talk, but you ought to listen. Your grandfather is good looking, good to talk to, whip-smart, and fully functional. That combination is a rarity."

She pauses and I hear her take a breath, then let it out as if she, too, is calming herself. I resist the urge to look at her. Nope. Not gonna.

"Eight of us share him," she says at last, and that stops me.

"Eight?!" I say, turning to gape at her as Bill saunters off to quieter locales. "So you're all part of some whacked geriatric sex club?"

She takes a sip of coffee, her expression once again neutral as if we're discussing what color leather interior she prefers for her next Camry. "In a manner of speaking, yes. He wants female companionship, we want... well... his penis." Her unwavering gaze holds mine, like a shimmer of steel lurking behind the detachment. "There are many lonely widows at the center, and we're thankful your grandfather—"

"So, he's your gigolo. Gotcha. I hope he's well paid."

"Amanda!" she barks. "There is no reason—"

"My name is Berkeley," I snap back.

"Fine. Berkeley. We're lonely. He's lonely. There are just more of us, so we share. Why is that so awful?"

"Because he loved my gram and she loved him. He's a good man, but you've turned him into a piece of meat."

"I loved my husband, Mary loved hers, Dotty, Helen... All of us. It's not about love, it's about being touched. Being held. Being *human*. We might be old, but we're not dead yet, Aman... *Berkeley*. And, frankly, this is none of your business any more than your sex life is his."

She's got me there. It isn't any of my business, and I know it. Doesn't make it sting less, doesn't make it any less gross.

"All right," I say, flipping my keys in my hand as I walk to the door. "Have fun, then. Tell Granddad to call me when it's safe to come back."

"Wait!" she says, and I hear the first flash of emotion in her voice. It's sorrow, and it makes me pause. "There's something else."

Oh gawd, I think, rolling my eyes before turning to face her again. "You're surely not pregnant."

This time, her gaze is soft. Sympathetic. All of her walls and defenses are gone. And I realize I might like her if we'd met under different circumstances.

She seems to struggle to find the right words. "That girl... the one you'd helped..." She swallows, and I hear Granddad walking around upstairs. "Kelsey?"

"What about Kelsey?" I ask despite the terrified slam of my heart.

"I volunteer at Hearthstone Hospice. Kelsey was admitted four days ago. I thought you should know."

Hospice? Frozen by the news, I blink back tears. Ellen stands and comes around the table. She hugs me and I try not to weep in the embrace of a stranger I want to hate, but can't. Her perfume is delicate. Spicy.

"I'm so sorry," she says, and I believe her.

"Me, too."

Hearthstone Hospice looks like an upscale ranch house, brick with an open front porch and a stone walk to a small parking lot. I park and, engine idling, listen to the wipers glide across the windshield. I wish they could whisk away the guilt I keep failing to pack away and bury.

Kelsey can't be in hospice. She just *can't*. She never had her life, how could it be ending?

Despite my shame, I need to go in. To see her. To say goodbye, at least.

I owe her that.

The rain-soaked stone walkway is textured for easy walking, and the porch is deep and welcoming, with wicker furniture handy for anyone who wants to sit and watch the muddy pasture across the street turn into a pond. Inside, the aromas of coffee and something cinnamony-baked overwhelm much of the sterile hospital smell. There's a guest book, the kind they have at weddings and funerals, so I sign in. I don't know what else to do.

"May I help you?" an older man murmurs from behind me.

I jump.

"Um," I say, my hand shaking as I put the pen beside the guest book. Despite his hunched and ancient age, I have to look up to meet his gaze. His eyes are comforting, the color of the rain, and they glimmer with patient understanding.

"Kelsey Jutland?" I choke out. My throat feels too narrow, too tight.

He nods and shuffles away, motioning me to follow. We pass a study, all books and leather furniture, where two middle-aged women sniffle into tissues, a youngish man sits red-faced and silent, and two teenagers stare at the floor. None speak or look up as my escort and I pass by.

The scent of cinnamon-and-coffee grows stronger and I glimpse a kitchen, the door barely ajar, a bathroom, then a bedroom with one elderly woman reading beside the bed of an unconscious elderly man.

My guide stops at a partly-closed door and knocks before easing it open.

Kelsey's propped in the bed, eyes staring at nothing, while her mom, Debra, moistens her lips with a pink sponge swab. I wonder how many times Deb's swabbed Kelsey's mouth these past ten years she's been in a stable vegetative state. Thousands, surely. I can't see a TV, but I hear Alex Trebek reading a statement about Lord Byron.

"Oh my God," Deb says, surprised when she sees me. She's put purple streaks in her dark hair—Kelsey's favorite color—and it helps me find my smile. "Berk? I can't believe you've come."

"Yeah, Deb," I say as my escort slips away. "I just heard you'd moved her to hospice." I take a deep breath and enter, feeling those long-cried tears surging back. "What can I do to help?"

"Sit with her." Deb comes around the bed. "Talk to her. She always enjoys hearing about your life."

I laugh a little. My life. No one gives a shit about my life, and we both know it.

Whether Kelsey can hear or not, no one really knows.

Her breathing sounds labored. Heavy. I swallow down the thickness in my throat.

Deb hugs me and I accept the affection, clenching her tight for a breath or two before letting her go.

I take a seat by the bed with my back to the door and grab Kelsey's hand. It's fragile and delicate, like a bird's wing, but manicured and warm, soft from lotion. Deb excuses herself to use the bathroom as I bend Kelsey's fingers around my hand and start talking about the idiot vocalist we got stuck with in Memphis and how her auto-tune kept fucking up so she sounded like a bicycle horn on the playback.

I brush a single strand of hair from Kelsey's brow with my fingertips then tell her about working in Manhattan at New Year's and playing a swank party for a publishing house with big shot authors and editors drinking *so much* booze. I tell her Dave and Lia's baby's almost four already, and tall, so tall, dark hair and dark eyes, gonna be a charmer, and his baby sister's just starting to crawl. I pull out my phone to show her recent pics. "They might get a puppy. Lia wants a Rottie mix, but Dave doesn't want epic shits in the yard."

I lean forward to whisper, as if divulging a secret, "I think they should just get a hamster."

Kelsey stares and breathes her heavy, fluid wheeze. I feel tears sting as I put my phone away then tuck her hand within mine.

No one's sure who did this to her, but I know, deep down where no one else can see, that I should have been there, with her, that rainy night a decade ago. That if I hadn't been grounded, if I'd snuck out to go shopping, if I'd done any of a thousand things to change it or stop it or alter her fate, then she'd be just fine. Somewhere.

I squeeze her hand and take a shaky breath as I shove my guilt back into its box.

If only...

Jeopardy gives way to the early news, so I take a breath and watch the TV high on the wall while wondering if Deb's deserted me for more than a potty break, not that I mind. More rain in the forecast takes the top story slot.

"Screw this rain. Right, Kelsey?" I say, smiling at her again. "How are the farmers gonna plant their beans if it keeps raining?"

Of course, she can't answer. It's always good to talk to Kelsey, so I tell her of the good things I've seen and the stupid things I've done since I last saw her. Since autumn before last. Since Gram's funeral. I talk about Myrtle Beach in the fall, and the birds and the sand, and the idiot tourists and the cheap shit they buy, painting the memory as best I can.

I hear Deb come in behind me, hear her footsteps pause beside the door while I explain to Kelsey how my little rental cabin was just a quarter mile from the beach, a nice walk on a bright September afternoon, and the air, sand, and sun were warm and sweet. "And the crab! Oh, Kelsey, the crab, so fresh it's a wonder they weren't still wiggling! They'd crack apart like little presents of yummy, and you can suck the meat right out of their skinny little legs. So good, especially with a cold beer on the beach."

The chair by the door creaks as Deb sits, sipping coffee, but I keep talking to Kelsey, holding her hand until my brain runs dry of stories. I grab a fresh swab to moisten Kelsey's mouth. "What happened?" I ask Deb as I swab. "I thought she was stable?"

"Pneumonia then a blood infection," a man says from the chair behind me.

Startled, I turn, the swab a puffy-pink weapon in my fist, to see Kelsey's brother, all grown up and sitting by the door, paper coffee cup in hand, while Deb's in the hall, whispering with a nurse.

"It stressed her liver and heart, ruined her kidneys..."

He's looking at Kelsey, not me, and he sighs at Deb walking in. His hazel-green gaze returns to me, his eyes so much like Kelsey's from before everything fell apart. "We decided instead of dialysis, it was time to let her go. The docs say it'll be just a few days. I'm glad you got to see her."

Max! I think, looking back and forth between mother and son. The same broad forehead, the same trim ears. Holy crap. I haven't seen him since high school, nearly a decade ago. No longer a geeky kid with glasses and over-sized t-shirts, he's all got-his-shit-together-man-stuff now.

Deb smiles at me, then Max, and she smooths his rain-rumpled hair. "Your dad wants to know if you can fix the sump. He won't be back until this weekend, he hopes, but with more rain..."

Nodding, Max finishes his coffee. "Sure, Mom, no problem. Anything else need fixing while I'm there?"

"Nothing that can't wait for your dad." Deb walks to the far side of the bed and settles into another chair. "So, Berk," she asks, drawing my attention as Max tosses his cup into the trash. "How often do you get to Myrtle Beach?"

❧

An hour or so later, I beg off. There just isn't much more to say. Max walks with me, past the kitchen and the study, now empty of mourners.

"How long are you in town?" he asks, opening the door for us.

We pause on the porch. I stare through the rain and breathe in the scent of spring worms. "A week or so, at most. My granddad's moving to a retirement home so I came to help him pack and prep the house to sell. His... His girlfriend mentioned Kelsey was here."

I turn my head to look at Max. We're the same height, give or take half an inch, and our eyes are level.

He says, "It's good to see you. Sorry I missed you at the bar. Had to run a couple of errands, but you were gone before I got back."

I stare past the rain again, to a clump of cows in a flooding pasture. "It's okay. Shit happens." My butt buzzes but I ignore Dave's latest freakout. I smile. "It's been a long time. Too long. Last time I saw you, you were a pale, skinny nerd."

He smiles and scratches one stubbled cheek. "Yeah, well, things change."

"That they do."

We watch drenched cows a moment more. I remember trick-or-treating in the rain with Kelsey and Max. The mud fight in their front ditch after a torrential downpour. Countless soaked spring soccer games. Sprinklers and swimsuits. Laughing while sprinting from the car to the school's front door with Max carrying my guitar because he ran fastest.

I smile for a moment, but it melts again. It rained the night everything went to shit. The night I failed my best friend and she nearly died. Check that. *Is* dying.

My throat tightens against a sob threatening to break free.

"You okay?" Max asks.

"Yeah," I lie, nodding, then swallow down my grief before glancing his way. "I'd better get back to the house. See ya later, gator."

I take one step into the rain before he says, "This isn't your fault, Berk."

Rain masks the sting of my tears when I turn back to look at him. I hope. There's no snappy comeback, only me and Max and the rain. "Okay," is all I can manage to say, and that, too, is a lie.

He sighs. I can't tell if it's exasperation with me or himself or anything else, but he steps down to me and offers his left arm. "Let me walk you to your car."

I nod and take his arm. His right hand is warm on top of mine in familiar formality. He'd asked me to prom a lifetime ago, a prom we'd skipped to take vigil in the hospital, and I think of that as he escorts me like a princess to my Mazda. I wonder what it would have been like to dance with him back then. Me, the outcast, with him, the regular guy everyone liked. How would we have danced? Would we have attended any parties? Would he have tried to kiss me?

The rain doesn't seem so dreary anymore.

It's a few quick paces to my SUV and, grinning, he frees my hand, bowing slightly as he lets me go. "Your chariot awaits, my lady."

I grin back. "Thanks."

"Anytime." He nods once then takes two steps away, but pauses and turns back to me. "Berk?"

"Yeah?" I say, smiling at him with one foot in my Mazda.

"One thing." He lowers his gaze a moment as he returns, leaning close as if to tell me a secret. He struggles for words.

"It's okay," I say, touching his arm. "Tell me."

He kisses me instead, his mouth firm and warm and tasting like home. It's a slam to my senses, unexpected and electric, and I feel his cheek stubble on my cheek and beneath my fingertips, his breath, one arm coming around me. The kiss lasts only a moment but leaves me reeling and I stand there, blinking, my mouth half open, leaning toward him as he draws away.

"Been wanting to do that for fifteen years," he says, his hazel eyes searching mine.

Fifteen? I think. Jesus, we would have been thirteen. Kids!

Middle school. High school. The two constants in my life then were Kelsey and Max. My best friend and her younger brother. He was always there, one leg of our trio. Kelsey was the brain, I was the kooky creative, but Max was the stable one, the one with sense, the one who carried my heavy gear for me and helped me pass geometry and brought me chocolate at midterms and let me bawl on his shoulder when my uncle Danny died in Iraq.

Max.

I manage to collect myself without dropping his gaze. "Why didn't you? Back then?"

His smile is sad and raindrops drip from his lashes. "I was going to. Had it all planned out. Then you left."

He shrugs and backs away, still watching me. "I gotta get that sump installed then get back to work. But come by the bar, if you can. If you want. We'll talk."

He trots to a little silver Cobalt. I watch him back out and leave, my head reeling and my cheek and lips still burned by his sweet stubble.

Intermezzo - Tenth Grade

I'm running late, again, scrambling to grab my crap before Kelsey starts honking and wakes the neighbor sleeping off his night shift. I do not need to see him on his steps in his tighty whities screaming at us to knock it the hell off.

Twice is two times too many.

Our cat Bill's sleeping, curled atop my coat on the floor by the TV. Despite his mrowing complaint, I tug it out from beneath him. Where the hell did I put my shoes?!

There. Beside the couch. I yank on my shoes and coat then rush to the kitchen where Gram's stacking Granddad's pile of brochures for security cameras he's adding to his service trucks. She's shaking her butt while singing to Creedence on her iPod. *Proud Mary.*

"Love you!" she calls out as I snatch up a granola bar on my way to the kitchen door. "Have a great day!"

"Biology test today, but I'll try. Love you, too!"

Backpack and sax-case clenched in the same hand and my guitar case slung over my shoulder, I knock the backdoor open with my hip and *sliiiide* down the icy driveway to Kelsey's car. Yeah, it's just a beige Taurus with a crumpled front fender, but it's *hers*. I can't even get my license for another seven months.

I am insanely jealous of her car.

I chuck my gear into the back seat, dumping it beside Max reading his Game Informer, then flump into shotgun. It's warm inside and Nickelback's *Photograph* is blasting on the speakers.

"You have got to be shitting me!" I say as I buckle in and she backs out to the street, skidding sideways at the bottom where ice always puddles and makes it slick. "Nickelback? They suck ass!"

She pops the car into drive. "I like this song!"

Grinning, I glance at her. My wacky beanpole self is just a single note in the dark, but she's a brilliant symphony. Drama. Art. Economics. Algebra—*who the hell likes Algebra?!? Kelsey*. And she's utterly oblivious how fucking gorgeous she is. I love her to pieces. There are days, many of them, I'm astounded we're best friends and have been since third grade.

School's nine blocks from my house and just a block from hers, easy walking distance for us both. We still do this roundabout commute every morning, because she has a flippin' awesome car!

"Can we stop at Hardee's?" Max mutters from the back. "I'm hungry."

"You already ate six Eggos and a bag of pizza rolls!" Kelsey glances at me and rolls her eyes.

"That was like an hour ago," he says, leaning forward, his elbows on the top of our seats and the top half of his face hidden behind his scraggly hair and glasses. "Mom gave me five bucks."

Despite being a grade behind us and nearly a year younger than his sister, Max is only about six weeks younger than me. We still treat him like a kid, though.

"And I have ten," Kelsey sighs, turning toward the highway that runs through town. "Fine, but you take your wrappers with you. I do not want my car smelling like hash browns all week."

"Whatever," he mutters, voice muffled by the gaming mag as he slumps back.

We're sitting at the stoplight on the highway, Hardee's in sight, when a rumbling blue vintage Mustang pulls up beside us. Smokin'-hot-yet-entitled-asshat Christopher *Do Not Call Me Chris* Duncomb's driving, but the car's crammed full of jocks. Cory Hildebrandt, who was a year ahead of us until he got held back and repeated fifth grade, is riding shotgun. He rolls down the window. He says something to Kelsey while Christopher and the three dudes in back laugh their asses off.

Cory fucks with Kelsey every chance he gets, which is far too often. There aren't many places to hide in this little town.

"Ignore him," I say, gesturing toward Hardee's. "Bacon Biscuit sammies await and I'm buyin'! I've got my debit card and ain't afraid to use it!"

I glance out of the corner of my eye to see Kelsey staring straight ahead, hands clenched onto the wheel. Something hits her window and we both look. A flood of green dribbles down the glass.

"Assholes," Max mutters from the back. I flip 'em the finger, but Kelsey rolls the window down about halfway.

"Why'd you throw a Monster at my car?" she snaps, and Cory jerks back enough for his buddies to start laughing again.

"You gonna go out with me or not?"

"Not!" She rolls up the window, cutting off him calling her a fucking bitch. Then she turns up her Nickel-crap to drown out everything else.

The light changes and the Mustang charges away from the light to zip into our lane and fishtail into Hardee's, but Kelsey sits there, her hands shaking on the steering wheel.

"You okay?" I whisper.

"Yeah," she says, still staring straight ahead. "We'll get Hardee's some other time."

She takes a breath and turns toward Midtown Park and school. I look back to see Max watching the Mustang as if he could incinerate it with his glare. The bruise on his cheek still hasn't faded from the last time he tried to kick Cory's ass.

Berk

By the time I cross town to Granddad's, the rain has stopped and the sun threatens to peek through the clouds. Ellen's Camry is gone. I drag myself through the kitchen doorway to find Granddad eating pasta at the kitchen table.

He's wearing his usual jeans and a pullover shirt, a definite improvement from his previous... attire.

Yeah, let's call it that.

"Ellen said you went to see Kelsey," he says, dragging a chunk of baguette through his sauce. "I expected you back earlier, but got hungry."

I know post-nookie munchies when I see them. A bowl and fork are waiting by the stove and I scoop up some grub. It's still warm. "No prob."

I sit in my usual place, back toward the corner, and an odd silence settles around us. I can't stop thinking about Kelsey dying and Max kissing me. Back and forth. Sponge swabs and rainy kisses. The smell of cinnamon over antiseptics alongside the intriguing scent of clean man skin.

The dichotomy's such a brain fuck.

"About earlier..." Granddad says, pushing his half-eaten lunch aside.

Thanks for reviving that image, Granddad, I think as GobbleGate replaces the luscious memory of Max's voice box thrumming beneath my fingertips so much like the strings of my standing bass. I jab at my pasta and try to shove the image away. "Don't worry about it. Your sex life is your business. Ellen was *very* clear about that. You're an adult. End of story."

"She told me she'd talked to you." He sighs. "I just want to assure you I love your grandmother. Still. I miss—"

"It's *fine*," I say, standing, bowl in hand, intent on reaching the one place in this house I can maybe hide in. The one room Granddad refuses to enter, not that I want to go in there, either. One peek inside feels like a gut punch. "I'm gonna go eat and pack up The Palace, okay?"

I'm already in the living room and hurrying for the stairs when I hear his chair scrape against the kitchen floor. Bill jumps down from the back of the couch and scampers to get ahead of me. He might be almost fifteen, but he purrs and weaves between my feet, slowing me down and thwarting my escape.

"Berk. Damn it, will you talk with me?"

I stop, sighing. Bill sits between my boots, purring, and looks up at me with his smug kitty smile.

Traitor.

I turn to my granddad and meet his gaze. It's tough, for both of us. At least it seems to be.

"I don't mind you having a girlfriend," I say, managing to hold my ground. "And, honestly, I don't mind the harem thing. What the hell. Enjoy yourself. Party on, Wayne, and all that shit."

He smiles, relaxing. "Party on, Garth."

I grin back. Gram bought a cheap Wayne's World VHS from McDonald's in Decorah when I was two, maybe three years old. By the time she realized getting something at Mickey D's didn't mean it was guaranteed kid-appropriate, I'd already watched it five times—thanks, Mom, for not giving a shit—and *loved* the movie, especially the head-banging of *Bohemian Rhapsody*.

I didn't realize how trashy it was until I saw it again in college, but my first guitar was an Arctic White Strat, just like Wayne's.

I write myself a mental note to lug Snow White—yes, I name my guitars. Doesn't everyone?—out of the attic before I head home again. It's beat all to hell from being a teenager's first guitar and the A string doesn't tune true ever since it fell over and smacked the head on the edge of my amp, but I don't want it to end up at auction either. "We're cool, Granddad. Really."

"I won't bring them to the house," he says, lowering his gaze. "You're only here for a little while, and I shouldn't—"

"*Seriously?* It's your house. I'm much more traumatized by the visuals, if you get my drift. I did not need to see—"

"No you did not," he interrupts and I notice his face is turning a hue best described as raw pork pink.

Eeew. Strawberry ice cream? No. Berry Smoothie? Uh... Chewed bubble gum?

Yuck. Let's just forget the food comparisons. He's blushing. My granddad is *blushing*, much like I was moments after I barged into his office and saw...

Nope. Don't need to think about that again.

"How about a signal?" I suggest, trying—and failing—to cram the whole thing back into an imaginary box marked DO NOT OPEN. EVER. BECAUSE EEEW. "Something visual, like a tie on a doorknob or a pipe wrench on the kitchen table. Shit, I dunno. Anything so I know you're entertaining your lady friends and I should make myself scarce. Hell, I even found a bar to land in while I wait."

He waves off my suggestion. "No. They won't be coming over anymore. I'll be in the senior apartments soon enough. They can wait until then."

I chuckle at the idea of a harem of frustrated old women cut off from their dick supply. Crazy, I know, but I can't help myself. I shake my head and walk toward the stairs, crushing my laughter as Bill weaves between my feet and tries to trip me. I'd pick up his squirmy pain-in-the-ass if I didn't have a bowl of pasta in one hand.

"What's so funny?" Granddad asks, following.

Free hand on the banister, I turn back and manage to corral my giggles. "You have eight horny women to contend with. Unless you buy them all vibrators and Sam Elliot erotica, trust me, they're not gonna wait two weeks to get laid. Might wanna keep them satisfied before they wander off."

He stammers and I sing *Just a Gigolo* as I trot up to the second floor.

Gram and Granddad's room's at the top of the stairs, with Danny's old room across the hall. My room's the smaller one next to Danny's and across from the bathroom. At the end is Gram's Craft Palace and her personal storage.

I hesitate at the door, my hand wavering over the knob. Other than the one assessment peek right after I got here, I haven't seen her studio since well before she died. For a moment, I think I smell hot glue and ModPodge.

Deep breath, and I open the door. Bill scoots in ahead of me and makes a beeline for the closet.

Gram's funky handmade curtains have faded in years of sunshine, and it smells more of dust and stale air than the more familiar glue-stick and lacquer, but otherwise looks about the same. Her once glorious Swedish Ivy has been left to wither and die, and a half-finished shell of a bunny-rabbit doll is still stuffed beneath the needle of her old Singer Featherweight along with various bits of bunny fabric on the cutting mat. Despite almost two years of obvious neglect and a definite layer of dust, the room's tidier than I expected. She must have had an organization binge right before she died.

I hear Granddad's boots *clumph* up the stairs as I look around, eating my pasta and trying to decide where to start. The piles of books and patterns? The fabric? The assorted wooden bits and paint? Markers and pens? Yarn? So much color, so much joy, all crammed into a twelve by fourteen room and overwhelming in its gleeful chaos.

Despite missing her, I smile. I always loved helping her in here. Never knew what treasures I might find or create.

"Thanks for tackling this," he says, his steps a warm patter down the hall behind me. "I haven't even opened the door since she..."

He trails off, but I remember. Gram'd had a heaping cart-load of yarn already picked out and, according to witnesses, was happily digging through crochet patterns when she collapsed like a dropped towel. She was gone before paramedics arrived. Brain aneurysm at sixty-eight. Quick, painless, and in her favorite craft store.

We all should be so lucky.

I hear Granddad behind me, his breath shaking. "Let's just tell the auction house to sort through this."

"We can't," I say, turning to comfort him. "There's no telling what she has stashed in here. I'd hate to have them toss her hand-written recipes or sell my baby blanket or my uncles Eric and Danny's medals."

He nods, tearing up. Granddad's a big guy, well over six feet, still solid at seventy-two, and he wipes his sniffles on his sleeve like a preschooler. "I used to get frustrated with her art-splosions," he says, his gaze downcast. "I always wanted to clean them up. Pins in the arm of the couch. Thread in the carpet. Paint specks on the kitchen table. My paintbrushes ruined by glue."

"Don't forget the yarn. Every Christmas. So. Much. Yarn."

"Yeah," he says, nodding and looking at me again. "Afghans for charity auctions. Afghans for the nursing homes. For the newborns in the hospital. For the homeless shelters. For the Veteran's Center."

I grin. "She'd start crocheting in September and not stop until Christmas Eve." I crochet too—thanks Gram!—and donate most of it, but don't tell anyone. I have a reputation to maintain.

He smiles, finally. "No matter what she was working on, she did beautiful work, always, and gave it all away."

I glance back to the piles of fabric, yarn, paper, and wood. "Do you want me to set aside some of the better stuff to donate? I bet school art departments and senior centers would love this stuff."

"Whatever you think best, Berk," he says, his voice catching as he walks away.

I watch him go, his head hanging, and something crashes in the closet as my butt buzzes again. Sighing, I pull the phone from my pocket to see I have five messages, all from Dave. I click to accept the call.

"Yo," I say, setting my bowl of pasta beside the sewing machine before climbing over a box of paint tubes and ribbon to find out what Bill's getting into.

"Berk! Where the hell have you been!" Dave whines into my ear. "I've got a line on a Cheetos radio commercial that's recording in Pittsburgh on Friday!"

"No. I'm here, sorting craft supplies and my granddad's cat — Shit, I just knocked over a stack of balsa wood cutouts. Shit! Goddammit! The stupid cat made something crash in the closet. Hang on."

"I can't hang on. It's two days away! We can totally manage it. It's only seventeen hundred to split between us, but it's *CHEETOS*! They even mentioned putting it on I-Heart-Radio!"

I'm not driving all the way to Pittsburgh tomorrow for eight hundred fifty bucks. Not gonna happen. I'm here to help my grandfather and I tell Dave so. I stretch to climb across a bundle of foam-core strips, and I reach the closet to see a tipped box of multi-colored pompom creatures stuck to magnets. Bill's lounging in them while grooming his already immaculate fur. The pompom critters are scattered everywhere, in pairs, because that's what magnets apparently do. Stick pompom critters together by their cute little magnetic feet.

There must be five hundred of the damn things, and at least half have fallen between and behind other boxes and piles of books. Bill licks the one closest to his ass. It's the color of a Cheeto.

I don't even like Cheetos.

I mutter "Shit," under my breath and haul Bill out of there then start scooping magnetized pompoms back into their box. "Granddad's moving into the retirement center on April first," I say, cutting off Dave's attempt to woo me to Pittsburgh. "I'm guaranteed available only after that. What does that mean, Dave?"

"It means we're able to take advantage of an unbelievable opportunity on Friday!"

"No. It means we're not recording a bassline for Cheetos in Pitt the day after tomorrow. *I am helping my granddad.* If you find a good gig in April, let me know. But otherwise, please stop calling. Please."

"We should have accepted Imelda and I can't believe you're—"

"Bye-bye, Dave. I'll check in next week."

I click off, but he calls right back. I let it go straight to voicemail.

One of the pompom critters is a penguin, a little black beak and teensy googly-eyes glued on. She put them on with tweezers, under a magnifying light. I'd seen her do it a thousand times. Seen her hand sew pea-sized buttons on doll dresses, seen her weave ribbons thinner than tines on a fork, seen her crochet threads into masterpieces.

And she gave it all away. All this luscious color, all this talent, all this joy, the scope of which is never to be seen again. Not by me, anyway.

My eyes sting and I can't see anymore, so I sit on the box of clippings she'd made about Kelsey's attack, printouts from every newspaper she could find, plus notes and diagrams of all possible variables, none of which ever proved good enough for the country prosecutor that Cory did it even though I saw him shake her lifeless body, saw him covered with her blood. I take a staggering breath and let myself cry over Gram and Kelsey and my uncle Danny. He'd be thirty-three this summer and probably have kids of his own if it wasn't for that fucking IED. I decide Gram's stuff, a good portion of it anyway, should go to kids. She'd want it that way.

By the time I fill the back of my Mazda, Granddad's left to see one of his lady friends. At least I think that's where he's going, surrounded by a fresh cloud of Old Spice and not looking at me as he scurries to his truck.

I wave at him as he backs out, and he waves back. Get 'em, Tiger. I knew you couldn't deny 'em long.

By the time I realize it's 5:42 p.m., according to my dashboard clock at least, I'm in the empty grade school parking lot and all the kid-wranglers are home grading coloring sheets and scribbled alphabets. Or something.

My SUV smells like craft supplies and memories of Kelsey and me folding baby afghans or putting dresses on the dolls, then packing them into boxes for the children's hospital. And of Gram painting wooden cars while singing along with classic and alternative rock.

She taught me to love McCartney and Flea and Geddy Lee.

For that, and everything else, I will be forever grateful.

I cry again. It's that kind of day.

Not knowing where else to go, I drive to Tony's. As I pull in, I wonder who in this muddy town can afford an orange Beemer roadster, and why it's taking two spots. Then I see the plate.

DUNCOMB

Oh. It's *him.*

Max

Max sat at his kitchen table in the apartment above the bar, phone crushed against his ear, and wrote in a ledger spread open on the dinette table before him. "Yeah, go ahead and send me the invoice," he said to his lawyer's secretary as he heard Gretchen muttering up the stairs. "There's nothing more anyone can do. Thank her again for trying."

Another $1387.00 blown on legal fees. Christ. Call clicked off, he took a sip of cold coffee and looked up at Gretchen's rap on the banister. She nodded her head toward the bar. "Dunkdoodle's here. Again."

Max sighed. Gretch hated Christopher Duncomb almost as much as he did. "You can't be calling the city planner Dunkdoodle. We've talked about this."

"Yeah, yeah, several times, but it still fits him. I'm about to be unemployed because of his stupid development project and he's lucky that's all I'm calling him. I still say you should tell the whole city council to stick it."

Max rolled his head until his neck popped. "I might, once this is done."

"Good. Then open a new bar over in Halstead or Murier. Shit, buy a trendy pub in downtown Decorah." She paused and grinned at him. "Somewhere close enough for me to commute to. Hire me back. It'll be awesome."

He sighed. Only one bar in the county was for sale, and it cost three times more than his business loan limit. Hell, after legal fees, he couldn't even pay in full for his sister's cremation, let alone make the down payment on a new bar. Or a place to live. "I'd love to, Gretch, but I don't think it's in the cards."

"I know, and it bites. You're the best boss I ever had." Gretchen turned toward the stairwell then paused, looking at him over her thick shoulder. "Want me to send Dunkdoodle up here, or have him sit in a booth and stew? I can ask Dwight to tell him war stories."

Max grinned. Dwight was their token combat Vet. Usually quiet and soft-spoken, he'd willingly reminisce about flamethrowers and charred or exploded corpses if offered a bourbon. Much of it was bullshit—other than a couple of sketchy months stocking shelves and coordinating shipments in Kabul,

Dwight had worked the remainder of his time overseas at supply depots in Germany or Kuwait—but it scared off the assholes.

Max's grin collapsed. Where will Dwight go after we close? he thought for the thousandth time. Henry? Mitch? Jack? Sherry? Everyone else in the neighborhood who's become my extended family?

"No reason to torture Dwight," he sighed. "I'll be right down."

She left Max to silence and his ever-dwindling ledger. Pay off the lawyer, he thought. The taxes, the suppliers, the utilities, and two weeks severance for Gretchen. That'll still leave enough to make a dent in Kelsey's cremation costs. I'll have to finance the rest. Somehow. Then what? Move into Mom's until I find a job—somewhere—and can rent a shitty apartment?

He downed the last of his coffee in a gulp. Goddammit, Heidi. Why'd you do this to me?

"Fucking bitch," he muttered, slapping the ledger closed.

Max grimaced while sliding into the booth across from Christopher Duncomb, Fayerville City Planner, Mayor's son, and overall Shitty Human Being. He snapped out one word. "What."

Gretchen set a glass of Coke with a lemon wedge in front of Max and he nodded thank you while still glowering at Duncomb. Despite the day's drizzle, the Mayor's son was perfectly polished in a tailored suit, tie with a matching pocket handkerchief, and impeccable white shirt. Everyone else in the bar, including Max, wore jeans and a pullover shirt, at best. Hell, Dwight was in stained sweats and flip-flops. With socks.

Duncomb kept his attention on Max, but said to Gretchen, "I'd like a scotch, on the rocks, with—"

"No."

As she walked away, Duncomb said, "One would hope a quality establishment like this would employ a better class of bartender."

Max pushed the lemon to the bottom of his glass with his straw and sipped the Coke. She'd added a splash of Jack. Atta girl. "Why are you here?"

"Money. It's all about money." Duncomb fished a slender notebook and pen from inside his jacket. "Time to finalize our business."

Max resisted the urge to roll his eyes. Jesus. Not again with the damned scribbles.

At the window table well beyond Duncomb, Mitch dealt fresh cards to Dwight and Karen. Dwight caught Max's attention, pointed at himself, and made a shooting gesture toward Duncomb. Max declined with a slight shake of his head.

"Finalize our business?" Max said. "I'd say three appeals, two court orders, and an injunction pretty much stamped *finished* on this."

Duncomb found his page and drew a wavy line. "The demo crew has an unexpected opening for next week, so let's get you scheduled for first thing Monday. Save us all a little time and money."

"No. The State Court of Appeals gave March 26th as the earliest demolition date, not the nineteenth. Want me to show you the Eviction Notice?"

Duncomb continued to scribble what looked like hieroglyphs. "If we begin first thing on the nineteenth, road crews take over that afternoon and the parcels—"

"I do not give one flying fuck about your damned development project. I will be out of here by midnight March 25th. Not one *moment* earlier."

"Maxie, let's be reasonable. Every day we delay in opening access to Murier Creek Development costs the city several thousand dollars. Surely you don't want to waste tax—"

"Waste *tax* money?" Max snapped. "You could have put the new road through a vacant lot, not a hundred feet from here, three damn years ago, *Chris*, without anyone giving a shit, and you'd have half of your house lots sold by now. Instead, your dad has a hard-on for this lot because he hated Tony. I bought Tony's bar so your father's destroying *my* life. Almost three years of bullshit court battles later, you come in here bitching about *tax* money? Fuck that. How much tax money did *you* waste by forcing—"

Duncomb stared at Max and a muscle in his cheek twitched. "A southern access would have been aesthetically—"

Max slid out of the booth and glared down at Duncomb while everyone in the bar turned to stare. "Fuck aesthetics. You might have scared a Honduran family out of their restaurant, but this is *my* bar, *my* lot, bought and filed legally whether your shitbag father likes it or not, and I'm *not* budging until midnight March 25th. If the city doesn't like it, they can kiss my ass and call my lawyer. Now get out."

Duncomb stood and buttoned his jacket. He smoothed the fine wool while giving Max a cool stare. "How does it feel, Maxie," he said, his voice as sleek as the fabric beneath his fingertips, "to know I'm boning the girl you married?"

Max smiled. "Great, Chris. I look forward to the day she takes everything you worked for, so we'll have that in common, too. Until then, fuck off and enjoy your sloppy seconds."

The front door opened and Berkeley walked in. The gang playing cards shifted their attention to her, but Max held steady.

She said, "Oh. My. Gawd! It's Chrissy D! How they hangin', bitch?"

"Who the hell do you thi—" Duncomb jerked away from Max's unflinching gaze then took a step back to bump his well-covered ass against the booth. "Berkeley Williams?"

"Yup," she said, flashing a huge grin.

"Didn't know you were back in town."

Berk started unbuttoning her jacket. "I'm a bad penny. But we all already knew that, didn't we... *Chrissy*? Two spots for a three-year-old Beemer? You're lucky I didn't key it."

Duncomb flashed Max a glare as if to say *we're not done*, then snatched his notebook and pen off the table and tucked them away.

"Whatcha drinkin', sweetie?" Gretchen called to Berkeley as Duncomb walked straight out the door.

"Calypso Street." Berk peeled off her jacket, dazzling grin fading. "If you still have any."

"We sure do, hon. Be right back."

Gretchen trotted for the cooler while Berk approached Max, cobwebs in her hair and sorrow in her eyes.

"You here to talk or drink?" he asked.

"Both?" she said, shrugging. "It's been a long day."

The screech of a car peeling out echoed through the bar and Max sighed. "That it has."

Berk

I thank Gretchen for my beer and wonder what the fuck I'm doing sitting at Tony's just to watch Max work. She flips Max a good measure of ornery yet respectful shit as he lugs a tray of glasses from the back, and the three regulars playing cards—who apparently live in those chairs—direct their drink orders to her, but everything else belongs to Max. He takes the phone calls. He unlocks the safe below the cash register. He tallies receipts.

Max definitely loves the place, and it's about to close. Which sucks. This is a great bar.

A few folks come in to loosen up after work, keeping Max and his assistant busy, so I flip through the juke and settle for *Hotel California*, the whole album for two bucks in quarters. Everyone loves classic Eagles, right? My Gram sure did.

My score sucks on the pinball machine, and I blame it on the pompom critters. That's better than my head still being fucked up in the undertow of geriatric blowjobs, kaleidoscope-colored dead grammas with their sprawling crime-solving charts, twenty-eight-year-old BFFs in hospice, and firm, rainy kisses.

I'd like today to end.

About halfway through my second beer, I'm sober enough to sing along with *Wasted Time*, but drunk enough not to give a shit if anyone's listening. That's a dangerous place for me to be, the place where my mouth charges right over common sense and gets my ass in trouble.

My butt buzzes again, surely for the gazillionth time today. I grumble and shoot the ball up to the twirly track on the left side. Can't I have one goddamn day to deal with my own shit, Dave? Why does it always have to be about you?

"Hey," Max says from behind me and I startle. Manage to save my ball, though.

"Hey." I flick that sucker back into play.

He comes around to stand by the pinball machine's deck. I can see him, he can see me. I resist the urge to smooth my hair.

"You okay?" he says. "You looked like you were crying when you came in."

"Yep. I'm fine," I say, pushing against the machine to help the ball swing... Shit. Almost waited too long and it rolls cock-eyed. "It's just been a helluva day."

"Yeah. No kidding. Thanks for disarming the, um, situation earlier. Me punching Brad Duncomb's son in his perfect nose wouldn't have helped anything."

"Punch for the throat," I say as my last ball exits the game. "A busted nose will just piss 'em off." I take a swig of beer and turn to face him. "Throat punches put 'em on the ground."

Dave buzzes—Jesus, dude, grow a pair!—and I try not to show my aggravation.

"You have experience with throat punching?"

"A little," I admit, more frustrated than I intended.

Max sighs. "I'll leave you to your game. Just..." he shrugs. "Just wanted to thank you."

As he turns to go, I say, "I thought you wanted me to stop by and talk."

He pauses, and his head tilts before he turns back. "You came to talk?"

"Yeah," I admit, "but you've been busy and I didn't want—"

"I *always* have time for you," he says, and I believe him. He turns, motioning for me to follow.

So I do.

⁂

There's a little loft apartment above the bar. Well, sort of an apartment. It's not much more than a storage attic with a bare-bones kitchenette, a hide-a-bed couch, a small TV, and basic dude-clutter, much like any college apartment I've ever been in.

At least I don't see any porn. Always a plus.

"Coffee?" he asks, gesturing toward the drip coffee maker by the sink.

I shake my head and waggle my half-full bottle of beer. "So. What do you want to talk about?"

"I... I dunno. You? Me? Kelsey? The missing decade? Why you were crying?"

Fair enough, I think, nodding. "You start."

"Okay." He sits on the couch, leaving plenty of room for me. "I worked crap jobs for a couple of years after high school, then decided to take some business classes at the community college with the intention to open my own business. Met a girl, got married, and bought a bar, she cheated on me so we got divorced, which led me to lose everything *but* the bar, only now I'm losing the bar, too." He shrugs. "Oh, Chris Duncomb's a dick and my sister's dying, but you already knew that." He sighs. "That's the short version, anyway. You?"

I settle onto the couch beside him. "For me, it's been college, bar bands, studio work, a neurotic business partner, avoiding Fayerville at all costs until I'm back to pack up my grandparents' house, walking in on my granddad whoring himself out, plus my comatose BFF's dying. Oh, and some guy I used to know kissed me in the rain, but you already knew about that."

"Yeah, I did," he says, giving me a sideways glance. "Sorry about that."

I set my beer on the dinged-up coffee table before us. "No reason to apologize. It was, by far, the best part of my day."

I hear him chuckle, but I don't dare look. Not yet. He's too damn cute and I've drunk too much beer.

We sit in companionable silence and my mind drifts to the emotional chaos of my day. I wonder, for a moment, if I should have accepted Dave's offer to do the car commercial and skipped most of the mess completely. Of course, my butt decides that's the perfect time to buzz. Again.

Damn thing. I pull the phone out of my pocket and toss it onto the table beside my beer. It hums against wood instead of my ass, with DAVE in big, blue letters on the screen.

Our companionable silence flips its switch to full-blown awkward, but I'm not sure why. Max says, "So. Bar bands and studio work? You're still into music?"

"Yep," I say as my phone goes quiet once again. "Upright and guitar bass, electric or acoustic. As long as the check doesn't bounce, I'll play whatever bass you want."

"Not guitar anymore?"

"Eh, I play a little, but not professionally. I'm passable at sax and piano too, but, again, not professionally unless it's for a local gig and they just need a warm body who isn't a total suckfest. Mostly I do studio work or chamber gigs." I really want to pick up my beer again, but I don't want to get too drunk. "I enjoy sight-reading a good bassline, and it apparently enjoys paying the bills." I decide to ask a question of my own. "Why'd you buy a bar?"

"Ah! Back and forth questions. Cool. I bought a bar because I love the sense of community it brings. You get to learn a lot about people, what they need, how to help them. It's sort of the heart of the neighborhood."

His answer makes me smile, but I manage not to look his way. "That sounds nice."

"It is, most of the time." The couch shifts as he settles into it. "Your license plates say West Virginia. Is that where you live?"

"Yeah, Charleston, mostly because housing's cheap and it's a reasonable drive to everywhere I need to play. Nashville, Detroit, New York, whatever." I shrug. "The town's great, but I get a little tired of the local country folk sometimes. They get kinda rowdy for me." My phone resumes buzzing and I flip it the bird. "My turn. Why's there a demolition sign in your window? Your place looks pretty cherry."

"Because the city's putting a road through here and there isn't shit I can do about it. I tried, but the Duncombs won, like always."

I roll my head to look at Max, who's already shifted around to watch me, the cheater. "That *bites*."

"Yep. With expensive lawyer teeth." Silence stretches a bit too long before Max says, "Who's Dave and why won't you pick up his calls?"

I manage not to laugh. "He's my neurotic, workaholic, *pain-in-the-ass*, drummer and business partner who cannot stand the thought of me refusing to drive to Pittsburgh to record the bassline for a Cheetos radio commercial."

"Seriously?"

"Seriously. Drummers be crazy. Especially ones named Dave."

I'm still pondering my next question when Max asks, "Are you dating him?"

I almost laugh. "*Dave?* Fuck. No. Strictly business partners only. I am godparent to his and Lia's two kids, though, which is by far the coolest part about having to put up with his crap." I flash Max a grin. "By the way, that's two questions, three if we count *seriously?*"

He nods and motions for me to continue. "All right. Ask me two."

"Do you know anyone who'd be interested in eight boxes of craft supplies? The back end of my SUV is filled with stuff from Gram's Palace, and I've barely dented the chaos."

"Can't say that I do, no." His laugh is warm and beckons me to join in. "Your grandma was something else, wasn't she? I still use the scarf she knitted me for Christmas my tenth-grade year. Peacock blue and lime green. It's starting to get ratty, but I wear it anyway."

I grin at him. "*Apple* green."

"Oh yes. She lectured me once on the difference."

"Don't feel special, she lectured everyone."

We laugh again and it's good. Cleansing. Safe. Like we were kids again. We've both scooched toward the middle of the couch, our shoulders just touching. Come to think of it, we'd frequently leaned against each other on couches while watching movies or playing Halo or whatever, way back when.

It's what we did, at least until life ran us through a shredder.

I sigh, finally relaxing, and lay my head on his shoulder to look up at him. It seems to be the thing to do, but he freezes for a moment then swallows. Silence stretches between us, lost among missing years and the green flecks of his eyes. His fingertips feel warm on the side of my jaw, and his gaze remains steady. Rock solid. Patient. Calm.

I can use a little calm.

"You still have one question," he says.

"Okay. If you'd wanted to for so long, why didn't you kiss me that time when we were fifteen?"

I'm sure he knows the night I mean. When it was just us two out in my grandparents' back yard cleaning up after a barbeque at twilight. All the adults had wandered inside for the Cubs game. Kelsey'd left hours before to make pizza at Casey's, but Max and I were told to pick up the supper mess and napkins the breeze had tossed against the fence. Of course, we goofed off. He dropped an ice cube down my back and I plucked a couple of pickles out of the dish and flung them at him. We'd chased each other, laughing, just kid stuff, but when he herded me around the shed, shaking a half-full bottle of pop to spray me with, I tripped over a loose paver and face-planted right into Gram's hostas.

Not my most regal moment, but I've survived worse.

Max immediately grabbed me by the waist and plucked me out of there, asking over and over if I was all right and helping me get leaves and grass clippings out of my hair. I'd laughed and hugged him for it, and I still remember the warmth of his hands on my back, his cheek against mine, my arms around his neck. No one in the house could see us behind the shed, and when I leaned back, when he still held me, he stared into my eyes and whispered my name.

Then he let me go and slipped away.

The now Max, all grown up and able to kiss the girl, smiles. "Which one? I have eleven times I still kick myself over not taking the chance and kissing you, as far back as sixth grade. I've lost count of how many others I didn't notice until it was too late."

Eleven? I don't know what else to think as his eyes search mine. "When I fell in the hostas."

He grins. "Ah. Number five. Your kitchen window was open and I heard someone at the sink. I worried they'd notice we were gone, come looking, and..."

"Find us making out."

"Something like that, yeah."

"Oh."

I'm trying to process all of this, figure out what my snappy comeback should be, but I keep coming up empty. The guy has left me speechless. Tingling.

Like I'm fifteen again.

But I'm not. There's been a lot of years, a lot of mistakes, and a lot of water under my bridge. Things change. People change. We're not fifteen anymore, nor should we be.

I look out to his apartment long enough to take one breath and maybe gather my nerve, then he says, "Can I kiss you? Not just a quick peck but for real? For all those times I chicke—"

I turn my head and silence him with a kiss of my own.

Good God, he can kiss.

We remain on the couch, but I've leaned back—duh!—and a lot of his weight's on me, my hand's under his shirt and on his skin. He's got a firm grip on my left boob, and our legs are tangled together. We're still dressed, which is notable, but I've got a slippery, tingly *need* happening between my legs, and the hard lump against my hip tells me he's feeling the same.

It's been a while since I've ridden a real dick, but between the beer, his kisses, and the rock rubbing into my hip, I'm confident getting back on that saddle will be fun, if not fantastic.

His knee shifts up and I straddle it, grinding against his leg. He smells *good*, no cloud of aftershave or body spray, just *man*. Skin and light sweat and testosterone. Hard dick, great scent, and a top-tier kisser. Man-stuff.

I'm in heaven.

He lifts up, releasing me from the kiss long enough to pull his shirt off. My hands follow over his stomach to his chest. Not as much hair as I prefer, but enough. Hell yes, enough, and I run my fingers through it, exploring and liking what I find. No longer a skinny kid, he's filled out nicely with a bit of definition. I'm cool with that, too, especially since muscle-bound isn't my gig. I want a little softness on my meaty men, and he's hard yet soft in all the right ways.

Hell, as sexy as he is, if he keeps kissing me like this there's not a lot of remaining variables I wouldn't be cool with.

Well, one.

Time to see what he's packing.

He tosses his long-sleeve Henley aside and I reach for his buckle. I've barely got the loose end pushed back when his hands grasp mine. His fingers are strong, capable, skilled, and I'm willing to bet good money they'll feel damn fine in me.

"We can't," he says. I look up at him, not believing the words falling out of his mouth. "Not right now, anyway."

I blink, the side of my palm riding comfortably on the bulge behind his zipper. "Why not?"

He stammers, letting my hands go, then says, "I don't have any condoms."

"You *what?*" I'm trying not to laugh, not at him but because it's just my luck to finally find a decent guy with a ready dick only he's not prepared to use it. Some days, my luck really sucks. "You're divorced, right?"

"Yeah. I just haven't—"

Seriously? Every recently divorced guy I've ever met is out trolling for poon before the ink's dry on the decree. Max has always been the ultra-responsible nerd, though. No reason to assume time would change that, but, shit, he's got me horny as hell. "Can't you *get* some? A gas station? The men's room downstairs? *Somewhere?*"

He grins. It's as if a light bulb finally turns on in his man-brain, starved of oxygen by activities down south.

"Yeah. There's a Kwik Shop across the street," he says, bounding off me. I sit as he reaches for his discarded shirt—That back! That butt! Damn!—then stops to look around. "Shit. What time is it? Gretchen gets off at nine."

I grab my phone. "Seven-twenty-three. We've got about an hour and a half of playtime left."

He's fumbling his arms into his shirt, one coming through the neck-hole. "Playtime. Yeah." I hear him swallow even though his head's still covered by the shirt, and I grin at my luck.

There's not one damn thing wrong with a little spit in the right place.

He's still getting his shirt on straight, so I stand and stretch. My undies are a mess. Sticky. But in a *really* good way. If he had a condom I'd already be on top of him, but good things come to girls who wait. "Do you have a shower up here?"

That stops him. He gapes for a moment. "A *shower?* Um, yeah, over—"

By then I can't see what he's doing—if anything—because I'm peeling my tunic-dress off.

"Holy shit, Berk," he mumbles.

I look down at my skinny self and chuckle. I forgot I wore my black lace bra today. It's old and actually pretty comfy, but it doesn't leave a helluva lot to the imagination.

"All right," I say, taking charge because little Max is enamored with my boobs and is stealing control again. "You are going to pick up a pack of condoms at Kwik Shop."

"Kwik Shop," he murmurs, his attention on my boobs, one fingertip tracing over the curve where a lace cup meets my skin.

I push his chin up with a finger until he looks into my eyes. "Yes. I'm going to take a shower while you're gone, then you're going to take one as soon as you get back. If you're fast enough, maybe we can share."

He grins. "And we'll both be clean."

I grin back, nodding. Atta boy. I knew you'd catch on.

Still grinning, he pulls me in his arms again and kisses me, deep and hard, meeting my tongue, one hand on my breast, the other in my hair. We both sigh as he draws away. "You'll still be there," he says, then he bolts for the stairs.

Max

Max sped down the stairs and through the door, banging his knee in a bright flash of pain as he made the pivot to the bar's hall too quickly. The shower turned on upstairs.

"Shit, fuck," he muttered, hurrying past the cooler despite the funny-bone pain throbbing in his knee. Nothing mattered but condoms, Berk in the shower, and the ticking clock that separated the two.

The hall seemed to run forever instead of fifteen feet or so.

Gretchen rushed to the hall. "You okay?"

"Fine. Just gotta run an errand," he said, pressing past her and into the bar.

"You sure?" She followed as he dodged people at tables. "You look flustered."

Dwight looked over from his cards. "Flustered? Looks horny to me."

"He did take a feisty piece upstairs," Mitch said with a wink. "Glad to know you're gettin' some, kiddo."

Two of the weeknight regulars whooped as he passed, still limping.

Gretchen joined in the teasing encouragement. "'Bout time you ended your dry spell!"

The embarrassment heating his face cooled as he ran into drizzle outside. He splashed across the parking lot to the highway, paced while waiting for a semi and a minivan to pass, then he sprinted across, not bothering to run to the corner to cross at the light.

Lori Sandersen worked the cash register as she did most weeknights, and he glanced her way before heading to the shelf of their so-called Medical Supplies.

Breath mints, he thought, searching, antacids, cold pills, lip balm, band-aids, and, hallelujah! There you are!

Durex, three pack. It'll do. For now.

He rushed to the cash register, his free hand pulling his wallet, and dropped the condoms on the counter.

Lori looked at the box as if it had bugs crawling on it. "Aren't you divorced?"

"Yep." Wallet open, he rifled through his cash.

"Don't know what you do in your bar, but, eew. Okay. Best to be careful, I guess." She picked up the condoms in a tentative pincer grip and held them in front of the scanner. She squinted at her cash-register's screen and winced. "Er, you can get these a *lot* cheaper at WalMart."

"How much?" Max looked up to the clock on the wall behind her. 7:27. Four minutes gone. *Just give me the price already.*

"A *lot*." Lori blabbered on, "I mean like a twelve pack, that's like twice as many, right, for like the same price. Walter and me had to use them between Jamie and Ethan because the pill made me—"

7:28. *Shit.* Max pulled a twenty from his wallet and slammed it on the counter. "Will this cover it?"

"Well yeah," she said, flinching as he snatched the box out of her hand and bolted for the door.

"Don't you want your chan—" rang through the rain then was cut off as the door swung shut.

Traffic cooperated this time, and he managed to stuff the condoms and his wallet into his pockets before reaching Tony's.

He flung the door open to cheers and clapping and lewd suggestions on what to do, but waved them off with a grin before jogging down the hall to the apartment entry.

When he opened the door, the running shower's familiar thrum filled the stairwell and, grinning, he charged up the stairs.

Intermezzo-Eleventh Grade

"Excuse me. I have to get to Chem," Kelsey said, shifting her backpack over her shoulder.

Two varsity football players, Bucky Sanderson and Troy Haddert, blocked the hallway. They wore their blue-and-black Fayerville Ravens jerseys, just like every Friday, but instead of getting high-fives from other students, they stood, arms crossed over their chests, and glared at Kelsey.

"Where is she?" Troy, the taller of the pair asked.

"You're going to have to give me more information." Kelsey managed to maintain an expression of calm detachment despite the rapid slam of her heart. She hoped. Bucky was as dumb as a dead battery, but she shared a lot of classes with Troy.

"Berk, you dumb bitch," Bucky said. "Where's Berk?"

Troy gave Bucky a hushing glare. "Calm down," he soothed. "Kelsey's okay."

"She cost my dad a fuck-ton of money a couple years ago, but her bitch bestie put Toph in the hospital *yesterday*. How the hell are we supposed to beat New Hampton tonight without Toph?"

Troy raised an eyebrow and gave her a *Well, how are we?* look as the other kids in the hall fell silent and stopped to watch.

Crap. Kelsey swallowed, held her head a little higher, and looked Troy in the eye. "So you're saying him playing tonight's game is more important than the girl he raped?"

"*Allegedly* raped," Troy said, while Bucky shifted with nervous energy beside him. "We all heard she was willing and everyone knows Berk has a tendency to over-react."

"Yeah," Bucky snapped. "She 'bout broke my nose last year."

You grabbed her boobs, Kelsey thought, but said nothing.

"Shoulda knocked her on her ass," Bucky spat.

"We need to win this game, Kelse," Troy said, pushing Bucky aside. "Where is she?"

Kelsey grit her teeth and took a step toward the boys. Bucky backed away, but Troy remained. "Paola, the girl he raped, is in the hospital too. Doesn't that matter at all to you? She was in your sister's Earth Science class. *My* gym class. He *raped* her, Troy. He's lucky he's not in jail."

"He had consensual sex with a fucking immigrant," Troy hissed, "and we're going to lose to New Hampton because Berkeley—"

"*Stopped a rape,*" a familiar voice said from behind Kelsey and she let out a tiny sigh of relief.

"Oh, fuck off, Scheffert," Troy said, shifting his gaze from Kelsey to past her right shoulder. "This doesn't concern you."

"Paola lives across the street from us," Jack Scheffert said from behind Kelsey. "She's a nice person and didn't deserve—"

Hands clenching, Bucky leaned toward Jack. "Some dirty Mexican living by the grocery store? I don't give a shit about any of them. I give a shit about us playing New Hampton tonight and the bitch who fucked over our team."

"Okay, fellas, break it up," Mrs. Bosworth, the accounting teacher, said, pushing beyond Troy and Bucky. "You're going to be late to class." Both young men turned to face her, and Jack grasped Kelsey's hand and dragged her through the crowd and around the pair of jocks arguing with Mrs. B.

"You all right?" he let her hand go but remained close beside her, arms barely touching. They passed through the clot of students and turned into a less crowded hall.

"Yeah," she said, braving a glance at his broad, bespectacled face as the tardy bell rang. His forearm was warm and she tried not to smile. "Nothing I couldn't handle. Bucky's an ass, but Troy can be reasoned with."

"Over academics, yes. Sports, no," Jack replied. He let her slip ahead of him through the gap between two gamer-heads focused on their PSPs and followed her to the deserted science hall beyond. "His mom's already been in the office yelling about tonight's game and some scout." He paused, one finger touching hers for an electric moment. "Lots of parents are pissed."

"I know," she said. "But Berk did the right thing."

"Yes, she did," he said. They paused outside the Chemistry lab door. "Wickerman's playing at the Viking this weekend. Wanna go?"

She grinned. "I can tonight, or after work tomorrow. I get off at three."

He backed away, smiling. "Let's meet up at five-thirty tonight. My turn to get the tickets, you can get the popcorn," he said, then turned to trot to Biology.

Grinning, she opened the door to Chem and didn't care she was tardy.

Berk

I step into the shower and the hot water feels really great after a day of being rained on. I stand here, water beating on my back and head, soothing away the day's chill. It's relaxing yet invigorating, and it gives me time to think.

I've known Max for damn near twenty years, more than two-thirds of my life, longer than almost anyone. He seems to still be a good guy, is cute as hell, and a helluva kisser, but is that enough to fall into bed with him?

I definitely could use a good snogging. Hell, I haven't slept with anyone other than my vibe in well over a year. Okay, fine. Two. And change. At least.

I remind myself I'm insanely busy, enjoy my solitude, and have no time or patience to dig through an ocean of man-gravel to find the one sapphire worthy of upsetting my routine, which tends to revolve around work and home-remodeling shows. I'm certainly not a virgin or prude. I love a good dick as much as any girl, but I've never moved quite this quickly, either. Is it me trying to escape my grief-filled day? The beer? My loneliness? His kisses? His good-guy vibe? His scent? His not trying to talk me into riding bareback?

Hell, they all try to go bareback. But not Max.

Crap. Five minutes ago I was up for almost anything, but now I'm not so sure. What the hell do I do?

I lift my face into the stream and start to second-guess both him and myself. Is he a bigger horndog than he seems? Is he infected with hawt-bartender STD?

Is he principled and kind and simply fetching condoms because it's the responsible thing to do?

I hear the rhythmic thuds of someone running up the stairs and it hits me. Micro dick. He's stalling because of a micro dick. Seen it before. Well, once, the day I tackled *Yes, I am a douchebag* Chris Duncomb away from sexually assaulting a freshman then stomped his balls. My crime-stopping earned me a two-week suspension filled with ice cream, a crap-ton of high-fives from my gram, and a new Wii, while Duncomb missed the rest of the semester and got a sex-crime notation in his resume.

I think I won that round but I *still* wish the girl had pressed charges. A couple years of jail time would have served the little pecker right.

Anyway, when I saw my first normal-sized dick in college, it actually scared me. I'd assumed they all were about the size of a thumb. Boy, was I wrong. Ultimately thankful, but wrong.

The bathroom door opens and Max comes in. No escape for me now. I brave a peek past the curtain to see him opening a Durex box, then he looks up to see me watching.

"Still want company?" he asks, setting the opened box aside.

I'm uncertain how far I want this to go, but I'm not really ready to say *hell no* either. My undercarriage is still thrumming with readiness and, damn, those kisses.

It's just been a really long time, and this is moving quickly, even for me.

He meets my gaze and blushes, and a lot of my hesitation rinses away. First, dudes with STDs don't blush, they bluster and deflect and repeatedly insist they're clean. Score another point in the Max column.

Second, just like Ellen said earlier today, sometimes it's about being touched, being human. And I want to be human with Max.

"Yeah," I admit, then watch him strip: shirt, shoes, jeans... Soon he's standing in Deadpool shorts and peeling off BB-8 socks. Once a dork, always a dork, I guess, and it makes me grin. "No Halo?"

We'd played a crap-ton of Halo in high school.

He laughs, bending a little to remove the shorts. "Nah, they're in the laundry. I *do* have Halo Five, but it's online co-op only. If you want to couch co-op, we could play Modern Warfare sometime, maybe Zombies. Gotta love undead splatter."

"Might as well play old-school House of the Dead at my granddad's house," I tease, but my voice fades when he straightens to toss his shorts in the hamper. He's not quite facing me, but there's no doubt he's sporting a thickish, standard-issue dick. It's beautiful to behold.

"You asking me on a date?" he asks, reaching for the shower.

"Maybe," I say as he steps in beside me. "My old Wii's still in the entertainment center. Probably still hooked up."

It's close quarters in the single-stall shower, and there's nowhere to hide anything anymore. Barefoot, I think I'm taller, not by much, but he's bigger overall. Thicker. Stronger. Heavier. And he's not looking at me. Well, not below my chin, anyway. I'm not looking down either.

"You shower with others very often?" he asks, tentatively placing a hand on my hip as I stretch around him to reach the soap.

"Nope. First time," I admit, rubbing the soap between my palms. His dick nudges wonderfully against my thigh, hotter than the water, and intrigues me in a delightful way.

He laughs, and I hear a plucked string of nervousness. "Same here. Why'd you suggest it, then?"

"I dunno." I hand him the soap. "It just sort of plopped out of my mouth." Then I grasp his dick in both hands.

The suds are slippery and his eyes grow wide and startled as I stroke him and soap his balls. He's definitely more than a handful, and that is just fine.

"Jesus, Berk," he manages to say, then he soaps his hands as well.

The water finally grows cold, so, laughing, we chase each other to the couch. I'm dripping wet and he has a line of soap on his cheek when he yanks the hide-a-bed open, the box of condoms in his other hand. He glances at the cheap sheets and a ratty floral comforter I recognize from his folks' house, from back when we were kids, then he winces. He mutters, "Fuck it," before reaching for me again.

We tumble onto the bed, damp limbs everywhere, then he's on top of me, body between my legs, kissing me, fingers magic and coaxing up my thighs. I hear rain pattering on the roof above us, and it's cozy, encouraging... erotic.

Our laughter fades as we grow serious, and he draws away. I assume he's grabbing a condom, but instead, he scoots down and devours me first.

⌒◠◠⌒

After, the sheets have dried our skin but our hair's still wet and we're tangled together, quivering and exhausted. I feel delightfully sated and he's snuggled beside me, cradling me in one arm while the other hand tilts my chin toward his kiss.

I wonder if he's questing for another romp, but he draws back enough to say, "So. House of the Dead at your place?"

"Sure!" I can't help but grin, there are so many great memories of playing that game with him. "As long as you bring the pizza."

"Pizza, huh?" He runs a finger over my breast, teasing my nipple awake again. "Seems fair. I have most mornings and all day Sunday open. Which work for you?"

"Any," I admit, stretching. "I'm always happy to take a break from sorting through papers and closets of dusty crap. My granddad doesn't want to look at anything, and I don't know what half of it even is. I've been here since night before last and don't feel like I've accomplished much."

Spending so much time with Max today hasn't helped me sort grandparent crap, but I don't mention that.

"Yeah, I remember how it was when my folks moved. We had to decide what to keep, what to trash, what to donate, what to sell. It's a lot of work."

And a lot of memories to sort through. "Your folks moved?" I ask, happy to change the subject. "I thought they'd live there forever."

"Yeah, well, Dad got downsized after the financial collapse, and Kelsey's bills started piling up, so they lost the house. They're over by the grocery store now."

Over by the grocery store. That's how folks from Fayerville say someone's living in the slummy part of town. I feel a pang of grief for Deb and Rick, good people who've lost their daughter, their home, and probably a lot more I don't know about.

I snuggle my head on Max's chest, yet one more thing I've never really done with a guy, and I hear his heart's steady beat beneath my ear. It's soothing. "So you're living here?"

"Yes," he sighs and holds me a little tighter. "I'd bought a bungalow across from the park, but my ex got it in the divorce. Along with pretty much everything else."

"That bites. Where will you go when your bar closes?"

"I dunno. Find an apartment or something, I guess. Mom and Dad don't have room, that's for sure. I don't even know if I'll stay here. Maybe I'll move to Decorah or Cedar Falls. Fayerville hasn't exactly been good to me."

"Me, either."

We both sigh and he turns his head to kiss me again, his hand still on my breast while I reach for his dick. It's relaxed some but pops right to attention at my touch, so I give it an encouraging squeeze.

"Be right back," I say against his lips as thunder rumbles from the storm outside, and he lets me go, watching as I scoot off the couch to fetch a fresh condom. My phone's on the floor, buzzing as usual, and the time above Dave's name says it's 8:22.

Thirty-eight minutes. Plenty of time to climb Mount Max again.

I rip the condom packet open with my teeth and wonder what life would have been like if we'd done this at seventeen instead of twenty-seven. If we'd been inexperienced, innocent kids.

If that rainy night had never happened. If I'd admitted I'd had a crush on him, back then. If he'd kissed me like he'd wanted to any of those countless times.

Maybe it's better this way, I think as I climb onto the hide-a-bed and roll the condom onto him. At least now we know what we're doing.

By the time we're done, it's pouring outside of Tony's and I'd be lying if I said I wanted to leave Max's little apartment. Or him. He feels like the only good thing in this soggy, fucking town.

Of course, I'm low on gas and have post-nookie munchies, so I scoot across the street to Kwik Shop. The awning mostly protects me from the rain as I squirt twenty bucks into my tank then dodge raindrops to buy something to fill the hole in my gut.

Inside, Lori 'rugrat plague' Sanderson's working the cash register. And she's glaring at me.

Greaaat. More drama.

I consider saying screw it and driving across town to Hardee's or some pizza joint, but I'm already in here and can't avoid her. I still have to pay for my gas.

There's not a lot of munchables to choose from. Oh, there are crunchy things and sweet things, but jack-diddly that actually tastes good. Like honey mustard pretzels. Or salted caramel anything. Forty-seven kinds of pop, but all the water's plain and the sandwiches are pasty-white-bread-blech.

Of course, there's plenty of beer, but I've had enough of that for one night.

Small town Iowa is nowhere to get decent gas station cuisine, just sayin'.

I grab some Gardetto's, a Snickers, and a Sprite, then set 'em on the counter. Lori looks at them, at me, at them again, then leans back, rubbing that skinny scar on her lip. "You just came from Max Jutland's bar, didn't you?"

I fish my wallet from my pocket, but she still hasn't rung up my snacks, or my gas. "Yep."

"He just bought rubbers. So. You fucking him?"

Pay cash? Credit? Which'll get me out of here quicker? I look up from my wallet and ask, "How much?"

She blinks at me. "How the hell am I supposed to know how much you're fucking Max Jutland?!?"

Jesus effing Christ. And I thought she was dumb in high school.

I finger the twenty folded beside my debit card, tempted to pay for the gas and walk out, just leave the munchables behind. "How much for my snacks?" There's a camera behind her, red light blinking at me.

And her.

I smile at it and think of all the prima-donna vocalists I've endured in my life.

She hisses, "If you think we're gonna stand aside and let you come back here and stir shit up again, well—"

"You asked if I'm fucking Max," I interrupt, holding the same bland smile. "Maybe I am, maybe I'm not. Maybe we chatted over a beer like the old friends we are, or maybe he fucked me up the ass right there on the bar while I blew the old hippie guy. You'll never know because it's none of your goddamn business, one way or the other. Hell, you're the one spooging-out sleaze-ball Bucky Sanderson's brats, the one screwing Bucky, the one sucking Bucky's oozy damn dick. Why should I care who you think I'm boinking?"

"His name is Walter," she snarls, leaning toward me.

"Bucky slept with every slut in school, including you and both of your bobble-headed friends, plus the meth-skanks over by the grocery store who'd banged every nasty-ass trucker passing through town. Everyone knew Bucky spread chlamydia, herpes, the clap... The dude was a walking plague, but you married him anyway. By the way, how'd his HIV test turn out? He got tested right before graduation, didn't he? *Everyone* was talking about it. AIDs. That's the big time. Did you and your BFF's get tested too? How'd that go? Are you all on maintenance meds?"

"Fuck you."

I drop the twenty on the counter to cover my gas. "How many times do I have to tell you that you're not my type? I like dick, remember?" I turn to go. "But *I've* never touched Bucky's. Eew. Nasty."

"His name is Walter, you skinny ass bitch!"

She cusses at my back as I walk out to the rain.

I'm still muttering when I cruise through Hardee's, and still wishing Lori would crawl into a hole and rot. Julia Gifford, one of Lori's best buds in high school is working the window. I just have that kind of luck tonight.

That's not fair, I remind myself. Max was pretty grand. My luck isn't so awful.

Jules barely glances at me as I hand over my debit card, so I have a moment to watch her. She looks rough around the edges, too thin, has a scribbly AC/DC tattoo on her thumb, and is missing several teeth. I wonder if she's developed a serious drug or drinking problem.

Not that I would be surprised. They did party pretty hearty, back when.

She's doing whatever fast-food window clerks do when running a card, then she stops, still staring at the computer screen, and her hand holding my debit card shakes.

Oh shit, I think as she turns to look at me. Her face has gone pale.

Then she bolts around the corner and out of my sight. The gray-haired woman working the counter cash register watches Julia scramble away and nearly drops a pack of curly fries. She sets the fries on a tray then follows Julia.

I wait while listening to Thorogood singing about being a steady rolling man, then a teenage boy hustles to the window only to duck out of my sight again.

He stands with my debit card in hand and the window opens.

"Sorry about that, Ma'am," he says, handing me my card. "We had a little mishap in the back. Your order will be right—"

The older woman trots up behind him with a bag in hand, and sets it beside him before filling a cup with Sprite.

The kid hands me my grub. "No charge Ma'am. Sorry for the inconvenience."

I take my grub and go, wondering why the hell I terrified Julia.

$$\sim\!\Omega\!\sim$$

Instead of going back to Tony's after my shower, I put a Talking Heads CD in Gram's player and get my butt to work. I bum-and-hum along to Tina Weymouth's rich bassline while creating order out of chaos in The Palace. By the time stuff's sorted into piles and boxes, it's well after midnight and I hear Granddad stumbling up the stairs.

I peek out of the Palace to see his walk of shame. Well, more like the stumble of exhaustion.

"Girlfriend a little rough on you tonight?" I ask, grinning.

"No more than usual," he says, opening the bathroom door. "Can you turn down your music? I need to get some sleep."

I turn it off—already listened to the album twice—then wander out to wait for him in the hall. He leaves the bathroom, yawning, and nods hello. "Sure you're all right?" I ask.

"Just tired. Had a bit more female companionship than I'm used to." He pauses to smile at me. "How about you? Did you have a good day?"

"The early parts sucked, but the evening was pretty good. Got to hang with Max Jutland."

Granddad blinks at me and smiles. "Max? How is he?"

"Good. Was nice catching up, but he's losing his bar."

Granddad nods, sighing, and he rubs his knuckle into his left eye. "Yeah,

Brad Duncomb's new development," he says, pulling the knuckle away and blinking before rubbing the eye again. "It's a damn shame. Your gram and I always liked grabbing a beer at Tony's after you kids' ball games."

"I remember," I say, and for a moment I want to go back to Tony's. Have one more beer, maybe sleep beside someone warm on a rainy night. Instead, I shrug and ask, "*Mayor* Brad Duncomb? I thought his kid—"

"No, it's all Brad, the Asshole of Fayerville," Granddad says, grumbling into his room.

I follow.

Granddad sits on the bed beside snoozing Bill who gives Granddad a one-eyed glare before snuggling beneath his tail again. "Remember Tony Hartford?" he says as he yanks off his boots.

"The guy who used to own Max's bar? Sure." Everyone knew Tony Hartford. A short, rotund fellow with a ready laugh, he played Santa at the holiday fair, co-sponsored the playground equipment in the city park, headed the music boosters, and was a sucker for any kid selling cookies or fundraising crap. He and his wife couldn't have kids, so they made up for it by helping the rest. All the kids knew it, too, so we all hung out at Tony's.

"Brad and Tony butted heads over Midtown Park, back when you were in middle school," he says, tossing his shirt and socks into the hamper. "Cost Brad a big development contract. Years later, he annexed that big field and went after Tony's bar out of spite, but Tony told him to bugger off then sold the bar to Max, supposedly for whatever he had in his wallet. Tony died not long after the sale, but Tony's remained open, thanks to Max."

"So why's it closing now?"

"New city council elections put Brad and his buddies on the council and they declared eminent domain on the whole side of the highway adjacent to the field. Everything had to be demolished so Brad's housing development could go in. Max told 'em to fuck off and refused to leave. Went all the way to the State Supreme Court, I heard."

"Shit. There's no way to help him?"

Granddad sighs and sits on the edge of his bed again. "I don't think so, and it's a damn shame. Rich assholes always seem to win, but their sewer lines clog up just the same." He rubs his forehead with a shaky hand.

"Sure you're okay?" I ask.

"Yeah. Just tired. Headache. Eye's a little blurry. Can you get the light?"

"Sure." I wish Granddad goodnight and make sure the door's open enough for Bill to get out before I go.

Thunder rumbles overhead followed by a sharper crack of lightning.

The hall lights flicker and Bill scrambles out of Granddad's room and down the stairs.

I hear Granddad's bed creak. "Berk! You all right?"

"I'm fine," I assure him, heading downstairs. "Gonna fetch a flashlight and get back to sorting."

The rain seems louder down here. It's lashing against the windows and rushing through the downspout by the kitchen door. I find the flashlight easily enough—top drawer by the fridge, the same place it's always been—and I walk to the living room windows before going upstairs.

The sky's a roiling, angry mess of purple-green clouds backlit by random flashes. The street out front flows downhill in a torrent and trees dance in the wind. Mrs. Flagg across the street is standing on her porch, gazing with admiration at the storm with her bathrobe clutched around her and a regal Springer Spaniel sitting beside her leg. She's smiling and I smile too, thinking of the times I'd watched clouds roll in with her. She'd make me a coffee and we'd discuss the coming storm and politics, which mostly meant I'd sip my oh-so-adult coffee and listen to her rail about politicians and pesti/fungi/herbicides killing the environment on purpose.

I never really agreed with her—except bees, all the dying bees worry me a great deal and Mrs. Flagg warned me about it before it ever happened—but she always treated me like I was smarter than I was.

Older than I was.

Like I was an equal, even when I was an eight-year-old kid. It's no wonder her kids grew up to be an off-grid organic farmer and a waterfowl migration specialist, which you have to admit sounds pretty cool.

At least that's what they were when we talked after Gram's funeral. They'd married, had kids, and seemed really happy.

The door behind Mrs. Flagg opens and her husband says something to her. The dog turns to go back in and she follows, giving one last hopeful smile to the sky.

Gram would like that, so I wipe the sting from my eyes and smile at the churning clouds.

Then I get back to work.

⁂

The power went out at some point because I wake to a blinking alarm clock, rain pattering against my window, and Bill pawing my cheek. I barely open my eyes when he mrows at me then scampers across my face and off the bed. My phone says it's not quite 6:30, damn cat.

Granddad's still asleep as I stagger downstairs. I reset the clocks on the microwave and stove while coffee brews. Bill munches away by my feet, softly purring, and I consider going back to bed. Instead, I sip my coffee and wander to the living room for the morning news.

I flump onto the couch and turn on the tube. A Kardashian got divorced,— like I give a shit—there is much yammering about men's basketball—again, I have no shits to give—and a bomb's exploded in some unpronounceable place in the Middle East. The President's running his fool mouth again, politicians gripe about other politicians being crooks and liars, Russia's moving tanks, China's fighting pollution, sushi is trendy, a woman in Louisiana's started a petition to outlaw curry—has she ever tasted curry? Yum!—and more houses are falling apart in Detroit. There's a preschooler who does motocross, an old couple prepare to hike the Appalachian Trail, Omaha and Sioux Falls are flooded, Nora Roberts has a new novel, then we're back to divorced reality TV idiots and basketball brackets before breaking for local news.

For us, that's KWWL in Waterloo. Once the breathless anchor teases a headline titled Cedar Falls City Council Crisis! they move to weather. Looks like pretty much the northern half of Iowa and all of the Dakotas are a mess, most of Minnesota is pouring-rain red, and the storm goes all the way to Winnipeg and beyond. Rain's not going away anytime soon.

Apparently, there's been some flooding. No surprise there. We've had a helluva lot of rain.

By this time, Bill's on my lap and is giving himself a bath. Don't remember him jumping up, but he's there and I'm already petting him before I notice. How do cats do that? One moment you have an empty lap and the next you realize you're petting them with no memory of anything between.

He's warm and purring, so I settle in and click through the channels. There's nothing interesting on, which reminds me why I don't watch much TV, but I guess an old Stargate rerun is all right. The ceiling creaks—Granddad on his way to the bathroom—so I escape from Bill's drowsy clutches and return to the kitchen to make breakfast.

I'm just finishing up when Granddad comes in, bright-eyed and freshly-shaven.

"How many ladies on the docket today?" I ask as I set a plate of eggs and hash browns before him.

He reaches for the salt and pepper. "None until tonight. Told them I need to get my garage straightened out and my tools packed before the auction folks come on Monday."

"You do know that's silly, right?" I say as I fork up some eggs. "How many tools are you going to take to the retirement center?"

"None. Well, maybe the bare-bones basics. Hammer, screwdrivers, a few wrenches. I'll be damned if I'll pay anyone to fix my leaky faucet or tighten my hinge."

I give him the *you have got to be shitting me* look. "You're renting an apartment at a retirement center. They're not gonna let you fix stuff."

"I'll fix anything I damn well please. Just last week, I unclogged Dot's sink drain. Couple of weeks before that, Maxine's car needed a new water pump."

"Are you using your handyman skills to woo the ladies?" I ask, laughing.

He gives me an ornery wink. "Maybe."

We eat for a while, then he says, "I really wish you'd take some of this stuff, Berk. Anything you want, it's yours. It doesn't all have to get sold."

"I have too much stuff as it is," I admit. "But I am looking as I clean, I promise. I found a couple of Gram's crocheted potholders I thought I could use, and I've set aside a casserole dish and some measuring cups. I might take the end table by the couch, maybe. Nothing too big, though. It all has to fit in my car."

"You're still taking Bill, right?"

I reach down to scritch his ears. "Yep. Not gonna let the old guy go to the shelter. Besides, I have plenty of moles in my yard. They'll keep him busy."

Thunder rumbles outside and we both sigh. It's rained every day I've been here and it'd be nice to see the sun.

By midafternoon, Dave's made my butt buzz more times than I care to count, but Max hasn't called.

Not that I'm upset about it or anything, I just expected him to. Sort of. I mean, he wanted me to stay over, even talked about bringing pizza and playing House of the Dead like old times. We hit it off, right?

Shit, I dunno, but he doesn't seem like a one-night-stand kind of guy.

The auction company had given Granddad a sheet of instructions explaining how to prepare for them to prepare for the auction, which, if you think about it, is rather circular logic. Right? I've read the crazy thing roughly sixteen times now, and I've been very careful not to throw anything away except actual garbage. I mean, seriously, who's gonna want Gram's craft-store receipts for wood glue and brads? Nobody, that's who. I've been careful not to set aside or remove anything from the house except what Granddad's taking to the retirement home and the few odds and ends I can use. I don't need furniture, Granddad's leaving most of his tools... I *did* remove the boxes of crafty scraps for school kids, which I really ought to deliver despite it still pouring outside, but I cannot for the life of me imagine anyone's gonna pay more than a buck or two for pompoms, half-used bottles of paint, old markers, or a big stack of colored paper.

Still, I don't know. Maybe I should bring them back in? Maybe I should drop them off then stop by to visit Kelsey for a few minutes?

Maybe I should call Max or drive over for a beer?

Something, anything, so I don't have to clean Danny's room.

I've been cleaning the house as I go, dusting, washing curtains, scrubbing light fixtures and baseboards, the whole nine yards, so the place is looking pretty spiffy, even with the boxes of stuff in each cleared room. With The Palace as done as it's gonna get, Danny's room is next. Gram and I tried, and failed, to clean it a few weeks after his funeral.

We never tried again.

I find myself standing outside his door with a steaming bucket in my hand, afraid to go in. He was, in a lot of ways, the first man in my life.

I've never met my father. Mom told me once he wasn't interested in a relationship with anyone, just a friends-with-benefits kind of hookup. As for a kid? Nope, not gonna happen. He knew about me but didn't care. I looked him up on Facebook a long time ago, and spent a few minutes scrolling through his public posts and pics. Still single, still no kids to claim, still living the party life, still couch-surfing and mooching off his friends. So no great loss there.

When Mom dropped me off here the summer between first and second grade, I was not quite seven and Granddad and Danny were the only guys I knew. Granddad worked all the time managing his plumbing crews and fixing pipes over several counties, so he wasn't home a lot. Danny, though, just twelve and an unexpected late baby for my grandparents, was about to go to middle school, and he showed me, well, pretty much everything. Bike riding, skateboarding, baseball, football, Doctor Who, video games, carrying stuff up ladders, and basic self-defense. He taught me how to spit and change a tire and dive off the high plank at the pool. All the important things.

An IED took him away from me, away from all of us, and I really don't want to revisit all that and start bawling again.

But I have to. Granddad's certainly not gonna do it.

So I reach for the door.

Miss you, Danny. Love you. Always.

～◯～

Between the rain, cleaning, and all this damned grief, I'm exhausted and kind of cranky by suppertime. Danny's room wasn't as bad as The Palace, but it still sucked sorting and cleaning his personal stuff; mostly clothes, video games, books, and movies. I thought about keeping a couple of old favorites—like a VHS boxed-set of the first three Star Wars films before Lucas screwed with them—but I decided not to. I don't have a VHS player, hell, I don't even have a DVD player anymore, so they'd just end up in a box in my basement or attic. I don't need more clutter, good memories or not, so I left them in the bookcase.

I am, however, perfectly willing to smoke Danny's decade-old weed he'd stashed under his mattress, especially if it helps me get out of this funk.

Granddad's staying over with some member of his harem tonight—I didn't ask who was tonight's winner—so I toss a frozen pizza into the oven and settle in to channel surf. There ain't shit on network TV besides fucking basketball. Boise versus Oklahoma State, which immediately goes to commercial.

I decide to go ahead and light that joint. It tastes like crap but beggars can't be choosers, can they? Here's hoping it lightens my mood.

I used to enjoy basketball, back when. I was a guard on our team, nothing extraordinary, but not shitty either. Started a few games, was the first sub on a lot more. We even had winning seasons my tenth and eleventh grade years. Never made it past district finals, but we were decent, I guess, and small towns in Iowa sure do love their winning high school sports teams. Fayerville is no exception. Half the town was football crazy the year our team was on the road to the playoffs, at least until I busted rapin' QB Chris Duncomb's left nut. Two Marches later, people literally danced in the streets and tour buses were booked to take damn near the entire town to Des Moines because the Fayerville Ravens boy's basketball team was *Going To State*.

They'd had a near perfect season and were favored to win the trophy. Was a huge deal for almost everyone.

Then I screwed up that championship too.

Commercials end and the game comes back. Cowboys 19, Broncos 15. Sounds more like a prime-time NFL score.

I flip through the channels again. Shitty network comedy reruns. Shitty network cop show reruns. Shitty Classic black-and-white TV rerun crap. And Nature: Aardvarks.

Three more minutes until pizza according to my timer, so I take another drag of Danny's shitty-tasting joint and click back to the game. It's either that or aardvarks. Shitty damn aardvarks and their shitty joints and shitty lifetime of clutter to sort through.

I wonder if any college teams are the Aardvarks and if they're in the tournament this year.

Surely that's the pot hitting me already—haven't smoked a single puff since college—and I giggle. Then some cute, bald-headed, black kid playing for Oklahoma gets a three-pointer.

Jameson Corey bumps the score to 28 - 17.

I fucking hate Cory.

Doesn't matter what the cops say. He took Kelsey away from me. Away from all of us.

Intermezzo—Ninth Grade

The hallway was starting to fill with freshmen when Kelsey jiggled her locker open and slid her Biology book into the stack between Geometry and Spanish, all tenth-grade classes. She yawned and glanced at the digital clock stuck inside the locker door. 10:24. Enough time to pee, if she hurried. She reached for her Creative Writing folder then jolted aside as a boy with a large hand slammed the door.

Cory again. Great.

"What?" she asked without looking at him and pushed his hand aside. She spun the combination wheel to reopen her locker. "I need to get my stuff then use the restroom. If I'm late, I'll get a zero on today's quiz."

"Friday. You. Me. Pizza. Shit, Kelse, I'll even pay for it all. A movie. Burgers. Stock car races in Cedar Falls. Weekend in the Caymans. *Anything*. Please."

She got the door open and snagged her folder and books for her afternoon classes before turning to face him. "I can't. I told you. Ask someone else."

"I can't ask anyone else. You know that."

She rolled her eyes and closed her locker. "That's BS and you know it. Gobs of decent girls would go out with you, no strings attached. Ask Gayle or Danica or—"

He leaned close and lowered his voice to a hiss. "No one in this school is going to believe I'd ask any of the loser girls out."

She whispered, "I don't know what you expect me to do if you won't take responsibilit—"

"One date. Just one," he whispered back. "We can say it was wild and awesome, then I can break it off because I need to focus on basketball and you can pretend you're crushed and—"

He stopped when she gave him a *seriously?* glare, her arms crossed over her chest.

"No."

She turned to go, but he followed.

"C'mon, Kelsey. Please," he said from right behind her. "You are the only girl—"

She grabbed his arm and dragged him into the alcove in front of the keyboarding lab's door. "Stop. Just stop. I'm not going to lie for you."

"A date isn't a lie, not exactly. It's just a date. One date. Hell, we're both in drama. We can even fake one kiss. Pretend it's a play and we're on a stage. It'll buy me some time to—"

"I'm not going to let you use me like this, when you need to stand up for yourself instead of hanging the lie all on me. I understand you're scared, but surely your folks will—"

"They won't."

"It's 2006, not 1956. Everyone will be cool. You'll see. Your folks won't mind that you're gay."

"Really?" He leaned back against the wall and said, "Tell that to Jake Milton."

"Oh come on. It's so not the same."

"It's exactly the same. Disowned by his family, beat up I dunno how many times—"

"I seem to remember you were part of one beating."

He continued, undaunted, "—three weeks in the hospital, then off to foster care. *Then* what happened, Kelse?"

"It's not the same. He was already an outcast. You're... You're Cory Hildebrandt, jock, class clown, popular—"

"What happened to Jake Milton?" he asked again, his voice soft.

She looked at the floor and swallowed bitter shame from her mouth. "He died."

"He took a bottle of hydrocodone, washed it down with cheap vodka, and eliminated himself from the problem."

Kelsey took a breath and raised her gaze. "You are not a problem. You're just you. But I can't lie for you. I'm sorry, I really am, but—"

"Cory!" a girl squealed from behind Kelsey and she turned to see the hallway mob make way for Lori Gilbert, grinning her annoying grin and bookended by her matching wing-girls. "I see you're slumming again."

"Not this time," Cory said, knocking Kelsey aside as he strode to the crowded hall. "Just trying to get answers to the English test. Fucking bitch won't share."

"We share," a wing girl said, grabbing his left arm, while her partner swooned against the right. One was Brittany Miller, the other Julia Gifford. Kelsey had known them since kindergarten but had been unable to tell them apart since they discovered bleached hair and neon-colored sweatsuits with JUICY across their butts.

Kelsey rolled her eyes. She had no idea why *anyone* would label their butt 'juicy'.

Lori, all of five foot two and disdainful of anyone not in her court of adoration, took a step closer to Kelsey. She, too, had bleached her hair to near white and it shone like a beacon over her black blouse and plaid Tripp miniskirt. She looked Kelsey up and down before smirking. "You ain't shit, brainiac."

"No, I'm not," Kelsey said, holding her ground. "I'm mostly water, some calcium, some iron, a smattering of electrolytes and amino acids..."

"All those brains, you'd think you could mind your own business," Lori said as the kids in the hall behind her fell silent. "And your mitts off Cory."

"My mitts are nowhere near Cory. I promise." And yours aren't either, she thought. You might be rich and your dad might help run this crappy town, but I'm the top of the class. Already have colleges calling me. I just have to survive 'til graduation then I'm pre-Med somewhere, but this is the best you'll ever be. An ignorant bitch in an over-priced trend.

Lori blinked once. Slow. "You got something to say?"

"Nope."

"C'mon, I got better shit to do than fuck with a nerd," Cory said. "You ladies wanna escort me to P.E.?"

Lori tossed her head and walked away, miniskirt swaying. The crowd parted for her.

Kelsey walked into the crowded hall, straightening her books, then turned headlong into Jack Scheffert, a year ahead of her and a fellow Talented-And-Gifted kid. The collision knocked books and papers from their hands to a sprawling, erratic mess of Math, Science, and Lit across the floor.

"Crap, I'm sorry," Kelsey said, kneeling and wondering if she'd ever get a chance to pee. She snatched up Jack's copy of *1984* before a Prep stepped on it.

"Not your fault," Jack said, his voice soft as he accepted the book from her. "I didn't dodge quick enough."

She'd rarely heard him speak except during their TAG classes. A couple of times a month they, and seven other students, were pulled from their classes to explore stuff outside of the regular curriculum. Trips to the science center in Waterloo or to see a ballet in Cedar Rapids. A writing workshop by a sci-fi novelist brought in from Massachusetts. Making a robot in the science lab. Just last week, they'd had a presentation from a surgeon about careers in medicine and taken a tour of the hospital's surgery wing. Jack, usually so quiet and still, always perked up and asked great questions during TAG. And it was the only time he smiled.

Which was a shame. He had a nice smile. A *kind* smile.

While other students rushed by muttering about nerds in the way, Kelsey and Jack spent a few moments trying to decide which Algebra II book was hers or his, or if the worksheets from Accounting were for his Accounting 2 or her Accounting 1, along with gathering and sorting the other papers and notebooks, most of which were hers. When they finished the sort, she gathered up her messy armload and he offered a hand to help her stand.

"See you in Algebra," she said, grinning as she backed toward her Creative Writing class.

"I'll be there," he replied, smiling at her despite getting nudged aside by a stoner muttering into a cell phone.

She bit her lower lip and, blushing, turned to go.

"Hey Kelse?" he called out through a thinning crowd.

She turned back. "Yeah?"

"Don't let The Bleaches get you down. They're not worth it."

Then he winked and trotted away.

Berk

Someone's knocking on the front door, and it's... Shit. Six fifty-four in the morning.

I haul my ass out of bed and stagger out wearing my oh-so-stylish Smashing Pumpkins t-shirt and ratty sweatpants. Granddad's bedroom door is wide open—his bed unslept in—so he's still out tom-cattin', my mouth tastes like shitty pizza and stale weed, and some motherfucking asshole's pounding on the goddamn door before the sun's even up.

"I'm a fucking musician," I mutter as I reach the bottom of the stairs. "This is past my fucking *bed*-time, not *get-up-it's-a-gorgeous-fucking-day*-time."

For the record, it obviously ain't gonna be a gorgeous fucking day since rain's still dashing against the kitchen windows.

I decide Granddad must've forgotten his keys as I undo the deadbolt and the pounding stops. I open the door, about to flip Granddad shit about waking me before dawn, but my words evaporate before I can start them.

It's Max. He's rumpled, drenched, and muddy, and he's carrying a Casey's breakfast pizza.

"Hey," he says, looking at the porch floor before raising his gaze to me. "I didn't want to wake you, but..." He sighs. "I promised to stop by."

He swallows and holds the pizza out to me. "And bring pizza."

"Get in here," I say, motioning him in and accepting the pizza. "What happened? Did Kelsey..."

He leans his hip against the wall by the door and wriggles off his soaked and squishy sneakers. "Kelse's the same, as far as I know," he says around a yawn before peeling off a sodden sock. "Storm sewer broke and my folks' place flooded the middle of the night after you left. I've spent all that time since getting what Mom and I could out of her house."

"Is she okay? Where'd she go? Where's your dad?"

He manages to get out of his coat and hang it on the coat tree. "Dad's in Houston with his new job and Mom's fine, other than being upset over losing half the furniture and almost everything in the basement," he says, shivering, and the toes of his pale, water-wrinkled feet dig into the carpet. "We're wet and exhausted and hoping Dad's job lets him come back up here. I told her she could stay at my place until we figure out what to do."

"You're gonna get warm, is what you're gonna do," I say on my way to the kitchen with the pizza. "Take a hot shower and I'll see if there's anything in Danny's room you can wear. You can stay here. Or your mom can. Or whatever. At least until stuff gets figured out. We certainly have space."

"A hot shower sounds *great*," he says, following me to the kitchen doorway but staying on the warm living room carpet instead of venturing to chilly kitchen tile. "Thanks, Berk."

I turn on the oven to preheat. "It's no problem at all."

When I stand and turn around he's still staring—and grinning—where my butt used to be. "So," he says, meeting my gaze. "Wanna help me take that shower?"

"Now that you mention it," I say, grinning back, "I haven't had mine yet."

"Might as well save water," he says, holding out a hand to me.

I take it. Sounds like a great way to start the day.

The sex is less frantic this time. Awkward at first then gentle and curious. Like we're figuring each other out, finding the little details of what works or what doesn't.

Now that I have a moment to think, I'm not sure if I like that. I mean, the sex was awesome after the first few nervous moments. Seriously. Awesome. I just have not made a habit of repeating partners. The one other guy I fucked two separate times during college ended up being a royal pain in my ass for months. Bastard thought he owned me, like his dick had laid claim to my entire life. Screw that, right? I just want to get laid and get on with my day, not have a goddamn relationship.

But this morning with Max, the sex rapidly became more *connected* than I've had before, which probably sounds batshit insane. Hadn't seen or spoken to him for a decade, then jumped on his dick a couple of nights ago to blow off some steam, but today I couldn't keep my hands off him while he looked me in the eye and took his time and figured out what *I* liked, like he was a potter and I was his clay. As for me, I just wanted to eat him up. Rawr, and all that shit.

Hell, I don't even know if Max came. I *think* so, but after I finished he kissed me and left me in my bed to quiver while he cleaned up.

I do not fucking quiver. Nor do I sprawl like a satisfied zombie in a puddle of my own making.

Yet here I am.

And I'm not sure if I like this either, now that I think about good-guy Max and how he used to be. Gawd, I hope he's not going to ask for a commitment or something because it is *not* gonna happen.

The sink finishes and I hear the toilet flush—I can only assume it's the condom's funeral dirge—then he's walking back to me, yawning. Still sexy. Still hard. And I still want to eat him up even though he's surely exhausted.

I don't do repeat sex. I *don't*. Yet here I am. What the hell's wrong with me?

"That was fun," he says, plunking down beside me.

"Yes, it was." I curl in his embrace and snuggle his chest like I've been doing it for forty-seven years or some shit. He smells yummy-man-stuff-amazing.

"Wanna go again?" he asks, eyebrows waggling.

I find it endearing. *Endearing.* Even with his fresh yawn.

Maybe I've entered the twilight zone, but I'm about to say sure, because *damn.* Then his stomach grumbles. "Aw, shit. The pizza!"

I scramble over him—taking one quick moment to slurp all of that lovely dick into my mouth while giggling at his startled gasp—then I yank on my tee and sweats before sprinting for the hall.

"Danny's clothes are on my dresser," I call out as I reach the stairs. "Take whatever fits."

"What if I want to stay naked?" he hollers after me. "Does that mean we can eat in bed?"

Images of a whole lazy day of cold pizza and napping and delightful Max sex flicker through my brain, but the ceiling creaks as he walks across my room. "Whatever you want to do," I holler back.

By the time I hear him come down the stairs, the pizza's piping hot and its aroma makes my stomach grumble. I set it on the counter and fetch a couple of plates.

"I just grabbed the clothes on top," he says on his way through the living room.

"It's fine," I say as I stack the plates on the counter near the pizza. "Do you want coffee? Pop?"

"You," he says, entering the kitchen. He's wearing flannel lazy-day pants and a thermal shirt, the same uniform Danny wore while camped on the couch playing Genesis all day.

Seeing Max in Danny's clothes makes my vision flicker, like they're both standing there.

Then it's just Max with a boner saluting me from beneath the flannel.

Torn between missing Danny and wanting Max, I flip open the pizza box and snag a slice. "Better eat up, Buttercup, and we'll shoot some zombies. Then maybe we'll go back upstairs."

⌒⌒⌒

After scarfing a couple of slices of pizza and wasting a couple of dozen zombies, I leave Max to play House of The Dead while I run upstairs to get his muddy clothes in the wash. I'm gone three, maybe four minutes, tops, but come back to find him snoring on the couch, Wii-Gun still clenched in his hand, and GAME OVER on the TV screen.

So I cover him with one of Grams afghans and let him sleep.

I consider going back to bed myself, but instead clean up the little mess we made in the kitchen and brew a fresh pot of coffee.

I'm definitely going to need it today. It's barely eight-thirty and Dave's already started buzzing.

About halfway through my first cup, Granddad walks through the kitchen door. His hair's a mess, his eyes are bleary, and he staggering.

At least he's not sopping wet and muddy. That batch of laundry's almost done.

"Ladies a bit harsh on you last night?" I tease.

"No more than usual," he says around a yawn. "Whose Chevy's parked in my driveway?"

"Max's," I say, peering innocently at Granddad from over my coffee cup. I pause, expecting to be fed a measure of shit but Granddad fills his own coffee mug and sits at the table.

"About damn time," he takes a sip of coffee. "Where is he? Did you break him?"

"No, I did not break him; he's asleep on the couch. And what do you mean *about damn time?*"

"I'm not blind or a fool, Berk. That boy's loved you since before his voice changed." He wraps his hands around his steaming mug and pauses, his head tilting. "Why's he sleeping here, let alone on my couch?"

I explain about Max's folk's place getting flooded and moving his mom to the bar, coming here, the pizza, laundry, and shooting zombies.

I skip over the boinking part.

Max

Max opened his eyes to a gray tabby cat on his chest, staring at him.

"Oh, hey, Bill," he said, petting the cat. "Where's Berk?"

Bill purred.

"You're no help."

Holding the cat, Max sat and stretched a kink out his neck. Someone had turned off the TV and Wii, but the guns remained handy on the coffee table. "Berk?" he called out as he set Bill aside and stood.

"In the kitchen!"

He found her barefoot and flipping sandwiches at the stove, stunning in scuffed jeans and an over-sized gray sweatshirt with her hair piled on her head in a loose floof. Grandpa Ted sat at the kitchen table with a cup of coffee and a stack of papers. Berk's phone buzzed near her usual sitting-spot with DAVE on the screen. Neither seemed to notice.

"Wondered if you were going to sleep through lunch," Ted said, motioning Max to sit. "Don't suppose you know anything about rental agreements?"

"No, can't say that I do," Max said, sitting. "Last place I rented was the shitty apartment I had after college. My name wasn't even on the lease."

"Was that the place with the roaches?" Ted asked

Berk set a plate piled with grilled ham-and-cheese sandwiches on the table. "That's gross, and it's lunchtime."

"Actually, it was bedbugs," Max said, watching her return to the stove. "I ended up leaving my bed behind and burning most of my clothes."

"Grosser," she commented, stirring a pot before rummaging around in the utensil drawer. "About the only thing worse might be earwigs. Maybe. They're *nasty*." She found a bright red ladle and dunked it in the pot. "Soup's done. Eat up."

She ladled herself a bowlful of soup and carried it and a plate back to the table.

Max breathed in the heady aroma of homemade cheesy sausage soup—

looked and smelled exactly like Berk's grandmother's—as he filled his bowl and returned to the table. He'd eaten little beyond takeout and microwaved crap for months and his belly rumbled in happy anticipation.

"The retirement home allows me only one parking space," Ted said as he returned to his seat. "I need three."

Berk rolled her eyes and dunked her sandwich into the soup. "You do not need your '67 Mustang or the damn trailer."

"I love that car."

Berk's phone buzzed DAVE again, but she didn't glance at it as she jabbed toward Ted with her soup-soaked sandwich. "You can't get out of it without help. It's too low and your knees are too shitty."

"Chicks dig 'Stangs." Ted slurped some soup and gave Max a conspiratorial wink.

"You have eight girlfriends already! How many *chicks* do you need?"

Max grinned, happily listening as they ate. He'd sat at this same table many times growing up, Berk's grandmother stuffing him and his sister full of food while everyone at the table bantered wherever the conversation shifted.

He was on his third sandwich—and Dave had buzzed in four times—when Berk's phone chirruped the opening of a Green Day tune.

Everyone fell silent and turned to blink at the phone.

"What the hell?" Berk muttered, picking it up. "No one calls me but Dave."

"Yo," she said, shrugging at the two men, then she broke out in a grin. "Oh, hey, Shel! Of course, I remember you. What's up?"

Max continued to eat but stopped when Berk's smile fell.

"Oh my God," she said. "Is she all right?"

Ted and Max shared a confused and concerned look as Berk got up from the table.

"Aw, shit. Goddamn. Okay," she said as she walked to the living room. "Of course I can."

Both men watched her pace just beyond the kitchen doorway, phone crushed against her ear.

"*Tomorrow?*" She glanced at Ted who gave her a thumb's up, then returned to her call. "Sure. I'll take care of it. No, it's no trouble, even the short notice. Absolutely. And you do have a venue, right?"

Berk stopped pacing. "Got it. We'll be there, I *promise*, so start telling people. We'll need to start setting up about two hours before show time."

She finished the call and, frowning, returned to the table, phone in hand.

"Well?" Ted asked. "Where are you going and when will you be back?"

Berk flumped onto her chair. "Back to Charleston and just for the weekend.

Remember my next-door-neighbor, Lois? She took a bad fall Monday and broke a couple of bones. Medicare's covering most of the medical stuff, but they're not covering the *life* stuff, let alone someone to help her take care of herself or refurb her house so she can get around in it." Dave buzzed on her phone, and Berk picked it up. "Her daughter wants to do a benefit for her tomorrow and asked me to rustle up a band. Turning down an unexpected cash job's one thing, but I can't turn down Lois. She watches over my house every time I'm out of town, collects my mail, waters the plants... Heck, she even bakes me cookies on the holidays. I need to help her."

She gave Max and Ted a stiff smile as Ted nodded and resumed eating his lunch, then Berk swiped to pick up the call. "Dave! Long time no chat!"

Berk ate while Max heard a faint male voice yakking a constant stream of pleading excitement from within her phone.

"Thirty-second radio ad in Poughkeepsie for three hundred apiece? Nah, not interested," she said. "What do you think, though, about a benefit concert in Charleston? They promised to feed us."

Berk took another bite of her sandwich and chewed until the yakking slowed down. "Just you, so far. I figured it was easier to wait for you to call back *again* before trying to call anyone else. Jesus, Dave. You called twenty-three times yesterday. Twenty. Three."

Max continued to eat while watching Berk and hoped he didn't look as bummed as he felt. She's going to be gone for the whole weekend?

"My neighbor had an accident. Lois... Yep, that one... Tomorrow at seven, set up at five. Can you get a keyboardist and a sound tech? I'll get the rest." She met Max's gaze and smiled. "Awesome. See you tomorrow!"

Then she grinned. "It's been forever since I played for an audience!"

Max wanted to ask, You're *sure* you're coming back for another week or so, right? But instead, he said, "Cool. Congratulations. What kind of music will you be playing?"

"Depends on which vocalist I can shake out of the trees. Pop or blues, most likely, maybe classic rock. If Chad's open this weekend we'll do requests all night and we could leap from Tony Bennett to Limp Bizkit to Beyoncé."

Ted chuckled. "I was there the night he did Liza Minnelli. Straight up perfect and funny as hell. You guys raised a lot of money that time, didn't you?"

"Yeah. About three times more than they'd pie-in-the-sky hoped, and his David Lee Roth, Garth Brooks, and Adele were perfect too. I'll call him as soon as I finish eating. Can't half-ass him like I can Dave."

Ted nodded in familiar understanding as he polished off the last of his lunch. "Yeah, he's popular and probably busy."

"Not so much busy as... *unique*." She leaned forward to say to Max, "Chad's really high maintenance." She sighed and leaned back. "Really high."

"Like no brown M&M's in the break room high?" Max asked.

Berk laughed. "No, that's to make sure venues read the safety part of a contract. Chad's more everyone has to treat him like he's hot-shit." Then she sighed. "He kind of is, though, at least for freelance live performers in Appalachia. Such a pain in the ass, but audiences love him."

"I'm meeting Dot at one. You kids be good." Ted stood, kissing Berk on the forehead before putting his dishes in the sink and heading out to the rain.

Berk finished her soup and took a breath. "Wish me luck," she said to Max as she scrolled down her phone screen.

"Get 'im," he said.

Berk put her phone on speaker and set it on the table beside her.

After two rings, a man said, "Berk!"

"Hey, Scott. Is Chad booked for tomorrow?"

"No, he's not. It's been almost a month and I'm about to skin him if I can't get him out of the apartment and my hair for a while. Whatcha got?"

"My next door neighbor took a bad fall and her family's doing a rush-rush-to-pay-bills bennie. They just called me."

"Your neighbor? The funny old bird or the talkative fat gal?"

Berk grinned. "Funny old bird. Payment's supper. And what's wrong with Abbie? She's awesome, too."

"Nothing! She's delightful! Chad just has a soft spot for chatty fat chicks, not so much old birds, so she'd be an easier sell." Scott paused, and Max heard a few odd clicks. "Supper homemade or catered?"

"No idea, but I'm betting on homemade."

Max picked up her lunch dishes and she nodded a thank you.

"Standard seven to midnight?" Scott asked.

"Yep, or whenever the band wears out. He's my first call, other than Dave. Let him know that, if you think it'll help."

"Okay, gimme a couple of minutes to grease the wheels. Might be tough, this short of notice. Hang on, okay?"

"You betcha!"

Berk stood and left the phone sitting while she gathered the last bits of lunch mess from the table and stashed the leftovers in the fridge. "I always want to play the Jeopardy theme while I wait."

"You can't call him back, or have him call you?"

"Oh hell no. *High maintenance*." She made air quotes as she walked to the sink. "Might take two minutes, might take thirty. If the call goes dead, it's a definite no."

"Ah," he said as she turned on the sink faucet. Seemed like a screwy way to conduct business, especially something so rushed.

She tested the temp with the back of her wrist and asked, "So. You wanna come with me to Charleston this weekend? I can get you back here by suppertime Sunday, if we leave before dawn Sunday morning. You'll only miss a day and a half of work."

"I don't know," Max admitted. "Between my folks' place, Kelsey, fighting the city..."

"I understand," Berk said, nodding as she squirted in some dish soap. "No worries."

"You'll come back, though. Right? For this next week?"

"I don't know." Berk shrugged before sliding silverware and three glasses into the dishwater. "I've cleaned and cleared most of the house, everything but the basement, attic, and Granddad's personal stuff," she said, running a scrubby sponge through a glass. "What's left is mostly digging through boxes and books looking for forgotten valuables. That's a tedious sit-down job and he doesn't need me for it. Hell, he could invite his harem over for a day and let them help."

Max didn't know what to say, so he grabbed a dish towel and accepted the glass from her sudsy hand.

Glasses finished, she slid in plates and bowls. "Can I admit something?"

"Anything," he said as he put dried glasses in the cupboard.

"I don't want to be here. The weather's shit, every room has been a slog through sad memories, Granddad's always out banging his groupies, and almost every place I've been in town, I've run into..." She shrugged. "People who hate me for, well, wrecking everything."

Silence dragged then she said, "It's like what's the point, ya know?"

"Oh," he said, drying a plate despite the bottom falling out of his gut.

She turned to face him. "You and your bar are the only bright spots in my entire visit. I have to help my neighbor. I couldn't look her in the eye ever again if I didn't step up, but I..." She sighed and managed a worried smile. "I like *feeling human* with you. Not sure I'm ready to give that up yet."

"What do you mean feeling human?"

"Part of it's the sex," she admitted, her cheeks brightening as she returned to washing dishes. "Part—a big part, actually—is I can relax with you and just be *me*. That probably doesn't make any sense."

"Nah, I get it," he said. "There's Berkeley Williams, edgy musician and town outcast, and there's Berk, who sorts through a lifetime of other people's stuff and holds my sister's hand while reminiscing about eating crab on the beach."

She smiled, sad and wistful, as she finished up the dishes. "I lied. Well, a little. Drank iced tea and ate a food-truck polish sausage on the beach, then scarfed crab and beer in a local crab shack on the highway. But it sounded, I dunno, more postcard romantic to have the crab on the beach." She turned her head to meet Max's gaze. "I only say good things to Kelsey, hopeful, happy things, even if I have to embellish a little."

"My mom does too. I always tell Kelse the bald truth. She's a good sounding board when I need to work out a problem. She just *listens*, ya know, and is a lot cheaper than a counselor."

Berk laughed and, for a moment, all was right with his world. He wondered how much extra he'd have to pay Gretchen to work the next couple of full days, and if he could afford the overtime along with the cost of a weekend getaway.

"What about your dad?" she asked, breaking his train of thought as she rinsed and dried her hands.

"He doesn't talk to her. He barely visits her. Hasn't for years."

"I'm sorry. That must be tough on your mom."

"She manages, I guess. He comes home for a long weekend a couple of times a month, but they argue and he goes right back to Texas a day or two later. I know Mom wants her marriage back, but Dad needs to move forward, yet Mom's tied to Kelsey, and round and round they go."

"Is that why they're not treating the pneumonia?"

"Probably. It's been a whole decade and we all know she's never going to get better. My sister died in that shed, the part that was *her* anyway. Dad and I wanted to let the rest of her go a couple of times before, but Mom always fought to keep her."

"So what changed her mind?" Berk asked.

A voice on her phone called out her name but she kept her attention on Max.

"Dad moving to Houston, I think. It's tough to be married when you're almost twelve hundred miles apart. Go," he said, motioning toward her phone on the kitchen table. "Bag your vocalist."

While Berk sat at the table and tried to woo the dude on the other end of the call, Max pulled his cell from the pocket of his borrowed pants and dialed Gretchen.

Berk had been on the phone with Chad for more than half an hour when Max, once again dressed in his own freshly-washed clothes, pulled on his coat and shoes. "Call me when you're done," he said and she nodded, scowling at the phone in her hand.

"I'm sorry," she whispered.

"I know. Just call as soon as you're done."

Then he walked out to the rain.

He drove to Tony's through dreary drizzle, berating himself for wanting to go, then berating himself for possibly leaving Gretchen to manage alone—assuming she could find someone to watch her kids—then for wanting to get the hell out of town on a—hopefully—cheerful weekend, then for not being there for his customers the last full weekend before he'd close. A weekend with Berk or the bar? Responsibility or fun? What the hell do I choose?

"Shit," he muttered as he pulled behind the bar and parked his Cobalt beside his mom's old Buick.

"Bout time you dragged yourself in," Gretchen teased as he walked through the back door. The regular gang nursed their regular drinks in their regular places, and a handful of occasional customers chatted over cards or beers. Silent Jack, again, sat scowling and alone in a booth, staring out at the street while steadily sipping gin and lime. Someone had decided to play Garth Brooks on the juke and Gretchen hummed along while pouring an orange daiquiri.

Max smiled. Was nice to see the place busy, even if he only had one more week of business.

"Had a pretty good day yesterday, considering," Gretchen said as she handed Karen her drink and scooped ice into a highball glass for her next order. "Seven hundred thirty-seven in the cash bag, after restocking the drawer. But we're out of bottle beer, less than half a keg of Miller Light left, and Dwight had a bad night so we're short on TP." She glanced Max's way before pouring in grapefruit and cranberry juice. "Doing all right on wells, though, and I think we're set on the good stock. Probably be enough of that left for you to throw a helluva a party after you close up."

"How many more orders do you have waiting?" Max asked as Gretchen reached for the well vodka and the limes.

"Just this sea breeze, then I'm good for now. Why? What's up?"

"We need to talk."

Max walked to Mitch and leaned over to speak privately. "Can you keep an eye on things long enough for Gretchen and I to have a quick meeting? Shouldn't take more than a few minutes."

"Sure thing," Mitch said as Max turned away. "How's your mom?"

Max turned back. "Fine, I guess. Considering. Got her moved in upstairs. Thanks for letting us use your truck, by the way. I didn't get much chance to thank you before."

"Don't mention it."

They shared a nod then Max walked to the hall, motioning for Gretchen to follow him to the office.

"Aw, shit," she muttered on her way down the hall. "You're letting me go, aren't you?"

"Not as long as we're still open." He held the office door open for her. "You said we have seven thirty-seven in petty cash?"

"Yep. Counted it last night."

He closed the door. "All right. You remember that girl from the other night?"

"Yeah, Berk, the skinny chick with the smart mouth," Gretchen said, leaning against the wall. "I like her."

"I like her too," he admitted. "I've liked her since we were kids."

Gretchen's brow wrinkled, but she said nothing.

"You don't need to know all the past history," he said around a sigh. "But she's heading back to West Virginia today because of her job and there's a chance she won't come back."

"That sucks," Gretchen said. "Not sure what it has to do with me, though."

"She invited me to come along, for the weekend, anyway."

Gretchen gave him a stern nod. "A couple of overnighters with your hotsy? Hell yes. You definitely need to do that."

"So I need *you* to keep the doors open, however you have to do it, so the Duncombs don't bulldoze this place with my mother and everything I own still in it." He paused, searching her eyes. "Is there someone who can watch your kids until Sunday evening or maybe Monday?"

She pushed away from the wall and crossed her heart. "I can hold the line until the official close date if you need me to. Go bang your hot chick. I'll keep your bar safe."

"Thank you. Five hundred of that cash is for you, to prepay for your weekend salary plus overtime. The other two-thirty-seven is for toilet paper or whatever else you need. Swing a deal with United Beverage to bring us some decent beer. They can bill me if there isn't enough petty cash. We're not gonna close limping on dregs of Miller Light. Your regular schedule's still in place for all of next week, but with Mom and Kelsey..." He sighed. "Even if Berk leaves again right after she brings me back, I'll probably still be scarce."

"I'll do whatever you need me to do," Gretchen insisted.

Max nodded his thanks. "I'm sorry this all went to shit. You've been amazing and I will give you the best damn reference for whatever job you apply for."

She grinned, but he saw dampness in her eyes. "Damn right you will. And you'd better call me if you ever open another bar."

"Deal," he said nodding as he leaned forward to open the office door. "I'll be around a little while. Go get at least a weekend's worth of toilet paper and whatever else you'll need. Just make it quick, okay?"

"You got it, Boss. Be back in fifteen, tops."

Berk

Goddamn, fucking, time-wasting Chad. The prima-donna dickwad sucked up a whole goddamn hour of my day for nothing, so by the time I head out to pick up Max I'm way behind schedule, still don't have a vocalist, my phone battery's low, and haven't even *started* trying to round up a guitarist or two.

And I still have to drive for more than twelve hours.

SHIT!

But Max is ready to go and waiting at the back door. It takes him moments to toss his bag in the back seat and climb into my SUV, then we're on our way.

Wish egotistical shitbag vocalists were half as considerate.

The drive starts out chatty and friendly, if awkward since I've never invited a guy on a weekend trip before. Max is all gentlemanly and stuff, plus he's great to talk to, so I'm glad he's along for the ride. So glad, we're already southbound on Highway 52 when I realize I can't call *anyone* while driving in a fucking rainstorm, let alone convince musicians to give up their Saturday.

I want to growl and snarl and start cussing like I tend to do, but instead, I say, "Don't suppose you can drive a stick?"

Max looks at me like I've sprouted purple tentacles. "Sure. What's up? Need a break already?"

"No. I still need to find a vocalist and at least one guitarist, but I'm driving."

"Happy to help," he says, and we agree to pull over in Decorah to switch drivers.

Ya know what? With Max driving, I feel like a big-shot manager, cruisin' down the highway while wheeling and dealing on the phone. My second-choice vocalist has a gig tomorrow, but the next is free and sounds delighted to help. Score some points for his kids being at their mom's this weekend. It doesn't take me much longer to round up a lead and rhythm guitarist. After a quick confirmation with Dave, the whole band's set up before we turn south just past Dubuque.

"I can take over," I say, smiling out at sunshine peeking through clouds.

Everything feels better already.

"Nah, I'm good," Max says. "We can switch when we stop for gas."

So we talk about old times and our families and how nice it is to see glimpses of the sun. About music and movies and politics and what great or sucky shows we've watched on Netflix.

After a bathroom-and-drive-thru pit-stop in Moline, I take over driving and listen as Max mourns his bar with crushing fondness, then I talk about late-night recording sessions, crazy saxophonists, and admit I keep a bowl of dog food on my back deck for possums and raccoons. We reminisce about stupid shit we did in school, then laugh about the first time we got laid and the scariest thing we'd ever tried to do.

Kelsey seems to be the only topic we avoid, but sometimes, when the evening light's just right, I see her reflection in the backseat grinning and taking it all in.

It's well after midnight Iowa time and we're heading toward Cincinnati, still a good three-and-a-half hours from my house. Dave has not buzzed once. We almost stopped in Indianapolis, but Max had insisted he was wide-awake and could drive. Two hours later, he's yawning with the window half down despite light drizzle, and I've already slept a ragged hour or so of Interstate. Time to find a bed to crash in.

The hotel is reasonably priced and forgettable, but the bed's wide and comfy. I'm already sprawled between the sheets and listening to the rain while he finishes brushing his teeth. He crawls in beside me and snuggles in, shivering, so we yawn and spoon to share body heat, his dick against my butt. Next thing I know we're humping like bunnies and the duvet's on the floor because we're slicked with sweat and saliva.

It's a good forty minutes later when we slump together, exhausted and drenched, his body warm against mine. I'm finally getting my cozy, rainy night sleeping beside someone warm.

I'm just drifting off when he kisses the back of my neck and slips away, out of the bed, but I reach for him and his luscious, fuzzy warmth.

"Get back here."

"Just gimme a minute," he says, laughing, and covers me with the sheet and duvet we'd kicked off forever ago before plucking his condom from the floor. He wiggles his butt on the way to the bathroom. "Gotta toss this and clear the pipes."

"Well that's a great vision," I tease as I snuggle into my pillow and watch his ass. But I'm tired, that utterly-relaxed-post-great-sex tired, and am nearly asleep before he starts to piss, then barely aware of him returning to slide into bed beside me.

I snuggle into his warm embrace on this rainy night, my head on his chest and his arms around me. He's stroking my hair and it's nice. Relaxing. My leg comes over his and my free hand finds his dick like it's reached for it a thousand times before.

We both sigh, then I yawn and twitch in his embrace, drifting away into one of my favorite memory-dreams, of me and Max and Kelsey at the lake waiting for fireworks on a sticky summer night before Senior Year. Kelsey and I are sitting on lawn chairs, our bare feet in the water, while Max has waded in, knee deep, to splash us. We're squealing and giggling with lightning bugs all around and our folks up on the bank finishing barbeque and beer.

But Max isn't looking at his sister or our folks, he's looking at me. Just me.

My dream blinks and he's there beside me, and we're sitting under a willow tree, hidden under a canopy of leaves giving us a shady break from summer swelter. I'm about to go into eighth grade and I've cut myself—on what, I can't remember, a sharp rock, maybe, I just know I still have the crooked little scar below my ankle—and Max has my bleeding foot on his thigh, examining it.

"It's not too bad," he says, smiling at me, and my heart feels funny. Fluttery yet heavy, nervous but not afraid.

Surely I haven't lost that much blood, I think, glancing at the red smear.

Max, still watching me, says, "A band-aid'll fix it right up. Let's get you in to your gram."

Then he leans over as if to tell me a secret and the moment stretches and stretches as I search his hazel eyes. This time, he doesn't look away and set my foot aside. This time, he whispers, "I still love you, Berkeley Williams," against my forehead, his lips warm on my skin and his hands firm on my back and his dick in my hand like it's been there forever. "I don't think I ever stopped."

"Me too," I whisper back, and, this time, he kisses me in my dream-memory under the willow until I drift into the nothingness of sleep.

He's up before I am, I can hear the shower running as I stretch in the big comfy bed that smells like us. It's almost 8:30 Ohio time, according to the clock, and while I'd love to roll over and go back to sleep, we still have a lot of driving to do. I manage to escape the covers and stumble to the bathroom door. It's open a crack so I call out, "Good morning!"

"Come on in, the water's fine," he says.

So I do.

We don't get downstairs to the free breakfast until almost ten, and we're still scarfing waffles and coffee when my phone starts ringing.

We make good time with Max driving and me handling the little details involved in playing a last-minute concert. The band's no problem—we independent and studio musicians are used to short notice on recording jobs or filling in for sick band members during a tour—but I have to confirm adequate electrical outlets for our equipment, status of the lighting situation, is our stage an actual stage or something else, where's the loading/unloading area, and stuff like that.

I want my peeps to know what kind of situation they're walking into, especially since they're doing this as a favor. Details matter.

By the time we reach Charleston's city limits, I know the show's gonna be kick ass!

Intermezzo—Eleventh Grade

Kelsey settled onto gym bleachers about halfway up, popcorn in hand, and watched Berk and the other girls practice free-throws while Max joked around with his gamer buddies near the gym doorway. Most of the cheerleaders milled together stretching or fiddling on their phones, but Lori and her entourage strode down the side of the court as if it belonged to them alone.

Kelse munched her popcorn and watched Berk or the main doorway, hoping to see Jack. He said he'd try to get to the game if he and his dad finished replacing the water pump in his mom's car.

I hope he comes, she thought, then someone large sat beside her, jostling her to the side.

She broke out in a grin and turned, expecting to see Jack had made it, but Cory Hildebrandt, basketball star and guy on a mission to get kissed by a girl, sat there, texting.

"Just a sec," he said, big thumbs smashing the RAZR's keypad.

Kelsey returned to watching the team pass basketballs around. "Did it ever occur to you that I might be waiting for someone?"

"You? No. Everyone thinks we're a thing."

Only in your delusions, Kelsey thought, sighing. Still no sign of Jack, and Max had apparently wandered off with his friends.

Cory finished texting and bumped into her as he pocketed his phone. "Okay. Here's the deal," he said.

She kept her attention on Berk's team. "There is no deal. There's never been a deal. Please stop asking me for a deal."

"You. Me. Tomorrow. Any movie you want. A nice dinner anywhere you want. Pizza. Fancy froufrou shit. Sushi. Dead-bug chili. Vegan Indian tacos in Alfredo sauce, I don't care." He paused as she gave him a grumpy glare. "Okay, fine. I'll throw in a hundred bucks. But I get to say we kissed."

"I am not your whore," she muttered then stood and excused her way down the bleachers to the second row where she squeezed into the space between a mom for the opposing team and a scrawny middle school boy she didn't know. They made room for her to sit, but the mom gave her a confused glare.

Since Cory was too large to descend through the gaps in a bleacher of spectators, she heard him excuse himself out of her original row and grumble down the aisle. She sighed as he worked his way closer to her, but a row behind.

A pair of grandparents with Ravens sweatshirts sat directly behind her, creating a barrier of sorts.

"Kelsey please," Cory whispered, leaning toward her despite Grandma *tsk-tsk*ing. "You're killing me here. It's just *one date*. What can I do to make it happen?"

"Nothing comes to mind. Leave me alone."

"I *can't*," he whispered back. "You know I—"

Kelsey stood and squeezed past the mom toward the aisle and descended to the gymnasium floor.

She heard him say, "Damn it!" from behind her, but she kept walking, pressing through the influx of parents and students and their snack foods until Lori blocked her path.

"Loser," Lori said, her two friends right behind her.

"Buzz off," Kelsey replied, shouldering past.

Someone grabbed her wrist and pulled her back. "Dammit, Lori," she muttered as she turned. "I don't have time—"

Then her head was held in two huge hands and her chin tilted upward. Cory kissed her, hard and sloppy and gross. She barely had time to gasp or struggle before someone else grabbed her shoulder from behind and yanked her away from Cory's sloppy-wet lips. She staggered back, wiping her mouth with her forearm, as her brother surged past her and punched Cory in the face.

Blood burst from Cory's nose and, eyes wide and startled, he took a step backward and crashed into Lori and her friends, knocking them and a couple of other people with soft drinks and popcorn aside. Pop, ice, and popcorn flew as Max punched Cory in the face again, this time splitting his lip.

"Keep your goddamn hands off my sister!"

Lori squawked as Cory stumbled over her, people scrambled away, and Cory, right hand full of blood, punched Max in the gut.

They wrestled and punched and gouged and kicked, smaller Max too close in for Cory to pull him off or shove him away. A backward step against Brittany sent Cory tripping and falling to the basketball court floor, Max on top of him, still punching, while Cory grabbed him by the hair and yanked him aside. With Cory's legs tangled over Brittany, Max slipped free and lunged right back. Coaches from both teams leaped into the mess, trying to pull the boys apart. As soon as he staggered to his feet, Cory swung at Max but clocked the Fayerville head coach in the neck when Max ducked, sending Coach Rawlins to the floor.

Berk ran up and leaped onto Max from behind, her forearms wrapped around Max's armpits and her legs around his waist like she wanted to be his backpack, and she shouted something into his right ear. He tried to shrug her off, but she held on. The opposing team's coaches stood together to halt Cory's advance, but he shoved them aside, leaving only chunky Coach Tyler, surely a foot shorter than Cory, in his way.

"Calm down, Hildebrandt. Take a breath and calm down."

"Fucker sucker-punched me," Cory muttered, wiping blood from his nose.

"Well you grabbed that girl and kissed her after she tried to get away from you!" the mom Kelsey had sat beside hollered, pushing into the open area where the boys had been fighting.

Murmurs ran through the crowd, but the mom pressed on, looking back-and-forth between the coaches, one still trying to get to his feet. "I saw the whole thing. That poor girl came down the bleachers from behind me and squeezed in right between me and my son. This big kid followed her, begging for a date and wouldn't take no for an answer. When she walked away, he grabbed her and kissed her. Right there. Right in front of everybody."

She took a step toward the other team's head coach. "You know me, Doug, you coach my daughter, and *that boy*," she said, pointing at Cory, "forced himself on her."

"She's right," a middle-aged man said from behind Kelsey. "The girl was sitting in front of us not bothering anybody until the tall kid sat beside her to ask her on a date. Wouldn't accept her no, so she moved down to sit with that woman and her son. I didn't see what happened after, but he definitely propositioned her when she was on the seat in front of me."

Kelsey felt scores of eyes upon her, and she cowered, her hands shaking. Berk had climbed off Max's back and was wincing at his bleeding cheek, Cory stood alone, shirt speckled with blood, head down but watching her, his eyes pleading. Lori, Brittany, and Julia stood whispering and pointing at her.

Aw, shit, Kelsey thought, looking for a way through the crowd. He got his kiss, right there in front of everybody like he wanted, but it became an even bigger mess. Maybe I should have just said okay to cover for him. Maybe I shouldn't have come to Berk's game. Maybe—

The woman she'd sat beside touched her arm. "Are you okay?" she asked.

"Yeah," Kelsey said, shaking. "Maybe I should have agreed to one date and—"

"No. You did the right thing."

But did I? He went from hiding in the closet to committing assault, because of *me*. How is that the right thing?

Kelsey turned and ran, pushing through the crowd to the main entrance of the gymnasium. She needed air.

She paced in front of the trophy case, struggling to wrap her mind around the mess Cory'd made and how to fix it, then Berk and Max found her.

"Kelsey, oh my God," Berk said, rushing to her. "Are you okay?"

Max followed. His face had started to bruise.

"No, I am not okay!" Kelsey snapped. "Everything was fine! I had it under control!"

"What?" Max asked. "He grabbed you and kissed you. That's like assault or something!"

"It was just a kiss and I had it under control until you jumped in and started throwing punches!" She stomped away, digging in her pockets for her car keys. "It was none of your business and I can handle him myself."

Then she walked out to the cold January night and cried all the way to her car.

Max

Delayed by a four-car pileup on the interstate, Max turned into the driveway of a standard white cottage around quarter after three. We have plenty of time, he thought.

"Well, this is it," Berk said as she opened her door and hopped out. "Nothing exciting."

"It's cute," he said, exiting the SUV to a clear, cold afternoon with a heavy bank of gray clouds to the north. "Always pictured you in something more... eclectic."

She laughed and grinned at him over the vehicle. "Nah. Eclectic can be a pain in the ass. My house is sturdy, simple, and all mine."

They unloaded their luggage and carried it to the side door. Berk unlocked it before elbowing it open for him. "C'mon in!"

Max entered the efficient white-and-chrome kitchen and Berk followed him inside.

She lugged her bag across the kitchen and through the archway to the living room. "C'mon. I'll give you the nickel tour."

Max followed as Berk pointed out the living room, bathroom, and home office on the way to her bedroom, every room modern white with bright-colored accents. She tossed her bag on the afghan of white, apple-green, and royal-blue granny squares covering the bed. "I have a guest room if you want it. Or you can stay here."

Max tossed his duffle beside hers. "Here is great. What can I do to help?" he asked, as Berk slipped into his arms.

Her hands found his butt. "It's been almost two years since I played in front of an audience, so how about a quickie to calm my nerves?"

He grinned. "Thought you were excited to do this?"

"Oh I am," She reached for his belt buckle. "Let me show you how excited."

Afterward, she showered first. He finished his shower to find her rooting through her bedroom closet wearing nothing but black jeans and a bra, her hair still wet but combed through.

Wearing just a towel, he stood in the bedroom doorway for a moment and simply appreciated the view.

"Should I do the leather jacket thing, or the lacy girly thing?" she asked.

He draped his towel over the back of a sapphire-and-lime upholstered chair. "What kind of music are you playing?"

"Probably mostly blues and Motown, maybe some classic rock," she said, pushing aside hangers one by one, "so I guess it's the leather jacket thing."

He lay on her bed, nude, to watch her. "What about that red blouse?"

"This one? Seems kinda skimpy to play bass in a church basement." She pulled it out and held it before her.

"Let me see it anyway. But take off your bra first." He grabbed his dick and stroked it a couple of times for her to see.

She turned, smirking an ornery grin at his flirtation. "We don't have time for that!" Then she dropped the blouse and hopped onto the bed to straddle him. They kissed, and she ground against him, his hands on her hips helping. "God, I want to, though."

"Go, get dressed," he said against her lips. "Be responsible. I can wait."

"Gah! Maybe I can't!" she said, rolling off him. "Okay. Focus. Benefit concert. For Lois."

She returned to the closet and rifled through. "Rockin', rockin'..."

Max got up and pulled on his own clean clothes, unable to take his eyes off her.

She selected a long, turquoise-blue t-shirt and a studded belt she buckled over the tee, leaving the shirt like a short dress over her jeans. She dragged on a waist-length, studded, black leather jacket with elbow-length sleeves over the tee.

She looked feminine tough, like the old Berk he used to know.

"I like it," he said as she walked to her dresser and pulled a silky bag from the top drawer.

"Me too. And it'll still look all right after hours on stage." She rummaged through the bag and pulled out black dangly earrings, put them on, then took them off again before returning to root through the bag.

A long pearl necklace came out, and she wrapped it three times to hang loose around her throat, then she put on silver-and-pearl earrings and a stretchy pearl bracelet. She kept layering black, silver, and pearl, finishing with a large turquoise ring on her right hand.

"You're gorgeous." He wrapped his arms around her waist and met her gaze in the mirror. "You look like you can play music *and* kick butt."

"Thank you," she said, smiling back at him. "I gotta get my makeup on, then we gotta go!"

They pulled into the church parking lot to see a short fellow carrying an amp inside while a massively obese man with a lopsided afro rushed toward her SUV. A pretty young woman with two small children shook her head and followed him.

"Berk!" the obese man yelled, grinning as she parked. "Have I told you lately how much I love you?"

She laughed and exited her SUV only to get crushed in a bear hug. "Love you too, Dave," she said as he spun around, holding her off the ground. "Just wish you weren't always such a pain in my ass."

"Ha! You'd think I was pissed if I wasn't driving you crazy." He set her down and noticed Max coming around the side of the SUV. "Hey!" the big man said while Berk hugged the woman with the kids. "I'm Dave, the drummer. Don't think we've met, but I am so looking forward to working with you. Just a quick FYI, Berk and I lay an awesome bassline for most any genre, so I'm sure we'll all have a great time tonight no matter what you play!"

"I'm Max," he said, his hand enveloped in Dave's paw. "But I'm not—"

Three precise pumps later, Dave let him go, then turned to the woman. "Max, this is my wife, Lia, and our kids Jeremy and Riley."

"They've gotten soooo big!" Berk cooed at the kids.

"Hi," Lia said, offering her hand while her husband turned to whisper with Berk. "He usually drags us to these things, but don't worry. Jeremy's used to them and I'll scoot out with Riley if she starts fussing. Don't want to interrupt the show." She smiled, and it lit up her dark eyes. "I don't think we've met before. What do you like to play?"

"I'm just Berk's friend from back home," he admitted, smiling back. "Not musical at all."

Dave sucked in a breath and gaped, turning to stare at Max. "Not the lead guitarist? *You're* a *friend* of Berk's from *back home!?*" He turned to Berk. "I thought everyone hated you."

"Not everybody," Berk said, glancing at Max. Her voice softened. "He's Kelsey's brother."

"Ooh," Lia nodded. "Gotcha." She gave Max a wink before turning to her husband. "C'mon, Davey-bear. Let's lug in the rest of your gear and get set up."

"I wanna carry something!" Jeremy said. "Can I carry something?"

Dave refused to budge. "How long have I known you, Berk? A decade?"

"Almost," she said, glancing at Max again. "It's not—"

"And, in all that time, in all our gigs over eight, nine damn years, how many men have you brought to any event we've done? How many?"

"Let her go," Lia said, tugging on his arm. "It's her business, and he's *fine*. Okay? C'mon. I'll tell you inside."

Dave didn't budge. "How many, Berk?"

"None," she said.

"Until today." Dave shrugged off Lia's touch and turned again to loom over Max, but Max held his ground. "I owe my life to Berk," Dave said. "My career. My marriage. Every single thing I hold dear. If she dragged you here all the way from flippin' *Iowa*, you must be something special. She better be, too."

Max stared him in the eye. "She is."

"DAVE!" Lia barked. "Quit being an ass and let's get the rest of your gear set up!"

Dave snorted then turned to follow his wife.

"Sorry 'bout that," Berk said as she opened the back of her SUV. "I didn't expect him to be so protective."

Max reached in for her amp. "It's fine. They both obviously adore you."

She grabbed her guitar case by the handle and slid it out. "Still. It was a bit much."

He paused to look at her. "No, it wasn't." He leaned over to kiss her. "Let's get you prepped to play."

Max soon lost track of names, but Berk knew everyone. At least it seemed that way. Her expected musicians arrived more-or-less on time, and the keyboardist, a diminutive Asian gal with electric blue hair, brought along her tall-and-buttoned-down sax-player boyfriend to add to the ensemble, along with their utterly charming seven-year-old daughter who ran right up to Lia and the kids. The lead singer, a bald, middle-aged black fella with a voice like spun gold, made a point to meet everyone's family, as did his wife who sat in the back corner of the church basement with Max, Lia, and the other 'band spouses'. The two guitar players—a scrawny white guy on lead and the short, stocky Latino on rhythm—spent much of the set-up time horsing around with each other. Both brought their girlfriends. Lead's remained focused on her phone, and the rhythms took it all in with wide, astounded eyes, especially as other folks started filtering in to set up food and tables for donations and auction items. She and the vocalist's wife hurried over to help, leaving Max, Lia, and the gal playing slots on her phone to manage the kids.

Dave paced near the spouses, his drum set half-assembled on the stage and his phone crushed to his ear. "How far?" he asked loud enough for most of the basement to hear. "Okay. See you when you get here."

He closed the phone and muttered, "Shit!"

"What's wrong?" Lia sighed.

"Lewis took 77 South and didn't realize it until someplace called Mossy. He's turned around, just passing by Marmet now."

"It'll be fine," Lia soothed.

"It better be. We can manage without him, but to really kick this, we *need* a sound guy!" He wandered toward the stage again, muttering.

"With all that equipment, they still need a sound guy?" Max asked Lia.

"Need, no, prefer, yes," she said as she wiped her son's nose. "Something about blending the tones instead of combating them, something, something, endless technical music babble. It's always endless technical music babble when you get more than two musicians together. I don't understand half of it; I just try to stay out of their way."

Jeremy scampered off to play with the other kids and Lia turned to Max, smiling. "It's nice to finally meet you, by the way. I've heard a lot about you."

"Oh?" Max asked.

"Yeah." Lia nodded once, then turned her gaze to watch the band prepare the stage.

Dave punched something into his phone, the two guitarists set up mics and stands, and Berk and the vocalist shifted amplifiers and cords to simplify the chaos on the small pallets-with-carpet-on-top stage while the keyboardist crouched beside them to tape cords down.

"Where's the dude with the saxophone?"

"Claude? Probably running power cords."

"I didn't know musicians played for free," he admitted.

"Most don't, but sometimes if a good buddy calls needing help, they'll show up. Berk has a lot of good buddies, and she's helped every person on that stage, some more than once."

"Chad—"

"Chad's a douche," Lia muttered.

"So I gathered."

"Don't get me wrong, he's an *amazing* vocalist and crowds love him, but almost no one wants to work with him unless they're well compensated. When Dave told Jen—she's the keyboardist—Berk was gonna ask Chad to sing, she was reluctant to come but agreed to wait for confirmation. When he called back to say Berk got Rich instead, she jumped right in and Claude wanted in too because he didn't want to miss a chance to work with Berk." She paused and nodded toward the stage. "Those seven musicians are near the absolute top of their fields. That's a *lot* of talent up there, but no one really knows because they're playing for commercials and movie soundtracks, not on hit bands. It's gonna be a helluva show."

And they're working for free, Max thought. "Berk has that much clout?"

"Nah, it's not clout. She's right up there with them. An equal. What she does have is heart. They're here, heck, we're *all* here, because we love her."

Lia turned her head to wink at him. "Including you."

The sound guy arrived about half an hour before the benefit was scheduled to start, and quickly ran through a *check one, check two* sound test of every microphone and another test of every amp.

Max watched from behind the church kitchen's beverage counter as each musician patiently played their chords or spoke into their mic without so much as a blink of irritation or boredom. Even the lead guitarist, who'd spent the afternoon buzzing around with nervous energy, settled right into his sound check.

Several dozen working-class people had already arrived and were walking past the tables of auction items. A scattered few had taken seats to eat their hot dogs and listen to the band finish preparing for the show, but most milled around the food and drink counters or chatted in loose groups.

Children scurried, laughing, and a pretty young woman pushed an elderly lady in a wheelchair down the ramp.

"Grandma Lois!" kids said as they ran to the old woman and she smiled, her white hair a halo around her dark face. Despite the cast on one arm and leg, she managed to find candies in her pockets and gave each of the kids a hug and a treat. Others came to see her, many holding her good hand as they gave her their best wishes or conversations. She graced them with beatific smiles as well.

Lois held court as her caretaker pushed her slowly through the rapidly growing crowd. Max poured ice tea and soft drinks into disposable cups and smiled at the delighted busyness of the event. He gave a little boy a cup of root beer then looked up to see Berk grinning at him.

"I see they put you to work," she said.

"Yeah. Someone heard I was a bartender." He filled three more cups with pop to fill the rows on the counter.

"Wasn't me," Berk said.

"I know," he admitted, winking at her. "I did it to myself when Lia asked what I did for a living."

They both laughed, then Berk said, "So, Mr. Bartender, can I have a couple of bottles of water, please?"

"Anything my lady wants," he said, retrieving two bottles from the cooler to his right.

Leaning forward, he handed them over. "Break a leg."

"Every time." She met his quick kiss.

The middle-aged woman working the beverage counter with him gave him a long sideways glance as Berk hurried back to the stage. "You and the guitar chick, eh?"

"Yep." He handed another drink to a kid who couldn't quite reach them.

"You're a cute couple. How long y'all been together?"

"Either fifteen years or four days. Take your pick."

She laughed, shaking her head.

The band took the stage, Berk off to the left side as he watched her settle her bass over her shoulder and across her hips. She tossed her head and her jewelry twinkled.

"Thank you, everyone, for coming to help us help Lois Glearden get back into her house," the vocalist said to wide applause. "Before we get started, I want to remind everyone about the refreshments by the kitchen," he said, gesturing to the two window counters while the keyboardist played a gentle note, "the donation jars near the door, and the items for auction. We're going to play a little music to give you time to look, then we'll auction a few items, play some more music, auction some more items, and so on until we're all ready to go home. How's that sound?"

Max grinned at the applause while, behind the vocalist, Dave tapped the edge of a drum four times. The women tagged on tap five singing *Do do do do do do do do do*, then the guitars and sax slid in behind, filling out a familiar 70's tune.

In less than thirty seconds, half the place was singing or dancing to *That's The Way—uh huh, uh huh—I Like It*. Three songs and ten minutes later, the crowd boogied to a flawless rendition of Robert Cray's *Smoking Gun*.

Donations flooded the jars.

"How'd you do it?" Max asked as he helped Berk carry her gear back to her SUV not too far past midnight. "Have you memorized all those songs?"

"Some, but not all. Most have a fairly simple repeating bass track. We decided on a playlist while waiting for the sound check and I loaded their tabs and chords onto my phone. I checked real quick between songs a couple of times, but mostly I just remembered from the days I worked with bar bands." She grinned and nudged him with her shoulder. "I sight-read basslines for a living. Popular music's usually a snap to reproduce."

"Cool." They reached her Mazda and he popped open the back hatch.

"Hey, Berk!" the keyboardist called out as she and the sax player walked past. "Most of us are going to IHOP off the turnpike. Wanna come?"

Berk slid in her guitar. She glanced at Max and shrugged.

"Whatever you want to do, I'm cool," he whispered before loading her amp.

"Yeah, we can do pancakes," Berk called back.

"Freaking awesome! See you there!"

Berk

The gig went great. Everyone was feeling the jam and having a blast, on and off the stage. That's one of the great things about playing with Dave, even though he's prone to freak-out modes. Whether we're hired to play techno-pop, old school jazz, or anything between, Dave and I freaking *click* on a bassline, and everyone else riffs off that. We set the tempo. We set the downbeats. It's like the foundation of a building supporting the fancy shit above. Everyone else handles the fancy shit, and it's easier for them to hit their marks if the foundation is rock solid.

I love playing a good bassline, and we hit it all night long.

Max grins all the way to IHOP, excited over the evening, and it's great to see. It's like he's forgotten about the bar and his family while serving soda and coffee and listening to us rock out. Sometimes it's nice to be part of something bigger than yourself. Forget about your own troubles.

We get to IHOP and pretty much everyone decides to meet-and-eat except Rich and his wife, so the waitress makes a huge table for us. We're all chatty and it's not long before Max is involved in a small-business-frustrations convo with Jen and Claude, who own a vintage clothing shop in Akron. All the little kids are passed out in the booth behind Dave and Lia, Riley snoozing in her car seat, the other two on the booth seats, and we adults discuss what went great, what we screwed up, and, mostly, what a great time we had.

"We really need to do this more often," Jorge says as the waitress sets his omelet in front of him. "Just play for the love of the music, ya know?"

Dave and Kev, the lead guitarist, nod as they shovel in food.

"Not too often, though," Lia says, winking. "We all have bills to pay."

Everyone laughs and agrees as the waitress sets my crepes in front of me, and Max gets his combo plate. She moves to Claude and Jen, then my phone rings. Weird. It's about 1 a.m. and pretty much everyone I know is right here.

Max looks at me while chewing his bacon.

The call's from an unknown number in the 563 area code. That's northeast

Iowa, same as Granddad's, same as Fayerville, so I pick up.

"Amanda?" a woman's voice on the other end of the line says. "Do I have the right number?"

I can barely hear her over Dave and Kev laughing at something Jorge said, so I put a hand over my open ear to cut down the background noise. "Yeah. But call me Berk. Who is this? Is everything okay?"

"Oh, honey, this is Dottie Jacobsen. One of Ted's lady friends. I'm so sorry to wake you up."

By now, Max has stopped eating and turned his head to watch me while everyone else keeps talking.

"It's fine," I assure her. "What's wrong? Is Granddad okay?"

"Well, honey," she says, and I lose the rest of it to Dave and Kev's background chatter.

Those two are louder than a table of drunks, so I get up and take a few steps away, the phone crushed against my ear. "What'd you say? I didn't hear."

"Your grandfather passed," she says, clear as a solitary mid C. "I called for an ambulance, then called you. I didn't know what else to do."

Things get lopsided after that.

I see a different waitress saying something as she kneels beside me. And Max is there, first on my left side and calling my name, then crouching on my right, holding my hand as he's talking on my phone. Claude's on my left helping me sit up.

Someone hands me a drink of water. Lia, maybe. And the lights are all weird. Too bright and curvy. Dave, of course, is pacing and fretting and scaring the regular customers.

Then I'm in a booth and Max is still holding my hand, but he's on his own phone this time. Mine's on the table in front of him, my contact list on the screen. Lia's sitting across from us, worried, while Jen and Claude are standing. Claude's on his phone.

"You gonna be okay?" Jen asks and I see tear-streaks through her makeup. "Berk? Are you here yet?"

"Where else would I be?" I say and, across from us, Lia winces.

"That's all we know," Max says beside me. "Yeah. She's still in shock."

"Who's in shock?" I ask Lia. This time Jen winces.

"You, sweetie." Lia squeezes my other hand and I look at it. I didn't realize she was holding it. She looks from me to Max, still on his phone.

"That's all I know, Gail," he sighs, "and I got every bit of that info from the woman with your dad. She sounded about eighty and upset herself so I do not have any more details. As soon as we know, you'll know."

"Why are you talking to my mother?" I ask, but Lia touches my face and I turn my attention to her.

"Your grandpa died," Lia says as Jen squeezes into the booth beside her and puts her hand on top of Lia's and mine.

"What? How?"

Lia glances at Jen who has no answer for her. "I... we don't really know," Lia says.

"Yes, we're heading back to Iowa as soon as Berk's good to travel," Max says, "and the minute we know anything we will call you. *Yes.*"

"Gawd!" He clicks off the call and drops his phone onto the table. "Always a fun time, talking to your mom."

"What happened to my granddad?" I ask him, my eyes stinging.

"One of his girlfriends called. He... Shit." Max rakes his hand over his head and through his hair. "He... He fell asleep after they were done... doing... *shiiit*. Old. People. Sex. He fell asleep after and..."

Lia squeezes my hand. "He didn't wake up."

"That's all we know," Jen says, openly crying. "I'm so sorry, Berk."

Then I start sobbing, but Max holds me and lets me cry it out.

I didn't know I had that many tears left in me.

Max

Max stayed close and watched Berk accept hugs and condolences from her friends.

Dave paced beside Max and wrung his hands. "Want one of us to come along? Spare you while driving back to Iowa?"

"I got it," Max assured him. "We'll be fine. I'm used to staying up all night." Berk had mostly stopped crying, and her color was better, not as ashen and pale. But her eyes were dull. Lost. Not that he could blame her. For all practical purposes, Ted was the last of her family. At least family that cared. Everyone else lived out of state and Max wondered if he should track them down and call them.

The big man beside him paused and leaned down, close to Max. "Lia told me who you were. Sorry I got all up in your business earlier, man. It's just, Berk's like my kid sister."

"I know, it's cool." Max watched itty-bitty Jen crush Berk in a hug.

"Seriously, though, if you need help getting her home or anything else, we can pitch in."

Jen left Berk and walked to Max, wiping at her eyes with the back of her wrist. "Can I see your phone?" she said with a sad smile. "Wanna give you our numbers."

"Sure," Max said and handed over his phone. Lia had already entered hers and Dave's.

"Call us any time if you guys need us," Jen said, her fingers rapidly tapping on his screen. "Funeral costs or whatever. You know we can get a band up almost immediately, and we've also done GoFundMe charity drives."

"Pretty sure expenses won't be a problem, but if they are, I'll call."

"Promise?" Jen asked, coming in for a hug.

Max bent to hug her back. "I promise."

"Send me a Snap. You've got my username. 'Kay?"

He let her go. "Yes, ma'am."

Most everyone begged off, their barely-touched breakfasts packed in to-go boxes, and Max shook hands as they left. Only Dave and Lia remained, gathering their sleeping kids.

Berk sighed beside him. "I don't want to go back to Granddad's."

"I know," he soothed, taking her hand. "Want me to just take you home? Figure out what to do in the morning?"

"Very much so." She met his gaze and flinched. "But I can't hide. And I can't run away. Someone has to be the grownup, has to handle all this, all this wretched business of death. And..." She sniffled and her lower lip quivered. "And there isn't anyone else but me."

She curled into his arms and he hugged her, held her, tried to soothe her.

Dave patted Max on the back and headed out the door with Jeremy asleep on his shoulder while Lia gathered Riley and her diaper bag.

"If it's okay with you guys," Lia said to Max, "I'd like to meet you at Berk's place and help her pack for an extended stay out there. I don't think she's gonna be coming home in a couple of days like she'd originally planned. If nothing else, she needs help unloading her equipment."

"That'd be fine," Berk said, lifting her head from Max's chest. She drew a shaky breath. "I don't even know what I'm going to need."

"Probably something nicer than jeans and leggings," Lia said, patting Berk's shoulder. "I'll help you pick stuff." She turned her head to look at Max. "I'm glad you're here. Thank you." She gave Berk one last consoling rub on her back. "We'll meet you guys at Berk's."

Then she carried her daughter out into the night.

The cashier informed them their food had already been paid for, so Max left a generous tip and walked with Berk to her SUV.

"I'll drive," he said and she handed him the keys without one breath of protest.

She stared silently out the window on the ride home.

✥

While the women sorted and packed, and Dave paced around the living room like a bear in a cage, Max brewed coffee and poured it into travel mugs. Then he made more coffee.

Berk's fridge was nearly empty of anything perishable, but the cupboards were well stocked. Tuna salad took a few quick minutes to prepare and spread into flour tortillas, then he put the tuna wraps into sandwich bags. She had no chips, but he found microwave popcorn, so he popped three bags. While they popped, he filled other sandwich bags with ice from her freezer.

By the time Lia walked into the kitchen at ten-till-two, he had nearly finished washing dishes and two reusable grocery bags stood on the counter.

"What's in the grocery bags?" Lia asked as she poured herself a cup of coffee.

"Food for the road," he said, running a scrubby around the tuna-salad bowl. "I figure if we stop only for gas and bathroom breaks, *and* I find fast-moving semis to follow so I don't have to worry much about speeding tickets, I can get her back there by one or so. Maybe noonish."

"You can stay up that long?"

"Got a pot and a half of coffee packed," he said, rinsing the bowl and setting it in the strainer. "I'm usually up until three or four in the morning anyway. I'll get her there."

Lia smiled and grabbed a towel to dry the dishes. "I know you will."

Berk talked and cried and reminisced until about ten miles after they crossed from Kentucky into Ohio, then she fell asleep, curled against the door in the afghan from her bed.

Max drank coffee and drove, the apple-green granny squares of Berk's afghan reflecting the streetlights of every off-ramp they passed. A semi blew past him on Kentucky-9 and Max followed, settling in about an eighth of a mile behind and doing a steady eighty-four until they hit rain in Cincinnati. Right at the speed limit through Cinci, then the semi sped up again until Indianapolis where it turned north toward Chicago.

Eh, needed gas anyway, Max thought, pulling off the interstate just west of Indianapolis. According to his map-app, trailing the semi saved them almost an hour.

"Berk?" he said as he stopped beside a gas pump. He reached over to touch her arm. "We're stopping for gas just past Indi. You want anything from inside?"

She stretched and blinked at him, bleary. "What time is it?"

"About six."

"Wow. Didn't know I slept that long." She stretched again and yawned. "I need to pee. Maybe grab a Sprite." She climbed out of her SUV and popped her neck before rooting through her pockets. "Lemme get you my debit card."

"I've got it," Max said as he unscrewed her gas cap and slid the nozzle in.

"But it's my—"

"I've got it," he assured her again. "Meet you inside."

He pumped gas and watched her trot across the rainy parking lot. He grabbed both travel mugs before heading in himself.

Berk paid for their meager munchies, then they were on the road again.

This time, a semi passed him right after they got on the interstate. They stopped for gas and a hot breakfast in the Quad Cities before Berk called the funeral director and drove the final leg home.

Intermezzo - Senior Year

"Miss Williams, who else would want to hurt your friend?"

I blow my nose and glare at the scowling detective sitting across the table from me. He's about my mom's age, smells like cigarettes, and stares at me as if I make no sense, like I'm a tuba solo dropped into the middle of a Beyoncé tune or something.

"Just Cory," I say again. "He's been harassing her since we were freshmen, trying to get her to go out with him." I glance at my gram who sits beside me, her hand on my forearm. "He even grabbed her at a game last year and kissed her, even though she'd been trying to get away from him. I didn't see it —I was warming up for the game—but there were a *ton* of witnesses that saw the whole thing."

The detective sighs—he sighs a lot—and flips through the folder of papers in front of him. "Then her brother—Maxwell, is that right?—punched him."

He flips another page as I nod. "Yeah. Served him right. Like I said, he's been trying to get her to go out with him for years. *Years.* Even though she always says no."

He sighs again and meets my gaze. "She refused to file charges that night. He refused to file charges against her brother that night, *and* against you tonight even though you beat him with a wrench. Can you explain that?"

Gram squeezes my arm and I admit, "No, I can't."

"All right," he says, tapping the pocket with the cigarettes then sighing and pulling his hand away. "He wanted to go out with her, but she didn't. Fine. Why then, did she text him and ask him to meet her?"

"What?" I say, starting to stand despite my Gram holding my arm tight and not letting me rise. "She'd never text Cory!"

"Yeah, but she did," the detective says. "We have her phone, Amanda. It shows she texted *him*, then she texted *you* with less than a minute between, asking you both to come to the athletic shed."

"That's not possible," I say. "You have my phone and her text to me says he was hurting her, was—"

The door opens and a Fayerville city cop peeks in. "Brian, the other kid's in surgery, but his father arrived with a lawyer and refused to turn over the phone."

"Maybe we need to do the same," Gram says, standing. "C'mon, Berk. We're done talking. Let's go home."

I wipe my eyes again and stand. "She was naked and bloody and unconscious when I found her. Cory was there, shaking her, and covered with her blood. I don't care what you say, *he* did it."

Gram drags me out to the hallway and *shh's* hard in my ear while the city cop gets out of our way. All I can think is how I should have beaten Cory's fucking head in.

Berk

I don't know how he did it, but Max got me back to Granddad's about twelve-thirty and I have plenty of time to get to the funeral home before they close at three. We carry in my crap and I notice his eyes are bloodshot and blinky from exhaustion and a constant stream of caffeine. He sets down my bag then he turns to go.

"I'm gonna go home and crash," he says on his way to the door.

"Your mom's living there," I remind him, "and your car's at the bar."

Plus I really don't want to be here alone, but I leave that part unsaid.

He sags and sighs, so I say, "Sleep here. Go on up to my room, Danny's room, the couch, wherever you want, as long as you want. I'll make those phone calls I really don't want to make, and I'll..." My voice cracks, then he's there, hugging me.

What am I gonna do without my granddad? The house feels weird, like it knows he won't be coming back. Like it died with him. Like it's hollow and empty and alone.

I start sobbing for surely the fiftieth time since I got the call from Dottie the Granddad Slayer. Max hugs me and we sit on the couch while I finish this bout of bawling-and-sniffles, then I get up and give Max a sad sigh before calling the funeral home to confirm my appointment.

I'm thankful I have time for a shower before I have to be there because it's been a long couple of days. I put on a nicer shirt than usual and watch Max passed out on my bed. Then I kiss his cheek and head toward the funeral home.

It looks exactly as it did when I went to Danny's and Gram's funerals, except the weather's currently rainy-March-gray instead of summery-green. Exactly the same. Do they ever update funeral homes? How could they get painters or carpenters to not interrupt the town's grief? Will I walk on the exact same tan plush carpet I'd walked on when we'd buried Danny? Sit in the exact same pew I sat in for Gram's service? Sing the same hymns? Listen to the same 'glory to God' spiel from the same forgettable minister who didn't really know anyone in my family?

Before I lose myself on the dark path my heart's aching to slide down, I take a lot of deep breaths while walking from my SUV to the vestibule.

A middle-aged woman in a bland, black dress welcomes me and has me follow her past a funeral to a meeting room with a long, dark table and comfy chairs for ten, even though it's just me. I sit as instructed, all alone in this spacious room, and wait. There are pamphlets, which I look at without really seeing, and a fresh pot of coffee in the corner. I pour myself a cup.

And wait.

I check my phone after my first cup of coffee. Thought my appointment was at two, but it's almost two fifteen. Granddad's already been brought here, and it's not like there are any other funeral homes in Fayerville. So I wait.

I hear muffled voices outside the door, and they sound aggravated. But I sip my second cup of coffee and wait some more. It's quiet here, at least. The Muzak is soothing and non-intrusive, the air not too warm, not too cold, the chair comfortable, and the room is spotlessly clean, with tissue boxes tucked within easy reach.

The door finally opens and a classically good-looking, thirty-ish man walks in. Brown hair, black suit, slender frame, wedding ring, perfect teeth showing behind a totally fake smile. Could be almost any salesman anywhere.

He's holding a leather-bound portfolio, which he opens when he sits across from me.

An older man in a better grade of black suit watches us from the hall, and he's scowling. The middle-aged woman glances our way as she scurries past with a handful of memorial flyers.

"I'm so sorry for your loss," the fellow across from me says, drawing my attention.

I accept his condolences and we fall into the ebb and flow of funeral decisions. Service time and size, burial or cremation, open or closed casket, and so on. I'm comparing caskets in the casket room and wondering if I should choose the same mahogany one Granddad chose for Gram when my sales rep says from behind me, "I really am sorry, Berk. Your grandpa was a good guy."

I pause and my heart slams once, then twice, before I turn. I made the appointment as Amanda Williams. I know I did. It's the name on my credit card and I didn't want any bullshit hassle about names not matching.

Yet this, this *death salesman* who slid right into service plan choices without giving me his name just called me Berk.

So I turn, lean back against the mahogany casket, and cross my arms over my chest, damp tissue clenched in my fist and my eyes stinging because, dammit, I have to bury my grandfather.

Funeral dude is not looking at me. In fact, he's barely looked at me the entire time he's been trying to upsell me organist and limousine services, or anything else.

"Who are you?" I ask.

He sighs and keeps his gaze on the floor between us. "Troy. Troy Haddert."

"Sunnavabitch," I mutter, keeping my voice low because I'm in a goddamn funeral home and someone's family and friends are mourning just down the hall. Troy Goddamn Haddert. The same shit who egged our house, wrote sexually violent graffiti on my locker, and stayed in his car while Lori and her fucking friends kicked me into the hospital. He never touched me, but he might as well have.

All those fucking jocks might as well have. And not one of them gave a single shit about Kelsey, only a goddamn basketball game they didn't win.

"I want someone else to handle my granddad's funeral."

"I can't do that," he says, still staring somewhere ahead of my boots. "I tried to pass your account to Jerry, but the boss—"

"I do not give one flying fuck what your boss says. Get me another sales rep or I'll haul Granddad to Decorah myself."

"Berk, please," he says, glancing at me.

"Berk please, Berk please," I snap back. "Where was the *Berk please* when your bitch girlfriend tried to kick my eyes out and you lied to the cops about it? Or your best bud Cory put Kelsey in a fucking coma? You had God knows how many chances to do the right thing but you—"

"I have three kids," he says, raising his gaze to mine. "One with a heart condition. Employment opportunities are shit here, you know that, and jobs with good insurance? Jesus, Berk. There aren't any. I've only been here three weeks. One more week and the insurance kicks in and we can get Cayden to a specialist. Please."

"Why should I care about your sick kid? You looked away from all the bad shit—"

"I was a kid!" he snaps back, his voice low as he walks across the display room to the door and shuts it. "And you don't know everything about that whole damn mess."

"I know Kelsey's dying soon and I know my left eye doesn't see worth a shit for precision work. So thanks for that."

He shakes his head and manages to hold my gaze for the first time this afternoon. "I never hurt you or anyone else," he says, then looks away again and starts pacing. "I know your mom dumped you off on your grandparents, everyone did. But did you know my dad left when I was eight? Left us four kids to manage on our own while our mom worked crap jobs to keep us barely scraping by? Did you know..."

He sighs again then stops to look at me. "I used to be mad at you, did you know that?"

"Big fucking deal," I mutter. "This whole damn town's mad at me."

"Not as many as you might think," he says. "I was, for a while, mad about Christopher missing those last couple of games. I was competing for a scholarship to Elmhurst. They were recruiting wide receivers and it was between me and a guy from Oklahoma. But it's pretty damn tough to catch passes when your quarterback's getting his dick fixed halfway across the country."

"Was his left nut," I mutter. "I saw it."

"Fine. His left nut. Doesn't matter. What I'm trying and obviously failing to tell you is I didn't get that scholarship. Didn't go to Elmhurst."

"So you're up in my business because you didn't get to catch footballs at some fancy-ass college?"

"No! Jesus, Berk, will you just listen instead of getting all pissy and defensive for one damned minute? My mother bawled. She'd worked ten, twelve hours a day, sometimes every damn day, so us kids had a shot. *She* was livid I didn't get to grasp the golden ring she always wanted for us. And I was pissed too, at first. Until the shit with Cory and Kelsey. But you tried to save her, just like you tried to save that girl Christopher raped. Then Jules, Lori, and Brittany beat the shit out of you. I was there, I was. In the car, just like you said. A scared kid with no money, no prospects, stuck stocking grocery shelves in a nowhere town with a slutty, nowhere girlfriend who kicks people in the eye, and I lied to the cops for them. I've *never* forgiven myself for that and for not dragging them off you."

"*What?*" I say, confused.

"I wanted to," he says, his eyes moist. "But I was afraid of being cast out. Stupid teenage shit. I knew inside I was better than that, but I was still terrified to buck the system like you always had. You faced life on your terms, least you did back then. Not trying to be something you weren't because of your overworked mother's guilt or because an airhead tramp gave you head to keep you in line. A lot of us, more than you might know, looked up to you.

Because you and you alone didn't give a shit what anyone else thought."

He pauses to meet my gaze, straight on, no bullshit. "You were *Berk*. Like a Norse goddess or something. Fierce. Kind. Untouchable. Pure *Berk*."

I'm not sure what to say. I've always considered myself a chaotic mess.

"Do you know why Lori and her friends hated you so much? I do. I heard all about it, over and over again from Julie, Brittany, and Lori."

"Why?" I ask before I can hold my damned tongue.

He laughs a little. "Because no matter what they did, you never cared about their bullshit. It was like they didn't exist, didn't matter. It drove them *insane*."

"You have *got* to be shitting me," I say.

"Nope. You never, ever, bought into their cult of personality at all, while Kelse openly mocked them. How to get you guys in line following them was a constant topic of conversation. Kelsey saw their imaginary line and hated it, but to you, there was no line to get into. That's all it ever was. Bitchy one-upmanship and mind games."

"Why are you telling me this?"

"Because I did hate you for a while, because of the Elmhurst scholarship thing and disappointing my mom. But I don't anymore. After the girls... after they beat you, I dumped Julie and got my shit together. Went to Kirkwood and took some classes. Met my wife there, which I wouldn't have done if you, well, hadn't been you. We have three kids–two girls and a boy. When our eldest daughter was born I understood. I finally understood."

He looks at me again, this time earnest and not at all afraid. "There she was, tiny and helpless and wriggly in my hands. And I knew right then, the moment I held my daughter, I'd kill anyone who harmed her. I finally understood why you defended that immigrant girl, why you went after Cory with that crowbar."

"Pipe wrench," I say.

He laughs and it's okay, like we're maybe on the same side.

"Thanks for listening," he says. "I just wanted you to know I'm sorry I didn't help when I could. Either time. I should have got out of that car and pulled them off you. Called the cops. Something. And I should have helped you with Christopher."

"You were there?"

"Yeah. I heard the commotion, peeked around the corner and saw you pummeling him right there by that half-naked kid, then I turned and walked away. It's haunted me ever since. I failed you, I failed that girl, and I failed myself. But no more." He stands a little taller and, for a few moments, I recognize the star athlete he'd once been. "I found my inner Berk the day my daughter was born."

"What about Kelsey and Cory?" I ask, my vision getting blurry. "Did you turn away from the mess with them, too?"

"Yeah. I should have helped him when he needed it. Listened maybe, I dunno."

He takes a shaky breath then meets my gaze again. "It was his Senior year, during Christmas break, I think, and I went over to his house to hang out. I saw this magazine in his room. Dudes on dudes porn, ya know? He tried to hide it, begged me not to say anything, and I never have, not until just now. And I've always wondered if... If I should have listened. If I should have told him it would be okay. Maybe Kelsey would be all right if I'd just told him I have a gay uncle and it was no big deal to me. If he knew he had someone in his corner."

He opens the door to let me go. "But I didn't. I turned my back on him instead. Shunned him, because I was a coward. And it haunts me still."

I follow him to the hall and, down near the entrance, a crowd of people mills around after the funeral service. The older man in the expensive suit frowns at us.

"I understand all this is probably too little too late," Troy whispers, "and you still have every reason in the world to hate me. Just, please, shake my hand for appearance's sake and when you call Monday, tell whoever answers that you decided to go with some other funeral home because they're cheaper. Then maybe I won't lose my job and maybe Cayden can see that specialist. Just... Can you do that?"

I smile and shake his hand, as requested. "How about you tell me what package my granddad bought when my gram died, September before last. And we can work it out from there?"

He grins, relieved. "That'd be great, Berk. Thank you. Come on back to the office and I'll pull the file."

I decide to call my mom on my way back to the house. I have no idea where on the planet she is, or what time of day it is there, but she needs to know when I'm burying her father.

Right?

It rings four times, then she picks up. Wherever she is, it's loud.

"Mandy!" she says. "I've been waiting for your call!"

I bite back my usual complaint about calling me Mandy and say, "Hey,

Mom. I don't know if you can get here or not, but the funeral's Wednesday at two."

"Well, crap. Already got my tickets. Won't be there until Friday. Didn't that man... Mark? Didn't Mark tell you?"

"Max."

"Yes, Marx. I just left a message on his voicemail. He should have told you, but maybe he's not that bright. I can't get there until Friday. Go ahead and reschedule the funeral for Friday evening or Saturday."

I stop at a stop sign and stare through the drizzle at a bleak and featureless sky. Don't do this to me, Mom. Not today. "I can't," I say. "It's already paid for and they've sent announcements everywhere."

"Mandy, just tell them I'm his daughter and I want to be there."

"Well, you're not here, I am, and I paid for it myself, picked the stuff myself, and am perfectly able to bury him myself. I agreed to Wednesday, and announcements have been posted. It's Wednesday, Mom. If you can't be here, that's okay. I'm managing just fine, just like I always do."

The background noise dims. "Don't start this again. You know I can't be there."

I don't know any such thing, but I remain silent and turn down Granddad's street.

"I have work to do, Mandy. I can't leave until after the shoot on Thursday or I lose this contract with NatGeo. I was able to push the Nepal shoot into next week, but the wedding in Darjeeling is Thursday, and they're scheduled for a two-page spread. If I don't shoot it, someone else—"

"I passed up at least five different commercials, but I'm here. It's all about choices, Mom. You made yours a long time ago."

"Mandy!" she says. "It's not the same thing. I'm a field photographer, and you play guitar."

I pull in the driveway and turn off my SUV. "It's exactly the same, and there's no need to come. I've got it handled. Have fun in Darjeeling."

Then I click off the call.

Mom calls right back, but I let it go to voicemail and lug my sorry ass inside. I need to find something for Granddad to wear, and pictures to have on display, and all of the other weep-heavy tasks on my 'preparing for a funeral' list, but right now, I just want to fall into a coma and stay there a while.

The house is quiet, no sign of Bill or Max. As I climb the stairs I wonder if he got a lift back to his place, then I hear him snoring softly from my room.

I stand in the doorway a few moments, watching him sleep. He's on his side, face pressed against my pillow, Bill curled behind his knees.

My two fuzzy guys. Looking at them makes me smile.

I strip and crawl in beside them where it's warm and safe and comforting.

"Glad you're home," Max mumbles against my shoulder as I snuggle in.

"Me too," I say, and he holds me until I fall asleep.

Max

Max woke with Berk spooned beside him and rain pattering on the roof. He needed to piss but didn't want to leave her warmth. His phone sat on the nightstand, blinking, so he grabbed it and found three missed messages.

His mother'd called twice, Berk's mother once. And it was almost 6 p.m.

He muttered 'Shit," and managed to slip out of bed without waking Berk.

He listened to the messages while the shower warmed and he brushed his teeth. Gail went on a ramble about a wedding and tea, something, something, Nepal, Friday, be cool Mark, then his mother asked when he'd be back to the apartment. Five minutes later but almost an hour and a half ago, she called again to tell him to call her right back because his father was in town and wanted to see him.

"Then Dad can call me himself," Max muttered, stepping into the shower.

While toweling off, he remembered he was stranded.

He dressed, grumbling under his breath to not wake Berk, then called his dad as he headed downstairs.

"Max? Where the hell are you? Your car's at your place, but you're not," his dad said when he picked up the call.

"Berk's." Max reached the downstairs. "We had to go to West Virginia the other night and just got back a while ago. What's up?"

"You need a lift?" his dad said, and Max paused, his head tilting.

"Yeah, actually I do. Was gonna call Mitch or Gret—"

"I'll be right there."

Then the call clicked off.

"Great," he muttered, and made himself a travel mug of fresh coffee.

Thankful for the overhang and porch light, Max sipped his coffee and watched the rain while he waited on the front stoop. He'd better not honk, he thought, eyes narrowing at every car driving down Berk's street. She needs to sleep.

He finally saw the familiar headlights of his dad's Explorer and waved before locking and closing the front door behind him. The Williamses never locked up their house when Berk'd lived there as a kid—all the kids knew about her Gram's no-questions-asked open-door policy for food and a place to crash. But Ted wasn't there to ensure safety, just Berk alone. Asleep.

Still felt weird locking that door.

Max hurried to his dad's Explorer and buckled his seatbelt as Rich backed out of the driveway, tires skidding through the puddle where the driveway met the street. "Thanks for picking me up," Max said.

"Thank you for finally calling back," Rich muttered. He sped to the corner, waited for a car to pass by, then sped toward the highway. "I got in last night and it's been a helluva mess."

"We got most of the clothes moved out of the house," Max said. "Pretty much everything but the furniture and some of the kitchen stuff. My car—"

"You did great with all that," his father said. "And I'd be insane to expect you to move a couch in your little car."

Actually borrowed Mitch's truck and it was too water damaged, Max thought then said, "Then why'd you need to talk to me?"

Rich turned onto the highway. "There's an opening at the refinery."

"Dad—"

"Just listen," Rich said. "It's a load operator job, filling tankers, but it starts at fifteen an hour, plus signing bonus and benefits. You'll have to live with us for a while, sure, but you wouldn't be on my crew."

"I don't—"

"Dammit, Max, it's time to grow up. Your marriage was a bust. Your bar's a bust. You need to face facts, stop chasing your pipe dreams, and move on to a real job."

"I'm not—"

"After you're at the refinery a year, assuming you don't fuck up, they'll train you to be yard foreman. You're smart and learn quick. You know all that computer crap. Maybe in a year or two after that, you can get into systems maintenance or something. Build a real future. Get back out on your own."

"I have a future, and it's in small business." Max stared straight ahead. "I've had a setback, sure—"

"Where are you gonna live?" his father asked, glancing at him as they pulled into the alley running behind his bar. "Everything you own is getting bulldozed next week. Do you even have money to rent a place? What are you going to do between the bulldozers and the first of the month? You mom's place is flooded out."

They pulled behind Tony's and stopped. Max stared at the back door and wished he could teleport through it. "I'll manage."

"Right. *You'll manage.*" Rich slammed his Explorer into park. "That's what you said when you caught Heidi cheating and needed a divorce lawyer. Well, you managed to get taken to the cleaners on that one. Twice."

Max reached for the door handle. "Thanks for the lift, Dad."

He'd barely left the SUV when Rich opened his door. "Maybe you should be careful about the choices you're making," he said, standing in the muddy parking lot. "Jesus, Max. You lusted after Berk in *high school.* Don't you think it's time to grow up?"

Max paused, his hand hovering over the back doorknob, then he turned and stared his dad in the eye. "Berk and I are none of your goddamn business."

He flung the door open to hear the familiar chatter of his Sunday night regulars and a Linkin Park tune on the Juke. The air smelled like beer and popcorn.

His mother sat on the stairs to his apartment and perked up when he entered his bar. "Max!" she said, scurrying down the last couple of steps to him while, from behind, he heard the back door open and his father lumber in.

His mother kissed him soundly on the cheek then she held his face in her hands. "You're gonna take the job, right?"

"No," he said, slipping away from her to walk past the bathrooms and cooler to the bar.

The guys at the window played Spades, Karen chatted with Gretchen at the end of the bar, and Dwight sang along to *Shadow of the Day* at the pinball machine, shaking his butt in time with the lyrics. Several other locals nursed their drinks while watching the NCAA tourney on the big screen, and a pair of UNI students argued politics in a booth near the door. Pretty busy for a Sunday night, and, as always, Gretchen kept the place immaculate.

"What the hell are you doing here?" Gretchen asked as Karen nodded hello. "Thought you'd be out boinkin' until sometime tomorrow."

I wish. Max eased past her and filled a glass with ice and Coke. "She had a family emergency so I decided to come in for a while."

Worry creased Gretchen's brow. "Everything okay?"

"No," Max said as he poured a generous splash of Jack into his Coke. He drank most of it in one long gulp then emptied the dishwasher and refilled drinks while pointedly ignoring his parents standing past Gretchen.

What the hell do I do? He thought, wiping dampness out of a freshly-washed highball glass. Dad's right, I don't have a job or apartment lined up yet, but, shit, things have been hitting hard and fast lately. I need to find something, yeah, but... *Texas?*

Shit!

Berk

I wake to darkness alone in my teenage bed, the faint patter of rain weeping on the roof above me. No Max. No Bill. No Granddad across the hall. Nothing but Dave making my phone buzz, three texts from my mother, and a hand-written note from Max saying he went to work for a while.

I have roughly seven gazillion funeral-prep things I'm supposed to do, but screw it. I've had enough of this shitbag of a day and I need to get out of this house. Maybe this whole damned town.

I drive through quiet, half-flooded streets, heading toward the highway back home, but, as I sit, blinking at the stoplights at the edge of town as they change to green to yellow to red for the fourth—Fifth? Seventh? Eleventy-bazillionth?—time, I realize I want to talk to Kelsey. Shit, maybe I *need* to talk to Kelsey.

But what if she's no longer here either? What if I missed my chance to say goodbye to her, too?

My Mazda's the third car in the hospice parking lot and I've been sitting here in the dark for a long time, silent except for the rain on my roof and my own random sobs. I'm afraid to go in. Deb's car's not in the lot; neither is anything with Texas plates. Rich used to drive a rusted out Explorer, but I don't know if he still does. I don't know anything except I might not be able to pick out burial clothes for Granddad tonight, but I *can* quit crying in my fucking car and tell my best friend goodbye before she goes.

I can.

I have to push the door buzzer. A soft-faced nurse lets me in then scurries off to tend to her patients.

Kelsey's where I last saw her, still staring at nothing while a stocky male nurse—the same guy I saw drinking liquor and lime in Max's bar—gently washes her face, neck, and arms, a fluffy towel covering her bare breasts. We share a nod. I still don't remember his name—Josh? Jeff? Something with a J—but he's focused on the task at hand instead of me. As I take off my jacket,

I realize I don't give a shit who he is.

Ancient reruns are on TV, some black and white Western barely loud enough to hear over Kelsey's heavy wheeze and the damp stroke of the nurse's washcloth. I excuse myself to get a cup of coffee.

When I get back, the nurse is gone and Kelsey's wearing a fresh nightgown. It's purple. Her favorite color.

"Hey Kelse," I say as I pull up a chair and fold her hand around mine. This time, her fingertips are cool but her palm's still warm and a little damp. "How about I tell you about my helluva weekend while I do your nails?"

I reach for the always-handy bottle of fingernail polish remover on her bedside table. "Do you want lilac tonight? Pearled Amethyst? Electric eggplant? Maybe something with glitter?"

She wheezes. I talk, like I always do, like I always can with Kelsey, about playing the benefit for my neighbor and losing my granddad and how Max drove all night to get me home.

I talk and cry and do her nails, and, for a while, everything's okay.

⚘

By the time Deb comes in, the Western's over and some old cop show is just starting. Kelsey and I have matching electric-purple nails with a glitter a topcoat. We look *marvelous!*

"Berk," Deb says, taking off her coat. "Didn't expect to see you here, what with your granddad and all."

I shrug. "Didn't want to be at the house so I thought I'd hang with Kelse for a while."

Deb nods as if this makes perfect sense, but we both know it's half insane. Kelsey's done nothing but breathe and stare and mess her diapers since Cory bashed in her head a decade ago. Sometimes I think she's still in there, somewhere, hearing and seeing and thinking. Other times... Other times, she's long gone, just an empty husk in a hospital bed, a make-believe illusion of her, a ghost with her face.

A flat out lie.

I just don't know, and it's hard. So, fucking *hard.*

God, I miss her so much.

I sigh and try to smile at Deb, to maybe show her our manicures, but I feel an awkwardness in the air between us and it makes me nervous. I'm not sure why. Maybe I'm imagining it.

Deb sits in the chair by the door and rummages in her purse before pulling out a partial pack of Juicy Fruit. "Gum?"

"No thanks. I'm good," I say, and Deb shrugs, sighing.

Maybe it's time for me to go.

"Well, Kelse," I say, forcing myself to smile, "I'm gonna take off. Maybe I'll see you tomorrow."

I squeeze her hand and gather my things.

Deb stands and approaches the bed while I shrug on my jacket. "Did you change her nightgown?" she asks me. "I'd put her in a fresh one this morning."

"No. A nurse was giving her a bath when I got here. He must have."

Deb finally smiles. "Oh! Jack came by?"

"Uh, I guess? He didn't mention his name."

She adjusts Kelsey's blanket. "Jack Scheffert. We just love him. He was her nurse almost every time she was in the hospital, off and on for six, maybe seven years, now. Always took the best care of her." She pauses and smiles at me. "She never got bedsores or infections when he was her nurse. And he *always* put her in a purple gown after her bath."

Ah. Now I remember him. Brainy kid, nice enough but I thought he was into mechanical things, not nursing. I walk around the bed. "He doesn't work here? At the hospice?"

"No. The hospital. Nice guy. Too bad he didn't know her before the accident, didn't know how incredible she used to be."

"He was a year ahead of us in school," I mutter. "So he probably did know her. Small town and all that."

Deb blinks at me.

I stuff my hands in my jacket pockets and sigh. I don't want to go back into the rain.

"Hey," Deb says as I reach the door. "Can you do something for me?"

I turn back at her. "Absolutely. Anything you need."

Her shoulders sag and she glances away before taking a breath and meeting my gaze. "I just... I don't care what you and Max do. You're both adults. Just... When you left right after high school, it broke his heart. Don't hurt him again. Please."

"We're just friends having fun," I assure her. "He knows I'll be leaving in a few days."

She nods and I turn to go. As I walk out to the rain I'm confident Max will be just fine. Me, on the other hand, maybe not so much.

My brain's half disconnected, but I'm about a block away from the hospice when my stomach reminds me I haven't eaten since breakfast in Moline, forever ago. And there isn't a lot of food at the house except canned soup and frozen corn.

I pull into the grocery store at nearly 9:30 on a Sunday night and scowl at the half-dozen vehicles parked near the doors. I really don't want to run into Lori again. In fact, I'd be just fine if I never saw her half-dressed, snot-nosed kids or her shitty heart tattoo either.

Suck it up, I think, stepping out of my SUV. I need milk, eggs, salad fixings, and sandwich stuff. Get in, get out, get home, and face Granddad's closet.

I grab a cart and put on my best do-not-mess-with-me face. I see a couple of half-sloshed guys buying beer, a short redhead chatting on her phone while trying to choose Hamburger Helper, two tall, bearded hipsters picking through lemons, a plump middle-aged woman happily examining cat treats in the pet food aisle, and some teenager comparing cold meds as if it's the biggest decision of his life.

No Lori. My mood improves immensely.

I cruise through dairy for my milk and eggs, snag some shaved turkey and provolone, then I'm on my way to the produce section when the hispter dudes come around the corner toward me.

The shorter of the pair swipes his phone screen while the taller pushes their cart and stares at the scrap of paper in his hand.

He has a scar running from his left eyebrow to his scalp and it parts his stylishly-scruffy brown hair.

He's the right height. The right age. The right everything.

No God. Please. Not Cory.

Not today.

"How do we make Herbs de Provence, again?" he says with the voice haunting my nightmares and everything within me twists and collapses inward like my chest has turned into a black hole.

"No. No!" I say aloud and Cory Hildebrandt stops to gawk at me while my heart slams so hard my hands shake the cart.

"Aw, Jesus, Berk," he says, his coppery-brown eyes unmistakable over his beard. "I knew you were in town but didn't expect—" He shakes his head and holds up his hands to me as his friend touches his arm. "I'm sorry. We'll go. We'll go."

"What about supper!" the other guy whines, showing Cory his phone. "We need savory and lavender, if we can find it, and some vermouth. That's it."

"We're going, Jacob," Cory says.

"But the *chicken*," Jacob says through clenched teeth.

Cory gives him a dark glare. "Screw the chicken, we have to go."

"Do whatever you have to do, just stay the fuck away from me," I snap, cutting through their argument.

Every voice in the rest of the store falls utterly silent but I do not care.

Jacob takes a half-step back and blinks as if he's just noticed me. "Who are..." he starts, then his eyes grow wide. "Ohmigawd. Is that her?"

"Yeah," Cory says, easing backward while holding my gaze. "And we're leaving. Right now. Because we don't need to cause any trouble. Okay, Berk?" he says, his voice soft and coaxing. "I don't want any trouble. Take your time shopping. We'll leave."

"No, we're not," Jacob says, taking a step toward me. "Do you know what you did to him?" he snaps. "Do you?"

"I didn't kill him like I should have," I snarl, staring at Cory and wishing I had laser vision or some shit to light his goddamn everything on fire. Then I'd dump lighter fluid on him. Maybe roast some marshmallows and make S'Mores. It'd be the highlight of my day.

"Forty-two stitches, a concussion, brain swelling, blood clots, and memory loss, along with *over a year* in therapy," Jacob says, his voice rising. "His right side's still weak, he has balance and memory problems, and for what, you goddamn bitch? For nothing! Nothing!"

"Jacob! Not now!"

"Kelsey's not nothing, and who the fuck are you, anyway?"

He stops just beyond my reach and crosses his arms over his chest, sterling wedding band around his finger shimmering in the overhead lights. "Jacob Hildebrandt, as if that's any of your goddamn business. We were here first, so you need to leave."

"Jacob!"

Jacob blinks at me and holds his ground. "Yes. *You* leave. I'm cooking Chicken Provençale tonight and we have every right to be here."

By now the gal with her Hamburger Helper has come to watch the show, as has a skinny dude with a case of Coors under his arm, and a teenager in a store-clerk uniform.

"Aw, shit," Coors says, rolling his eyes. "Just the damn queers." Then he walks away, leaving Hamburger Helper and the clerk to witness whatever's about to happen.

Cory watches me, his eyes pleading, while Jacob stares as if he'd like to light me on fire.

"Fine," I say, turning to stomp away. "I hope you both choke on your shitty

French chicken."

Jacob hollers after me, his voice echoing through the store, "He never touched her, you stupid bitch! You wrecked his life for nothing!"

"Kelsey isn't nothing!" I holler back before returning to the rain.

Intermezzo-Summer Before Eighth Grade

Kelsey rode bikes with Berk and Max to the splash pad at Midtown Park under a scorching August sun. All three waved hello to Tony Hartford huffing and sweating while mowing his front yard. Tony smiled and waved back before shoving the mower beneath his lilac bush.

"Wonder if he'd pay me to mow his yard?" Max said, glancing back at Tony.

Berk grinned at him. "Probably. Whatcha need money for?"

"Just to have," Max said. "Never hurts to have a side business or two."

Kelsey rolled her eyes. *You're suddenly an entrepreneur because you want to see Kate Beckinsale in tight leather when Underworld opens.*

They reached the park and all three groaned at the clot of daycare kids hogging the sprinklers.

Berk mumbled *shit* as she skidded her bike to a stop, then she turned and said, "You guys wanna try for the pool? I can cover it."

"No, we're okay," Kelsey said. "This is *fine*." She gave Berk an assured smile and dismounted at the bike rack. "Right, Max?"

Max's face had fallen, but he nodded and stepped off his bike. "Yeah. They'll leave soon, anyway."

Frowning, Kelsey watched him shove his bike into the rack. Mom had lectured them that morning about not letting Berk pay for *everything*. Just because their dad's hours had been cut didn't mean Berk needed to supply their summer entertainment. Midtown Park's splash pad was free, the pool was not. End of story.

Besides, after admission and snacks, it'd cost fifteen, twenty bucks, easy, Kelsey decided. Far too much to dump on Berk.

Berk inserted her bike beside Kelsey's. "Mom sends me a pile of money every month and I'm glad—"

"Wet is wet, and we're good." Max peeled off his t-shirt and crammed it into his backpack before walking toward the sprinklers.

"Really," Berk said to Kelsey. "You're my friends and it's cool. We don't have to hang around the can't-wipe-their-own-ass set all the damn time."

"I know," Kelsey said as they fell in together. "Let's just have fun anyway."

They peeled off their tank tops and shorts beside the restrooms then followed Max to an empty bench shaded by a nearby tree. Berk pulled a super-soaker from her backpack and giggled as she jogged toward the big sprinkler but Kelsey paused to put her hair into a ponytail and smear on sunscreen.

"Excuse me, Miss," a man said from behind her and she jumped, turning to see a city worker rolling a measuring wheel toward the restroom. "You're right where I need to measure."

"Oh, sorry," she said, stepping aside.

She watched him roll the wheel to the end of the restroom building, then he paused to write in a little notebook.

"Oh good," she said. "They're upgrading the restrooms!"

He chuckled and shook his head before turning the wheel to roll directly toward the parking lot. "Nope. Ripping it all out for retail shops."

She followed. "What kind of shops? A lot of people use this park!"

"Not sure. That's a long way above my pay grade," he said, nodding toward the far side of the park. "I'm just supposed to get a rough measurement for the boss."

Kelsey turned her head and squinted in the sunlight. The mayor and Bucky's dad, Mr. Sanderson—who owned the crappy downtown discount store and the equally crappy movie rental store—examined the large sheet of white paper Lori's dad, Mr. Gilbert, held in front of them. The mayor pointed west of the splash pad while Mr. Sanderson nodded.

They can't rip this out for more scummy stores! Kelsey thought, glaring at the three men.

The mayor pointed past the restrooms and their gaze passed right over her as if she wasn't there.

That made her madder still.

Later that afternoon, while Berk and Max played some punch-kick-flip combat game on the PlayStation in the living room, Kelsey sat in the kitchen, nursing a Dr. Pepper and watching Berk's gram chop veggies for stir fry.

"What's on your mind, Kelse?" Beth asked. "Something's bugging you."

"Nothing I can do anything about," Kelsey said, shrugging.

Beth dumped chopped broccoli into a bowl. "Maybe, maybe not. I've been around a while and might be able to help. Let's hear it."

"The city's gonna rip out Midtown Park," Kelsey muttered, spinning her glass in her hands. "It just sucks."

"What? Why would they do that?"

"Pretty sure Mr. Sanderson wants to build another crap store. I saw him, the mayor, and Mr. Gilbert there today. Some worker guy was measuring the park while they looked at plans. The guy said they were putting in retail."

Beth turned to scowl at her. "He said that?"

"The measuring guy? Yeah. Gonna rip out the park and put in retail."

"Goddammit," Beth muttered, reaching for the kitchen phone. "Not this shit again."

She punched in a number then leaned back against the counter while Kelsey watched.

"Hey, Hannah? It's Beth. You and Tony busy? Put him on the other line." She covered the receiver and gave Kelsey a consoling smile. "Hang tough, hon. We'll get this sorted out," then her expression changed to fury.

"Hey. Wanted to let you know a little bird just told me Bob, Walter, and Brad were at Midtown Park today with construction plans and a surveyor measuring for retail. Is that on the council meeting agenda or last week's minutes? I don't recall reading it. Yeah, I'll hang on."

She covered the receiver with her hand again. "Tony's checking."

Kelsey nodded and sipped her Dr. Pepper.

"No, I'm not gonna tell you who," Beth said, glancing at Kelsey. "But I will say they're utterly reliable. We all knew they'd try this shit again. They can't stand to see profit slip away. Bastards."

She nestled the phone on her shoulder and began chopping an onion. "So nothing on record. Then it's not official, right? Uh huh. Yeah, I can get two hundred signatures, probably more. Yep. Email me the form and I'll start canvassing right after supper. I'll hit every house on our end of town by meeting time Monday. Promise! Thanks, guys!"

She hung up the phone and continued to chop. "Tony Hartford's the go-to guy for this stuff. He's blocked Bob Gilbert and the mayor's building schemes before, and we'll start gathering signatures tonight. So. You coming along to knock on doors with me if I clear it with your mom?"

Kelsey grinned. "I'd love to!"

Max

Max lugged a fresh tub of popcorn from the office and grumbled, "No parties!" at Gretchen rushing to answer the ringing phone. "I'd like to get a little sleep tonight."

"Me too," she sighed as she picked up the receiver. "Tony's!" she said, more cheerful than she looked, then nestled the phone between her shoulder and ear. "Yeah, hang on, he's right here."

She held the phone toward him and bent to fetch a bottle of Sam Adams from the fridge beneath the bar. "It's for you, and we have four Sam left."

Crap. Hope they last the hour 'til close. The pair of students in the corner had grown to five, all whooping at UNI sinking a three-pointer. They'd gorged on popcorn and a _lot_ of beer, thankfully most of it on tap, and the guy wearing a _Drink Up, I'm the DD_ ballcap had been throwing back Cokes. Max set down his popcorn tub and grabbed the phone. "Can I help you?"

"Hey," Berk said from the other end of the line. "I tried calling your cell—"

"Oh, it's back in the office," he said, giving Gretchen a cheerful thumbs-up as one of the students dropped a ten on the counter and carried away the entire tub of still-warm popcorn. "Did you get any sleep?"

"Yeah. I guess. But right now I wanna know if you're hungry. I'm starving."

"I can eat, sure," he said.

"Great. I'll bring food. Your folks still up?"

"Yeah, Dad's watching the game and Mom should be back soon."

"Cool. So, you, Gretchen, your folks... How many customers?"

"You don't need to feed everyone. Hell, we're closing in about an hour."

"Oh, yes I do," she muttered. "How many do you have right now?"

"Five rowdy tourney fans and three neighborhood regulars. But you really don't have—"

"Okay, cool. Food for thirteen. Be there in a few."

The call clicked off.

He stared at the silent phone for a moment then put it back on the hook.

"Was that your *girlfriend?*" Gretchen teased on her way to the cash register.

"Just friends," he said. "And, yeah, it was her."

Gretchen winked at him and stuffed the ten in the till. "Y'all've been boinking for the better part of a week. Hell, you even left town together. That's a bit more than *friends.*"

"She's leaving in a few days. And I'm apparently going to Texas."

Gretchen graced him with her you-have-GOT-to-be-shitting-me eye roll as she walked to the next kid wanting a beer. "Uh huh."

"Yeah, I don't like it either," Max muttered, nodding to Dwight who wanted another glass of below-the-well bourbon.

⌇⌐⌇

Berk showed up about fifteen minutes later with an armload of steaming pizza boxes and breadsticks. "I got a variety," she said, maneuvering the stack onto the bar before waving a 'come on over and get some' greeting to the cheering basketball fans and the guys at the front window. "You got plates?"

"I'll get 'em," Gretchen said then hurried away.

Max sighed. "What do I owe you?"

"Not a goddamn thing. And we're done discussing it." She flipped open a pizza box, pulled out a slice, and snagged a bag of breadsticks before stepping aside to make room for hungry students. She eased onto the stool at the end of the bar. "How long 'til close?" she said over the chaos.

Max glanced at his watch. "About forty-five, fifty minutes."

"Cool." Berk munched pizza and glowered at the game, leaving Max to arrange the pizza boxes and refill drinks.

Gretchen set a pack of foam plates on the bar and handed one to Berk, who'd waved her over. The two women talked, heads close together, their voices lost beyond the UNI students hollering over a bad call. Berk handed Gretchen a twenty, then they fist-bumped.

Gretchen turned toward Max, grinning. "Guess what?" she said, pocketing the twenty before pulling a Sam Adams from the fridge.

"You're embezzling right in front of me?" Max said, shaking his head.

Gretchen laughed. "Nope. It's a tip." She removed the beer's cap. "Your girlfriend's putting everyone on her tab until close."

"*What?*"

"Yup." Gretchen delivered the beer to Berk and said over her shoulder, "She said she's throwing a pity party and everyone here's invited."

Dwight slid a couple of pieces of pizza onto his plate. "Did Gretch really just say your hotsy's paying the tab?"

"No."

"Yes!" Berk snapped back, toasting with her beer. "Anything y'all drink between now and close is on me."

The regulars nodded, Max's dad grinned, and the students cheered. Max wanted to throw his head back and curse at the ceiling.

He stood in front of Berk while she stuffed a breadstick in her mouth and gave him the same, defiant *watch what I can do* expression she'd had the first time she gave him a blow job.

"Berk, look, I can't let you—"

She chewed the breadstick and washed it down with a mouthful of beer. "You can't stop me. I had to make Granddad's funeral arrangements with Troy Haddert, who, honestly, wasn't anywhere near as much of a douche as I expected him to be, came home to crash then woke up alone in a dead-empty house, so I went to see your sister who sounds like she has a train in her chest, had to talk sex with your mother, thankfully briefly, then ran into Cory at the grocery store. *And* his boyfriend got all up in my face."

"Husband. They married almost two years ago. And, yeah, Jacob's kinda confrontational."

She gave him a *you are not helping* glare and polished off the beer. "Gimme another one."

"You sure? I have Sprite on tap."

"Give me another fucking lager, if you still have some. If not, I'll take Jack and Coke."

He fetched Berk's beer. Only one left in the fridge.

The regulars left at their regular times, each thanking Berk for the booze and pizza before heading out to the rain, and Dwight snagged a couple of slices for the road. Max's folks carried their pizza and beer upstairs and didn't come back down, but the students continued to watch the game. With only 2:28 left in the game at his usual Sunday close time of 11 p.m., Max agreed to let them stay until the final buzzer.

Berk had taken her second beer to a booth where she talked and cried while Gretchen held her hand and listened as if they were lifelong friends.

Max, meanwhile, munched on a slice of sausage and mushroom and tidied up, prepping to close once the bar cleared out. The UNI students alone had bought more drinks than his usual Sunday night crowd, but Berk covering the final hour really pushed up the numbers.

"Last call, guys," he said to the students riveted on the double free throw with a minute and thirty-four seconds left in the game. UNI was down by five. Not impossible, but tough to get in a minute-and-a-half against Oregon.

One free-throw in, the student with the designated driver hat said, "Just another pitcher and one more Coke ought to do us," then he groaned and threw up his hands at the second ball bouncing off the rim. "Goddammit!"

"Just need two. We'll get there," the girl sitting next to him said without looking away from the screen. She wore a Panthers sweatshirt and purple barrettes in her yellow-streaked hair.

Max fetched their beer then paused at Berk's booth. "You ladies want anything before I finish up?"

"I can freshen my own coffee," Gretchen said, scooting out of the booth.

Berk leaned back and regarded him. "How bad's my tab?"

He sat. "Not too bad. The kids were pretty sloshed before you got here, so they only had two pitchers and a couple of Cokes, plus a handful of drinks for the guys. So you're looking at fifty-two bucks."

She chuckled. "Is that all? I was expecting at least twice that."

He shrugged. "We're not exactly hopping on Sunday nights, especially now that everyone knows we're closing."

Oregon dropped a three-pointer and the students groaned.

Berk shook her head and toyed with her nearly-empty beer bottle. "It's a great bar."

"Yeah, well. Doesn't matter. It's getting bulldozed in a week."

"There has to be a way to save it. Has to."

"Nope. Sometimes things just *are*."

He held her gaze for the couple of moments until Gretchen returned, steaming mug in hand.

"Want me to finish cleaning up?" she asked before taking a sip.

"Nah, you went off the clock forty-five minutes ago," Max said. "You can head on home."

Gretchen rolled her eyes and walked away. "You sit. Eat some pizza and chat with your girlfriend. I got it."

Berk chuckled again, drawing Max's attention. "I like her. And I'm not your girlfriend."

"Yeah, I told her."

Silence stretched a couple of moments too long.

Max broke it. "Do you want *anything* else?"

"Besides you? Nah, I'm good." She reached into her pocket for her wallet and pulled out three twenties. "Here. Put the rest in the tip jar."

He sighed. "You don't have—"

"Are you staying at... at Granddad's tonight?" she interrupted, her lower lip curling in.

"Was hoping to. It's either that or sleeping in my car."

She nodded, dropping her gaze, and took a shaky breath. "Good. Thanks."

He reached out to grasp her hand as the final buzzer sounded. "You okay?"

"No. I don't think so. Mind if I stick around until you close up? Then you can follow me to the house?"

"Don't mind at all."

He slid from the booth while the group of UNI students stood, grumbling, and gathered their coats.

"Hey, dude," their designated driver said. "Thanks for letting us watch the game. I know we got kinda rowdy."

"Nah, it's all good," Max said. "Thanks for coming in." He grabbed a bus tub and bar towel, then waved goodbye to the students as they headed out into the rain. The table was an absolute disaster, but they'd left a scattered collection of bills and change totaling almost thirty bucks and a fifty-dollar Amazon gift card sitting on top of a napkin.

He lifted the card and chuckled, shaking his head at the note written beneath.

> *Mr. Bar Man, there's only $34.87 on this, but it's all I got.*
> *Cale was right to watch the game here. We had a blast!*
> *Have a happy!*
> *Keri!* ♥

I'll do my best, he thought, adding the card to the stack of small bills and coins.

Berk

Max followed me to the house like he promised, but I'm crying by the time we get there. I don't want to go in, but what's the alternative? Standing forever in the rain?

At least he can't see my tears, right?

My hand shakes when I try to insert the key. His hand covers mine, and it's warm. Comforting.

"I got it," he says and I lean against him as he unlocks my grandparents' back door.

We're dripping and drenched. The air inside's warm and smells like Granddad. Bill scurries from the living room, chirping hello. Of course, he makes a beeline for his food dish, which I forgot to fill today.

I know it's understandable, considering, but seeing that empty food dish and Bill sitting so patiently beside it starts me bawling again.

"I'm sorry. I forgot," I say pulling his bag of cat food from the cupboard while Max takes off his coat. "It's been a really bad day."

Bill dances around the dish, mrowing the way cats do, and I end up dumping some of the food on his stripy head when his eagerness to eat puts him in the way. The kitty-kibbles scatter on gram's white tile floor, and they remind me of Kelsey's blood on the athletic shed's walls.

Of Danny exploded.

Of Gram and her aneurysm in a pile of yarn.

Of Granddad, cold in some strange woman's bed.

Everything feels sideways again, but Max is there, cradling me, whispering my name against my brow. "It's okay," he says. "Everything's okay."

"No. It's not." I wipe tears away. "The funeral's Wednesday. Can you... Can you come? And sit with me so I won't be his only family? So I won't be alone."

"Absolutely. Of course," he says, helping me out of my wet jacket. "I can even call your aunts and uncles if you want. Your mom. Anybody."

"I already tried, I did. I called gram's sister while I waited for the pizza. She can't get off work that day but she promised to send flowers, and she said one brother's in the hospital recovering from heart surgery, and her other brother's on some cruise for two weeks, so they're out, and I haven't seen my cousins since I was a kid, so I can't imagine them coming all this way but she said she'd tell them. So then I... I called both of granddad's brothers, even the one he can't stand."

He holds me, cradles me. "Berk..."

"I told his wife who I was and that granddad had died, she said good, he can rot for all they care," I sob. "And his other brother just wanted money."

"Shh. It's okay."

"And my mom, my own damn mother, she won't be here until Friday because of some stupid photo shoot. And I can't, I can't do this all alone. I just *can't*. Not with everything else."

"I'm here, and I'm not going anywhere. What can I do to help?"

I know what I want, but... It's not real, just stress and grief, I tell myself. He'll probably laugh at me, but the idea doesn't let go. It's like its roots are deep, burrowed into stone foundations I never look at. I take a shaky breath and steady myself. "I, I hate to ask. Shit." My fortitude is fragile and crumples like tin foil while the roots still insist, sending shoots that thrum my own bassline, the one I'm afraid to hear, the one that insists I don't have to be alone. Torn, I pull away from him. "Never mind. Forget it."

"What?" he says, turning me back to him and searching my eyes. "What do you need me to do? I'll do it."

"It's stupid. I know. But..." I take a shaky breath and manage to meet his gaze. "All of my life, I've had no real family except for Granddad and Gram. You've always been a good friend, but... Shit." I hesitate, but his firm gaze doesn't let me pull away. "Can you make love to me? Not just sex, but... but like I really was your girlfriend and you love me? Maybe just hold me, I dunno. I need to feel like I matter to someone. So I'm not *alone*. Just once."

He pulls me into his embrace and rocks me, still standing in Gram's kitchen. "Oh Berk, you've *always* mattered to me."

His fingers tilt my face toward his and he kisses me like he has dozens of times this past week, but I tell myself it's different somehow. He is a helluva kisser, after all, and it's easy to pretend that he loves me and I love him even though I know it's all a delicious lie.

He kisses my neck, opens the collar of my sweater to trace his tongue along my collarbones, and I'm breathless when he scoops me up like I'm not crazy tall, like I'm petite and as light as a handful of fragile petals in his hands. He carries me up the stairs and I giggle despite myself, feeling like a newly-minted princess carried away by her prince in an old black-and-white movie.

He's laughing too, all the way to my room, to my teenage bed, a bed I've shared with no one but him. He makes us naked and his hands and lips are warm and coaxing, familiar and adoring as he opens me up for him and his face and his tongue.

It's not long before I cry out, I've never come like this, and, off in the ether, muffled against my thighs, I hear him say, "I love you, Berk. God, I love you," but I know it's not real, it's not. It can't be. Then he's over me and in me and loving me slow and deep, as if I'm priceless to him, and him to me, like it's always been this way. Forever. Maybe since we were twelve and he almost kissed me under the willow tree. Maybe before, when we were eight and he sprained his ankle falling out of a tree in Midtown Park and I supported him as we hopped to his house. Maybe long after, when we were fifteen and he almost kissed me behind the garden shed with bits of hostas in my hair. Or any of the countless times it was just *us*.

We've humped like rabbits for days, but it's different now, something's different, something's changed. When he shudders within me and groans out my name, which he's never done before, ever, I realize it's all him this time, no condom, just Max, *my Max*, my lifelong friend, the foundation of my childhood. He tilts my hips and I feel it, I feel him come and the sudden wet heat within me and, oh God, now I'm going again.

And I believe him. In that one raw moment, I believe him. And I believe me. And I believe us. That I matter to him and he matters to me and this is real.

But then I'm in my old room with rain on the roof and him exhausted and panting and rolling off me, cradling me even as the illusion fades. I don't want him to leave me, I don't want this one precious moment to end, so I snuggle in. He does too, his face against my shoulder and our legs sprawled together as he pulls the blanket over us. His arm is comforting and heavy across my belly and his breath so warm on my skin.

I wish we could stay here forever.

"You forgot the condom," I whisper, pressing closer to him, reaching for him. I'm warm and cozy and safe.

"Aw, shit, I'm sorry," he mumbles against my neck.

"Don't be," I whisper, fading fast. "Made it seem more real."

Morning comes and I manage to get out of bed without waking Max. I glance at Granddad's room on my way to the shower and his death hits me in the gut again. I wonder if it always will or if it, like every other loss, will fade over time.

In the shower, I decide I don't want to face choosing his forever suit or dig through photo albums or devise some pithy thing to say. Nope. Later maybe, but not first thing, not when I'm this pissy. Maybe what I need is a good stretch. It usually helps my mood.

I'm in the midst of a yoga DVD, pressing into a revolved side angle to my left, when Max comes down the stairs.

"Wow. No wonder you're so... bendy," he says.

The DVD leads me into a downward dog. "I started doing yoga in college. Lia dragged me to a class and I loved it. Zumba, too." Another shift to an extended-hand-to-toe, balancing on my right foot this time, and I glance over to see Max grinning and enthralled.

"Ever done yoga? I can show you," I say, easing my left foot to shoulder level and outward as he walks toward me. "It's great stretching. This one really helps tight leg muscles and overall balance."

I bring my foot down and back, then bend, twisting into triangle pose as I extend my left hand toward the ceiling and my right to the floor. "It's not that hard," I say pressing into the stretch. "Just takes some practice."

"Oh, it's plenty hard," he says, grasping my hips and thrusting against me, almost knocking me off balance. "And I'd love more practice."

"Hey!" I say, giggling and swatting toward him. "I'm trying to stretch here!"

He keeps humping my butt and his voice is husky, seductive. "Me too."

I sigh and stand, turning to face him, while my DVD plays on. "Okay, cool. You're horny. Right now, *I'm* doing yoga."

"Awesome," he says, still grinning, and he unzips his jeans. "Go right ahead. I'll watch until you've finished."

"Urgh! No! I'm working out, then I have to dig through Granddad's clothes."

He frowns at me. "Okaaay. Just trying to figure out the new parameters here."

"New parameters?"

"Since we're like officially dating now, what am I supposed to do? Ignore you looking all sexy-bendy hot? Forget I woke up with my face smelling like your vagi—"

I blink. "Thought we agreed we're not dating and, last I knew, the parameters haven't changed."

"Oh really," he says, pointing to the kitchen. "Last night, *right there*, you asked me to be your boyfriend and to make love to you. See your coat on the back of that chair? You asked me right there. I carried you upstairs, and, frankly, I fucked your brains out. Pretty sure you came twice."

"And you left a slimy, stinky mess for me to clean up this morning," I mutter while my DVD moves on to horizontal work. "But that doesn't make you my boyfriend!"

"You didn't seem to mind last night. Said it made it more real. Hell yes, it's real and you asked me—"

"To pretend to be my boyfriend!"

"Bullshit," he says and takes a breath to say more, but someone knocks on the front door.

"Not bullshit," I say on my way past. "I had a bad day, and a weak moment—"

He follows. "Asking me to love you is a *weak moment?*"

"I asked you *to pretend!* I'd had a really shitty day and just needed some comfort," I mutter as I yank the door open.

Two women and a man stand there, the man with flattened boxes, and one of the women holds a pair of clipboards.

"Good morning!" the older of the two women say to Max behind me. She's short and thick, with gray-streaked dark hair and glasses. Her name tag says Judy. She looks past me to Max. "Theodore Williams?"

Granddad's name hits me like a stone in my gut. "No, he just passed away. Can I help you?"

"We're here to prep for the auction this weekend." She glances from me to Max then back to me again. "Did we come at a bad time?"

"I don't think there's any such thing as a good time," I sigh.

"Apparently not," Max mutters on his way to the kitchen. "I'm going to work."

"Wait, what? You can't go!" I say, following as the auction people enter the house.

He's already yanking on his coat. "Oh? Why not? It's not like we're a couple or anything."

I mutter, "Goddammit," then say, my voice low so maybe the auction people won't hear, "I never asked to be a couple and I don't want a relationship."

He turns to face me. "You think I do? After Heidi fucked me over I swore off women. Three years, Berk. Three goddamn celibate years, then you slide into my life after I thought you were gone forever. And it was great. Incredible. I knew you'd up and leave again, but, shit, I accepted we could just have some fun, no strings, no worries, nothing important. Just fuckbuddies, like you wanted."

"We did! We are!"

"No. Lovemaking isn't *fun*, it's fucking *serious*. And it fucking *matters*. At least to me. But obviously not to you."

I stammer, not knowing what to say and clean up this mess I've created.

"See you around, Berk," he says, then he's gone, slamming the door behind him.

My hands shake and I feel tears sting my eyes. I don't know how to fix this, if it's even possible.

Someone clears their throat behind me and I turn to see the three auction workers watching me. "Sorry, ma'am," Judy says, checking the papers on her clipboard. "But we have a contract with Theodore Williams. To sort and assess the contents of this house, everything as is, except whatever Amanda Williams decides to keep. If Theodore's deceased, where would we find Amanda?"

"I'm Amanda," I sigh. "His granddaughter."

She looks at the other two, who shrug and lower their gaze, then she's back to me. "Ma'am, um, that young fellow called you Berk." She taps her pen on the clipboard. "If you're not on Theodore's approved list, you *can't be here.* We're bonded and—"

"My middle name's Berkeley," I snap. "Everyone calls me Berk."

The other two nod and pull on gloves as they walk away, but Judy watches me with bland disbelief. I sigh. Why do so many people insist on calling me Amanda? I fucking hate being called Amanda. "Goddammit. I'll go find my license."

"No need to cuss, Ma'am," Judy scolds as I climb the stairs.

My wallet's in my jeans, tossed somewhere when Max removed all of my clothes and actually made love to me. For real.

To him, it's all for real.

What the hell did I do?

Intermezzo - Summer Before Eleventh Grade

Jack carried two bags of food and Kelsey carried her grandmother's quilt into a tiny scrap of woods a mile or so southwest of Kiester, Minnesota.

They found a grassy place, almost flat, and he helped her spread the quilt in the shade.

She smiled. It was quiet. Peaceful. Private. Birds sang and a squirrel chittered at them before scampering away through the trees.

"Just got a chicken bucket meal from the store. Hope that's okay," Jack said, his hands shaking as he unpacked the grocery bags. "Dew for me, Diet Pepper for you..."

"It's wonderful," she said. "And we don't have to do anything except have lunch."

"I know," he said, pulling the bucket of chicken from the bag. "I don't want you to feel obligated to sleep with me, just because we've been dating..."

She put her small hand on his thick one. "I'm ready for this next step."

He took a breath and turned to look at her. "You can do better than me, Kelse. You're brilliant, you're gorgeous, and you're gonna go places. I'm just a fat kid who might, maybe, be able to get a Pell Grant and go to community college to become a diesel mechanic."

"Jack..."

He took a breath. "You should save this for somebody who matters."

"*You* matter," she said. "You matter to *me*." She kissed him, her hands on his face. "I want to tell the world about us. How I found the kindest, smartest man."

She looked into his eyes. "You're graduating, salutatorian no less, this coming spring. Maybe valedictorian. And you'd get offers from colleges if you just *applied*."

"My family's trash, Kelse. I'll never—"

"You will be a *Structural Engineer*." She nodded once, as if putting an end to that discussion, then pulled off her t-shirt. She'd bought a new bra and panties for today. Lacy and delicate. Not utilitarian.

Jack stared at her chest, then her eyes, then her chest again as she slid into his embrace and onto his lap.

His gaze returned to hers and she draped her arms over his shoulders. "You will get your engineering degree and will apply for a job with NASA. *NAA-SAA.* Because that's *your* dream, not your dad's. Are we clear?"

"Yes, ma'am."

"And by then I'll be ready to apply to med school in Houston or Central Florida, wherever they put you. Then we'll get married, have the requisite 2.4 kids..."

He grinned. "Not sure how you get four-tenths of a kid. Is that a new kind of trig?"

"Nah. Just statistics. We will achieve all this quickly and efficiently, and will be utterly happy. All right?"

He settled her in his arms and cupped her left breast, marveled over it. "Yes, we will. I love you, Kelsey Jutland."

"And I love you, Jack Scheffert. Now get me out of this itchy bra, make love to me, and let's get this life-plan started."

Berk

That Judy bitch is a pain in my ass. She keeps tapping on the stupid contract Granddad signed and telling me they have to be here, but I really wish they—especially she—would march right back to the hole they crawled out of.

She started their 'sort' by going to Granddad's office and doesn't want to leave it alone because of the fucking contract even when I tell her to. I stand my ground and order them to sort the kitchen, garage, or the two cleared rooms upstairs instead or I'll rip up that contract myself.

There's money here, in Granddad's office, maybe some Treasury Bonds. And the photographs I need to find. Who knows what else, and I'll be damned if I let any pushy-ass, clipboard-holding-bitch screw with me today.

I'm still upset about Granddad dying the night before last—that's all the longer it's been!—and upset about Max and the endless rain and the snotty bitch who tsk-tsks my cussing and ARRGH!!

I hate this goddamn day.

But I'm sitting here at Granddad's desk, my head in my hands, staring at an envelope with my name on it.

Maybe I should clarify. With *Berk* on it.

I pick it up and hold it over his blotter/calendar/thing, where he's written the names of various women on various dates, his past encounters this month all crossed out with large X's, including deep-throat Ellen.

Dottie isn't crossed off and I hate her even though I haven't met her.

The envelope wasn't exactly propped up and waiting for me. I found it underneath advertisements for tools and small business seminars and male enhancement pills—shudder—but I've been staring at it and my name for too damned long.

Long enough for scowling Judy to unlock the office—

She's here. Again.

Jesus, bitch. It's your fourth stop and it's only been eleven minutes. Just sort out the goddamn garage already!

I glare at her, but she has zero shits to give.

"We really do need to get to work in here," she tells me in a no-nonsense voice that I can only assume works on other people. "And, again, we're bonded by the county and state to handle and catalog estate valuables. I promise, as an auction professional and a good Christian, your important papers and memories will be safe with—"

I flip her both of my unicorn hands. "Fuck. Off."

She purses her lips in reply. "*Amanda*, need I remind you that such rough language and gestures are unbecoming of a lady and it's quite distressing to myself and my staff to hear those horrid words coming from such a lovely face."

She smiles and it reeks of all the similar superior grins when someone's told me women can't play jazz bass at all—let alone professionally—as if ovaries do the string plucking, or I mustn't hang out with Dave and Lia because what would people think of a pretty white girl like me slumming with those filthy blacks, or how dare I hand out sammies to homeless people whenever I have to record in New York or Boston or wherever because—gasp!—they might survive another day, or any other stupid ass reason I do not meet their closed-sphincter expectations of what *my* reality should be.

Or they ask me not to break their son's heart, again, yet that's what I goddamn do anyway a couple of hours later.

And I don't know how to fix it.

I slam my envelope on the desk. Again. And glare at sphincter-lips Judy. "Good. Then you all can fuck off right back to your fucking office and come back fucking later. Long after I've fucking gone home to West Fucking Virginia so you don't have to fucking listen to my vulgar fucking language."

The *you bitch* was, hopefully, implied.

"The auction is scheduled, posted, and advertised for *this coming Sunday* so we must clear the entire home, including this office, *promptly*, or we will not be ready on time," Judy says through her pursed lips. "Please finish your business in here and let us do our jobs."

She starts to walk away, then snorts out a harsh breath and turns back to me. "It helps, *Amanda*, if you open an envelope to see what's inside. Doing so would make this all go much smoother for everyone."

I stomp around the desk and slam the door in her face.

It's a useless gesture. She has a full set of keys, and we both know it.

So I slump behind Granddad's desk again and take yet another shaky breath as I pick up the envelope, again, and stare, again, at *Berk* written in ink the same blue as the Star Wars shirt Max wore this morning.

Before he left me because he'd thought I loved him.

Damn. I sure can make a god-awful mess of things.

My breath gets shaky and my vision blurs, but I rip open the envelope before I get all lost in grief and shame again.

It's just one piece of laser-printed paper and is dated the day I arrived to help him move.

> *Berk,*
>
> *If you're reading this, then you're still here and I'm thankful. It's so good to see you again after so long. You remind me of your grandmother. Your defiance, your strength, your creativity, your clear core of what's right and wrong no matter what anyone else thinks, and even your conversational cussing. You definitely picked that up from her, not me.*
>
> *I miss her so much.*
>
> *I'll keep this short. As short as I can, anyway.*
>
> *Almost two years ago, before she died, we found out I had severe coronary artery disease. She didn't want to lose me and we'd decided I'd get an angioplasty to prolong my life. We had the appointment scheduled in Iowa City, but she died. Her, not me. After the funeral, after you left, I decided I didn't want to live on without her. I canceled the angioplasty, quit taking my meds, and almost killed myself twice. Once with my pistol, once with my truck at eighty heading for the oak tree down at the T-intersection by the Hampuer's house. I chickened out the first time and missed the damn tree the second.*
>
> *I honestly don't know how. The sheriff said there was a dip in the dirt just off the road and it sent me to the left instead, but there wasn't a dip there when I checked it myself a couple of days later.*
>
> *Maybe it was your Gram saving me. I don't know. All I know is how much I miss her.*
>
> *About a week after the truck incident, I'm at the coffee shop, you know, the one on Wilson? And Maureen Rinatelli walks in. I'm sure you remember her. She and your gram used to swim together at the community center and go to crocheting retreats? Maureen and I got to talking. She was lonely too, her Bob had died six years ago and she lived alone at the retirement center. We had a nice visit, but that's all it was. At first.*
>
> *I was so lonely. Months rattling around this big house by myself.*

Then I saw a thing on TV about blocked arteries and heart attacks, and how older men with the condition, like me, shouldn't have sex because they might die.

I watched it and decided that would be a better way to go than eating a bullet or crashing into a tree, so I called Maureen. The first time I slept with her, I imagined she was your gram, the love of my life.

But it felt so good to be human again, Berk. Maureen said so too. Then Dottie. Then Nancy and so forth. And, to me, every one of them was Beth calling for me to come to her, but to spread a little affection and kindness before I go. A little humanity. A little less loneliness.

I told them, all of my lady friends, that I wasn't taking my heart meds and I wanted them to help me be with my wife again. And they understood. So don't hate them, or be angry with them. They did it because I asked them to. And because they understand the loneliness and emptiness of life without love.

I'd appreciate it if you looked for them at my funeral. They promised whoever sent me to Beth would wear purple. Please give her a hug from me, from Beth and me both, and tell her thank you.

I hope you mean it when you do.

Your gram and I loved you more than you can ever imagine and I hope, too, that someday you understand.

Forever yours,
Granddad

Below, he'd written in the same blue ink as the envelope:

ps: Max Jutland's divorced now and owns Tony's. You should look him up. Your gram would approve.

I set the letter down and start bawling again.
I feel like such a shit.

I drop off granddad's clothes at the funeral home and make a detour to the hardware store before heading to Tony's, but I can't make myself go in. So I sit and cry in Tony's parking lot in the pouring rain and give myself hell for being, well, *me* while Stanley Clarke is cranked up full blast on my stereo.

I was a college freshman the first time I met Stanley at a Master Class workshop in Chicago. My guitar teacher insisted I go, even pulled some strings to get me on the list. Everyone else had years of experience playing bass while I was a clueless newbie, but that one first workshop opened my eyes and changed my life. I never knew such brilliance and variety was possible with four simple strings.

Since then, I tend to listen to Stanley when I'm facing a tough decision. Usually, he helps, but not so much today.

Tony's' door opens and the scraggly guy with the MakeLoveNotWar button comes out, flipping up his collar against the rain, and walks right to my SUV. He tries the locked door-handle before tapping on the passenger side window.

I hit pause on *Bass Folk Song #10* then unlock. He slides right in and closes the door.

"Okay, kiddo," he says, wiping rain off his face, "I dunno what happened with you two, but you're obviously not happy about it either since you've been sitting out here for at least twenty minutes."

"Seventeen," I say, my hands clenched on the steering wheel.

"Whatever." He opens the door again and steps one leg out. "He knows you're here, so I suggest you shit or get off the pot."

Then he gives me a wink, shuts my Mazda's door, and trots back to the bar.

He's right, and I know it. Time to face the music of my own screw up.

I finish listening to the track while I gather my courage, then I step into the rain.

⚬⌒⚬⤙

A handful of folks are having Liquid Lunch and the usual three people are in the window playing cribbage. MakeLoveNotWar nods my way when I come in, and I nod back. Max is alone, no sign of Gretchen, so I find myself a booth and settle in.

Jack Scheffert, Kelsey's nurse from last night, sits in the next booth directly facing me and he's steadily drinking clear liquor with a lime wedge. We, too, share a nod. Since Max is ignoring me, I decide to fiddle on my phone.

I'm focused on level fifty-five in a forgettable bubble-popping time-waster game when Max says, "Whatcanigetcha," to my left.

I jump and almost drop the phone. That's me, always keepin' it clutzy. "Um. A Sprite?" I say, managing to smile. "And to talk to you when you get a minute?"

"Sprite. Okay," he responds then leaves to fill my drink order while two other people raise their glasses for refills.

Since I'm obviously gonna be here a while, I go back to the phone. Got nothing else pressing to do today.

By the time I switch over to matching sweets instead of popping bubbles, the lunch customers have filtered out to the rain but the three cribbage players remain. Doesn't sound like Sherry's surgery went well. I don't even know her, but it sounds bad. I hope she gets better.

My phone chirps from a double-gummy-bonus-bonanza as Max slides into the seat across the table from me.

"I don't know what there is to talk about," he says as I turn off my phone and set it aside.

I reach into my jacket pocket. "Just want to say I'm sorry. I screwed up. And I have something for you."

He sighs as I slide a pair of freshly-cut keys on a rubber 60's-Batman keyring—the geekiest key ring the hardware store had—across the table to him.

"What's this?" he says, frowning at them.

"House keys. Front and driveway. I don't have keys for the patio doors."

The frown kind of fades; at least I tell myself that.

"Berk…"

"No… No strings or expectations," I say. "You can have Danny's room, my room, the couch, Granddad's, any bed you want. I'll sleep in the tub if it'll help you stay."

This time, he sighs, "Berk."

"I know I have attachment issues, but I cannot, *will* not, let you sleep in your car when I'm in that big house all alone. Please. We are still *friends*, right?"

I realize the rest of the bar is silent. No jukebox, no cribbage banter, no anything.

We both glance toward the window. Two of the guys stare at their cards as if they hold the secrets of the universe, but the little guy in sweatpants and flip-flops apparently stalled while turning away from us. MakeLoveNotWar smacks him on the upper arm and sweatpants completes his turn.

"Yeah, we're still friends."

I wonder if it's true. He still hasn't looked at me.

"Then can we just talk about all this?" I say. "Maybe? I know I screwed up.

It's all my fault, I overreacted, and I'm sorry. So fucking sorry."

"C'mon," he says, sliding out of the booth. "We'll talk in the office." He picks up the keys but doesn't pocket them.

I grab my phone and follow him to the hall.

The tidy office is small, barely large enough for a desk, two chairs, and the stand-up popcorn popper. Several neatly stacked papers lie clipped together on a shelf above the desk and tavern-supplier catalogs are stuffed in a wire rack on the wall.

I sit in the chair beside the popper and resist the urge to draw my knees to my chin like a terrified employee about to get fired.

Max sits, still frowning at the keys in his hand. "We need to be perfectly honest," he says at last. "Both of us."

My heart slams, wondering what he's going to ask me, but I take a breath and say, "Okay."

He tosses the keys onto his desk and turns his chair to fully face me. He's looking at his knees, then his eyes drift closed as his expression softens. "I remember the day you first came over to play with Kelse. It was fall, late October, probably, because it was after my birthday but we had pumpkins on the front deck. I opened the door for you and your gram, and the sunlight on your hair glowed like an angel's halo. I couldn't speak, you were so beautiful. Your gram asked if you and she were at the right house, then Kelsey came, squealing, and dragged you in. I stood there like an idiot, dumbstruck by the glowing goddess in my home."

He opens his eyes then and looks at me with an intensity that slams me square in the chest. "I was seven, Berk. *Seven*."

I don't know what to say, but I feel tears. I've cried so much, yet somehow I still have some left.

"I watched you grow up. You're closer to my age than Kelsey's, we're just, what, a few weeks apart, me and you? I was ten the first time I realized I wanted to kiss you. Just you. And twelve when I knew I loved you."

"Oh, Max," I whisper. "I didn't know."

"My dad thought I was weird to prefer to hang out with you and Kelsey than neighborhood boys. He even asked me twice if I might be gay. When he finally realized what was going on, he informed me you were out of my league and I needed to move on. To settle for someone more appropriate, some working-class nobody like us, someone barely scraping by, not lose my soul to the well-off, golden Valkyrie from the nice part of town."

He laughs then, shaking his head. "I told him no. Actually, I told him to fuck off, because that's what *you* would say to someone who wanted you to kill your life's dream and make you leave the person you loved."

His eyes are strong. Passionate. Unflinching. "I was fifteen and he punched me. Knocked me down like I was nothing. And that's exactly how I felt today when you told me it was all pretend."

"I'm sorry, Max. Everything just hurt so, so bad. This whole trip has been awful, every last moment of it, except *you*. I needed to quit hurting, just for a little while, and I thought—"

"Been thinking all morning how your friends, back in West Virginia, they were shocked when you brought me. Dave, especially, he got all protective. Except for Lia, your college roommate. She knew who I was right off, didn't she?"

"Yeah." I don't know what else to say, and I lower my eyes.

The pause stretches until he says, "Do you date? *Anybody?*"

I can't look at him, can't speak, so I just stare at his shoes and shake my head.

"You told me you'd slept with nine guys. How can you do that without dating?"

"*Really?*" I ask. "It's pretty easy. Go to a bar, have a couple of drinks and pick one. The acceptance rate of guys in bars is pretty high."

"Well, yeah, but..."

"But nothing. I'm no saint, Max. Sometimes I want a little dick, but that's it. I don't let people in. It's too much trouble."

"So you've never had a real boyfriend? Anything lasting more than a single night?"

"Yeah, well, a lot of that's your fault."

"My fault? How the hell can it be my fault?"

"Lemme tell you about every guy that *mattered* to me after I left Fayerville. The first guy, just a day or two after I had to testify at the trial, I'm in the dorm cafeteria and right there, in line about six people ahead of me, was *you*."

"What?"

"No, he obviously wasn't *you*, but I was behind him and he looked like you, at least from behind. Same crappy sweatshirt and jeans, same hair, same gamer shit, same watch. So weird. And I couldn't help myself, it just happened, I ran up to him and hugged him and called him Max.

"He laughs, startled, and he's obviously not you. His name was Steve, and he was a Junior. We struck up a conversation and he asked me on a date. I said yes. Because he looked like you."

"Berk, I—"

"He wasn't *you*, but *I* wanted him to be. And I didn't get to see you when I was here to testify, you were off at school and your mom said you had a girlfriend, but *I* wanted him to be *you* so, so bad I got drunk enough so I could pretend and... And afterward, he brushed me off because I didn't matter. I was just another lay."

"Aw, shit."

"And then, like a year later, there was this guy named Oliver in my Music Theory class. I was lonely, he was cute, so what the hell, ya know? So we went out a couple of times, fucked once, and went our separate ways. Only I went home that next Christmas break and your mom said you'd broken up with that one girlfriend, then two others, but went to Colorado with the current one to ski. So, sorry Berk, but he's not here. And I was really blue for a long time after that. At least a couple of months. If it wasn't for Lia and Dave, I probably would've dropped out my Junior year. But, anyway, I came home for one weekend in March—"

"I was down in Des Moines for a concert. Mom told me you'd stopped by."

"Yeah. Kenny Chesney. *Barf.*"

"Hey, my girlfriend thought—"

"Exactly. You had a new girlfriend. Again. How many did you go through before Heidi? Fifty? Sixty?"

"Eleven."

"Eleven. You go, Casanova. So, anyway, I get back to school and who do I bump into who then volunteers to carry my gear to my dorm room? Oliver from Music Theory. And I'm pissed and lonely so I fuck him again, only this time we don't go our separate ways. He decides since he's balled me twice, I'm like his personal property or some shit."

"What?"

"Yup. Stalked me, cut me off from my friends, hit me, forced me to blow him, and threatened to kill me whenever I tried to make him leave me alone. Took me until fall term, a restraining order, three cops, and Dave literally busting his leg to get him to fuck off. And *that* was the end of me dating. Anybody. Hell, I couldn't even do a repeat hookup with some guy I thought was a friend without things going to shit."

"Oh my god. What the fuck? Is he the guy you lived with?"

"No. That's Fernando, my vibrator. He resides in my underwear drawer and is a hell of an excuse when pushy guys won't accept a no. *Sorry, dude, I belong to Fernando, so buzz off. Ha ha!* They usually leave me alone after that. If they don't, Dave'll come charging up after I holler *Fernando!* He's a pretty big guy and no one wants to mess with him. He's like my get-away-from-horny-assholes card."

Max grimaces, shaking his head.

"So. Prior to us humping on your hide-a-bed, I'd had one guy who balled me and tossed me aside like I was garbage, then another who tried to control every moment of my life because I was his property to use as he saw fit. Picked a couple of winners, didn't I? But I learned my lesson and kept it all anonymous after that. Cute guy and I'm horny? Bang him, get what I want, and walk away. No names, no phone numbers, no nothing. One and done and I'm out the door."

"Wow. No wonder everyone was so surprised when you took me to West Virginia. And Dave was so over-the-top protective. He thought I was another abusive shit."

"Yep. So now you know." I stand and open the door. "Stay at the house if you want, or not if you don't. It doesn't matter. And don't you *ever* accuse me of not loving you. You're the only guy I ever have. Only you broke off our dates and left me to grieve Kelsey all alone, didn't even visit me after Lori and Julie put me in the hospital. You disappeared when I needed you, so maybe loving you back then was a fucked-up failure too."

I'm already in the hall before he stands and follows me into the bar. "Berk, wait!" he says, but I walk right out the door to the rain.

⌐◦⇥

I drive down to Decorah to go to the grocery store because I really need fresh stuff. Max has sent me four text messages, which I do not want to deal with, so I turn the phone off again.

I take my time shopping, checking prices and sniffing oranges, all that shit. The only familiar face I see belongs to Brittany Miller, the bitch who held down my legs while Lori Gilbert and Julia Gifford kicked the shit out of my head. The one who never even got charged as an accessory. She's wearing nurses' scrubs and starts to say something but I give her a *do NOT speak to me* glare. Britts backs away then runs out of the store. I see the blue heart tattoo on the back of her neck, right below her short brown hair, and I want to incinerate it—and her—with my eyes as she flees.

I also want to yell *bitch!* at her back, but I don't need more grocery store drama. I huff out my anger while checking cantaloupes for ripeness instead. Then I sample cheese. Compare yogurts. Dally over donuts. Ponder pork chops.

Basically, I waste time at the grocery store until the manager starts watching me like I'm casing the place. I do not want to go back to the house. In fact, I don't want to go back to Fayerville at all. But I'm burying my grandfather the day after tomorrow so I'm kind of stuck here, at least until that's done.

It's cool enough outside for me to leave my groceries in the car, so I take myself out to the fancy Japanese/Korean restaurant downtown. I went there with Gram and Granddad a couple of years ago at Christmas and it was soooo good. I order the spicy sushi combo and take my time eating it while playing one of my phone's time-waster games and pointedly not looking at Max's four texts. At least he didn't keep texting and texting and *texting* when I clearly wasn't going to answer.

That's something right?

I finish my sushi and tell myself I need to quit screwing around and face the house as well as the possibility of Max in it.

So I drive back to Granddad's, in the dark, in the rain, Talking Heads' *Fear of Music* blasting on my stereo. The house is quiet and dark, the driveway empty except for Granddad's boat under its sun-faded tarp, so I lug in my perishables.

Much of the kitchen is an erratic chaos of boxes and piles of dishes or pans or appliances.

"God, this sucks," I mutter as I put the couple of bags of groceries away. There's a posty note on the fridge informing me everything needs to be eaten or donated by 6 a.m. Thursday when the Auction House begins their final prep, and I need to be out too because they're selling the house on Sunday.

So it'll all be sold in one fell swoop, then it's done.

Maybe that's for the best, I think as I toss the posty into the trash. Maybe I'll just head home after the funeral Wednesday. Maybe tell Mom to just forget it and stay in Darjeeling. It's not like there's a reason to be here any longer than that.

Bill's thrilled to see me and I pick him up and carry him to Granddad's locked office, which is also in shambles. A single box sits on his chair with *Amanda* written on the forward side. I sigh and open it.

It's full of photos and coins and an envelope of cash, mostly twenties I'm sure Gram had stashed somewhere. Assorted valuables cover the desk, including Granddad's pistol, a couple of hunting and fishing knives, some rings and necklaces, a diamond tennis bracelet in its box, and an antique wooden ballerina doll sitting atop the pile of jewelry like a hen on a nest.

I pick up the doll and smile. Gram showed Belinda to me when I was maybe nine, said her gram had brought her over from Germany, and someday, if I wanted, she'd belong to me. Then she put Belinda away, buried her deep within her dresser. I smooth the doll's aged and faded skirt then tuck it into my box of money and photos.

I find Gram's wedding rings in the pile and keep those too. I already have Granddad's wedding ring and pocket knife from his bag of personal effects Troy gave me at the funeral home. It's upstairs in my luggage. I hope Judy and Co. have left that the hell alone.

She'd probably have a coronary if she found Fernando.

Smiling at the thought of her convulsing on the floor with a rabbit vibe in her hand, I start sorting through photographs. Some are really old; my great grandparents, aunts, uncles, and cousins I never met or barely remember. Most, though, are of my mom as a kid and her two little brothers. They grow up, then I come along. There aren't many photos of Gram—she was usually the family photographer—but I find several good ones of my granddad and his plumbing trucks and crew. I set those aside for the funeral, along with a few family shots.

There are at least a couple of dozen of me, Kelsey, and Max, more than I expected. I linger over them, sometimes touching our young faces. About a third are the three of us, four are just Kelsey and me, but about half are me with Max, goofing off or playing games or whatever while Kelsey might be in the background with her nose in a book. Maybe. Or more likely writing a letter to the editor of the local paper, a practice she picked up in Middle School.

One photograph's just her, sitting in our backyard at the picnic table, her face aglow in the setting sun with soft-focused autumn leaves fluttering downward behind her. She gazes slightly to the right, a confident smile on her lips, the Kelsey I remember. Like a lot of my Gram's photographs, this portrait's a delicately composed work of art and I hope the original file or negative still exists. Somewhere.

There's a sealed manila envelope at the bottom of my box with my name on it, written in Granddad's familiar hand. It's full of papers. I try not to groan as I glance at bank and investment statements along with the house deed, vehicle titles, savings bonds, and insurance policies. There's also a safety deposit box key for Cornerstone Bank, and a business card for Kyle Newbend, an accountant in downtown Decorah.

Call Kyle and make an appointment, Granddad had written on the back of the biz card. *He has my will and all the papers you need to sign.*

So that's that. I stand to gather the photos and hear the kitchen door open.

Bill looks up from licking his ass then stretches and trots to the living room, mrowow-ing happily.

"Berk?" Max calls from the kitchen. "You here?"

"In Granddad's office!"

"Jesus, what a mess," he mutters on his way to me and I sigh as he stops just outside the doorway, holding Bill in his arms.

"Yeah. I guess this is called *sorting*."

"More like making a jumbling mess, if you ask me," he mutters then pauses to put Bill down. "You okay? You didn't answer my texts."

I shrug and drag a finger through the crap on the desk. "Didn't want to talk to you. Don't suppose you're interested in a fishing knife with a mother-of-pearl handle or an onyx-and-silver necklace? Or how about Avon Vintage Car After Shave? Mint in box and there are like eight or ten of them. Take your pick!"

He chuckles and shakes his head. "No, can't say I want any of that stuff." He holds my gaze for a warm moment then turns to go. "Glad you're all right. I'll get out of your hair."

"You don't have to leave," I say and he pauses before turning back.

"I kind of do. Was worried about you so I called Gretchen in to cover for a few minutes. Just want to make sure you're all right."

"I am. And I'm still really sorry."

"Don't be. It's my fault, too." He sighs then smiles. "I'll come back after work, if that's okay."

I nod. "It is."

"Feel free to come by the bar, if you want. Your drinks are on me tonight."

"I might," I say, and he smiles. "But I do need to deal with this mess."

"No worries. See you later tonight, either way."

We share one long, last look, then I watch him leave.

Max

The last of his customers left around 10:30 and Max closed at eleven, an hour early but he didn't care. He drove through nearly-deserted streets and pulled in the driveway behind Berk's Mazda. The house was dark except for a light in Ted and Beth's old room.

"Oh, Berk," he said, exiting the car and hurrying to the kitchen door. He maneuvered through the mess and up the stairs to find her sitting cross-legged on her grandparent's bed in a long nightshirt, a bottle of Sprite beside her hip, and a box of film negatives in her lap.

"I can't find it," she said, holding a negative up to the light before setting it aside and reaching for another. "I have to find it."

"Find what?" he asked, sitting beside her.

"This."

She handed him a single 4x6 inch photograph of teenage Kelsey, smiling in the setting sun.

"I've never seen this one before," he said.

She held up then discarded another negative. Then another, her voice coming in ragged sobs. "I hadn't either. It was in with my gram's photos, so I'm pretty sure she took it. I want to get it enlarged for your mom. Went to see Kelsey tonight, after you left, and she's worse, so much worse. They think she's going to die tomorrow. Maybe Wednesday, at the latest. I need the picture to take to her funeral, so people remember how amazing and beautiful she was."

He took the fistful of negatives from her hands and drew her to him. Cradled her. "Shh. It's okay."

She clung to him as he rocked her. "If only I wasn't grounded that night, I could've been with her. Protected her. If only I'd driven faster when she'd called, if only he hadn't had time to hurt her so badly, maybe she'd—"

"None of this is your fault. You need to stop blaming yourself. I carry enough for both of us. I'm the one who didn't put gas in the car and left her stranded."

She looked up at him. "I know, but it was *her* car."

"But I drove it last and didn't put gas in it, did it all the time, but this time she got hurt so it was my fault, well before it was your fault. She'd had a fight with Mom at supper then stormed out the door about an hour before she got hurt. Maybe if she'd stayed home it never would have happened, so it's Mom's fault. She got a B on her Advanced Math test that morning. She insisted it'd obliterate her GPA, which made her mad, and sent her to a fight with mom, then to leave in a car that was low on gas, so maybe it's Mr. Jacobsen's fault. Or maybe a million other random little dominoes, all falling in their relentless pattern that dragged her right to that shed, and dammit, Berk, not one bit of *any* of it has *anything* to do with you."

He held her a little tighter. "Bad shit happens. Sometimes it just *does*. And there's nothing we can do."

"I want to kill him," Berk said. "Granddad's gun's right there on his desk. He taught me how to shoot it."

"Don't," he said. "Because then I'd lose you too, and it still wouldn't bring her back."

She shifted to look at him, and he smoothed her hair from her brow. "Kelsey died a decade ago. We're all just now catching up to that truth, and we gotta let her go. Maybe then we can remember her for *her*. Maybe we can finally move forward."

Berk nodded and snuggled against his chest.

He held her for a good while, relishing her warmth in his arms. "You ready to go to bed? I dunno about you, but I'm exhausted," he said.

She chuckled and eased out of his embrace. "Sounds great. But I have some bad news."

"Aw, crap. What now?" he grumbled as he helped her off her grand-parents' bed.

She grimaced and gave him a sideways glance. "Started my period tonight. Never in a million years thought I'd ever admit that to a guy."

He laughed. "That's probably the nicest thing I've heard all day."

He kissed her, and she him, then he took her hand and led her to her room. "Let's get some sleep. We'll face tomorrow when it gets here."

Intermezzo - Senior Year

Kelsey crawled across white butcher paper with a blue paintbrush in her teeth. She'd already written *Ravens Going To STATE!* in pencil, but still had to paint the letters. Then do it again. And again. And again. Eleven times. At least.

Because Lori insisted every flippin' business in town needed the same boring banner and the other Senior cheerleaders backed her up.

"Maybe we should mix it up a little," Kelsey said when Lori stood over her to watch. "I dunno. Different messages? Some other colors besides blue? If all the banners are the same—"

"Then they'll look coordinated," Lori snapped. "Don't you know anything?"

I was thinking more like *boring*, Kelsey thought but said nothing as she finished painting the capital E and refilled her brush.

"You think you're so smart," Lori said, "and we all know you don't like sports. So why are you even here helping?"

Two straight lines for the T, add a little flip at the ends to give it serifs... "School organization participations look good on my scholarship and grant money applications," Kelsey said, crawling backward to start the A.

"That's totally stupid," Lori said, then bent to whisper, "And I should kick your ass for what you did."

A done, on to the second T. Kelsey refilled her brush and glanced at Lori. "Because I didn't pass you the answers in history last year and you flunked? I thought we'd already discussed that."

"No. Because that stupid presentation you gave at the county courthouse last week cost me a graduation vacation to Martinique."

Kelsey finished the T and began the S. "Oh? Did your dad get caught skimming development money again?"

"He might lose his job and it's all your fault. Again."

"No, actually, it's his, both times. There *are* ethical urban designers. And ones smart enough to not leave a paper trail a high school kid can follow. If the council doesn't fire him, I'll catch him the next time he does it, too." She gave Lori a bright smile and reached to refill her brush again. "Next time, I'll send my letters to the *Des Moines Register* instead of the local paper."

"Kelsey!" Berk called out, running into the lunchroom. "Guess what!"

"Bitch," Lori muttered before flouncing off to harass someone else.

"Whore," Kelsey whispered then continued to paint as Berk sat cross-legged beside the banner. "Whazzup?"

Berk leaned close and whispered. "Max. And I. Are gonna go out for pizza Saturday!"

"Okay, cool. Um. But you guys have pizza and video games all the time."

"No! You don't understand. *He asked me out.* On like a real date!"

Kelsey managed to keep her expression neutral despite knowing full well Max had been gathering his courage to ask Berk out since roughly seventh grade. She whispered, "I know you two decided to crash prom this year, but he asked you on a *date?* Are you sure?"

"Yes, I'm sure!" Berk whispered back, grinning. "And just because we're going as Rose and The Doctor does *not* mean we're crashing."

Kelsey painted another letter. "I've told you. Prom is not a costume party. People here take that stuff seriously."

"Rose and Ten are serious! Plus, we're gonna dance. Once. We agreed. And I'm gonna *totally rock* Rose. But. Irregardless—"

"Regardless," Kelsey corrected.

"Fine. *Regardless* of our amazingly awesome prom plans—the pics are gonna be *so sweet!*—we're going to Waukon for pizza. On Saturday. At the Main Feature."

Kelsey rolled from her knees to her butt and gawked at Berk. "Shut the town!"

"Seriously! A real honest-to-God *date!*"

It's about time my stupid, chicken-shit brother got his act together, Kelsey thought, grinning. "Congratulations!"

Berk squealed and pounded her feet on the floor, saying aloud, "I know, right? This is so cool!"

"What's so cool, dork?" Lori sauntered toward them. "Pokémon doing Jedi Card Tricks in Nerdville?"

Berk scrambled to her feet. "Bite me."

"You wish, *Amanda*," Lori said as nearly everyone in the lunchroom turned to look. The other cheerleaders gawked and a couple of girls turned on their phone cameras. "Everyone knows what you do."

Berk pulled out her ponytail and dragged the hair-tie over her wrist as she walked across banners to Lori who was armpit-tall to her. "Oh? What exactly are you suggesting, *Lori?*"

"Everybody knows she's a filthy dyke, so you must be one too," Lori snarled, glancing at Kelsey. "She's *disgusting.*"

Oh no, Kelsey thought, coming to her feet. Oh no. No, no, no!

Berk took one more step toward Lori, barely far enough apart to pass a palm between them. "Say whatever the fuck trash bullshit you want about me," Berk snarled, looming, "but don't you fucking *dare* talk shit about Kelsey."

Lori stared back. "Did she drug you the first time? Surely you didn't go willingly; we all know you're hot for her little brother instead."

Berk punched Lori square in the mouth before flinging her to the floor. "You fucking bitch!"

Everyone else gasped, but Kelsey ran toward them. "Stop it!" she said, pulling Berk away. "Dammit, Berk! Stop!"

"See? What'd I tell you?" Lori sat and wiped her swelling lower lip. "Look at them! Perfect-dyke and her pet pitbull-dyke!"

The group of girls behind her murmured and milled together, watching.

Berk, however, jerked in Kelsey's grasp. "I'm gonna bust your nose for that one, you fucking skank!"

"Hey!" Cory yelled from the doorway, still in his practice uniform, and boys on the team trotted up behind him. "What the hell's going on in here?"

Someone in the crowd of girls said, "Lori called Kelsey a dyke so Berk's kicking her ass!"

"Yeah." A freshman girl in the front stepped forward. "Berk's right, Lori, you are a damn skank! Also, my sister's a lesbian, and she's awesome, and so is her girlfriend. So fuck you!" She flung her paintbrush onto Lori on her way out the door.

"You're a bully, too!" a faint voice called from the back of the group. The rest murmured their agreement. "Just because you're rich doesn't mean you can treat us like crap!"

Lori scrambled to her feet. "Who said that?"

"Doesn't matter," Cory said, walking to them. "They're right. You are a bully. Now apologize to Kelse and Berk."

Lori wiped at her mouth. "*What?* That skinny band geek hit me! Why should I apologize?"

Mr. Thompson, English teacher and assistant basketball coach, pressed through the team and demanded to know who hit who.

"She. Hit. *Me,*" Lori said, pointing at Berk.

"That true, Berkeley?" Mr. Thompson asked.

"Yeah," Berk said, walking to him, her hands out as if awaiting cuffs. "But she asked for it."

"I'm sure she did," Mr. Thompson sighed, his hand on her back as he led her out of the lunchroom. "Let's go to the office."

"I wanna press charges!" Lori called after them, then she turned to glare at the remaining crowd of girls. "Back to work!"

Berk

My dream makes no sense. I'm on stage, playing *Simple Man* with Skynyrd and having a blast doing it, but, somewhere, a phone's ringing.

A land-line, with a bell. Who has one of those anymore?

"What the hell?" Max mumbles, rolling onto his back and rubbing his face. "What time is it?"

Shit. The kitchen phone must still be working. "I dunno. Let's-wake-'em-up-o'clock?" I mutter, dragging my sorry ass out of bed. "It's probably my mom losing track of time zones again. I'll get it."

I stumble down the stairs to the kitchen, my bare toes curling on the chilly kitchen floor. Here the ring's loud and clanging, and my ears are thankful when I pick up the receiver. "Hello?" I say around a yawn.

"Berk, it's Deb. Is Max with you? He's not answering his phone."

"Yeah. He's asleep. I'll get him, but gimme a minute. Gonna get the cordless from the garage."

I set the phone on the counter then open the garage door. Holy crap this floor is freezing and, of course, the phone's on the far side of Granddad's Mustang.

"Shit, shit, shit," I mutter there and back, cordless in hand until I return to the now-welcoming warmth of the kitchen floor. I click on the phone. "You still there?"

"Yeah. I'm here."

Kitchen phone hung up, I finally realize no one calls in the middle of the night just to chat. "Is everyone okay?" I ask as I climb the stairs.

"Just let me talk to Max."

He's back asleep, but I nudge him awake. "It's your mom."

"What? Okay," he says, accepting the phone without opening his eyes. "Yeah, Mom?"

I'm not quite around to my side of my bed when he says, "Aw, shit. We'll be right there." I stop, my heart dropping to my gut. "Yes, she's coming with me."

Then I hear a couple of beeps and the phone's golden light disappears.

He sits, then stands, little more than a silhouette against streetlights brightening my window. "It's Kelsey."

We dress quietly, quickly, and rush out the door.

It takes Kelsey until morning to die, every slowing breath like gurgling soup.

I'm not there when it happens. Rich won't even speak to me, and Deb... she scowls at Max holding my hand. So I sit in the waiting area, mostly. Or fetch coffee and cinnamon rolls. Or sit on the floor outside Kelsey's door wishing with every ounce of my heart I could have saved her.

Jack, Deb's favorite nurse-dude, rushes in around 5 a.m. and I sigh when he's still in there and speaking quietly with Kelsey's parents ten, fifteen, forty minutes later. At least Max mostly sits with me except when his mom calls him back to Kelsey's room because he's been gone too long. But he mostly sits with me.

When it's over, I hear Deb wail. Max stands, promising he'll be right back. He is, and we sit again, silent beside each other in the waiting area out front. We don't talk, and, now that it's done, I can't seem to cry.

Jack comes out next and he's openly weeping. He walks right past and out to the rain without even looking at us. I don't know what to say about that, so I say nothing. Max's grip, though, tightens as he watches Jack leave.

Then it's Rich. His mouth is frowning but his eyes are relieved and he pulls up a chair to face us. Well, face Max, but I'm right there, too.

I swear, it's like I'm invisible.

"So," Rich says, clasping his hands between his knees. "All the arrangements have been made and we're holding a small service on Saturday. Would you be willing to say a few words about your sister? Your mom would really appreciate it."

"Yeah, sure," Max says, his hand tightening around mine.

"Great," Rich says, glancing toward Kelsey's room, then back to Max. "We're leaving for Texas this weekend and there's room in the U-Haul for your stuff."

"Oh, um, about that—"

"I've told Jim you'll be there next Wednesday. That'll give you a day or two to settle in."

Max releases my hand and stands. "*Wednesday?*"

Deb comes around the corner, sniffling, a hospice nurse at her side, and motions for Rich.

"Gotta go," Rich says, standing. "We'll talk later. Nice to see you, Berkeley," he says without looking at me, then he walks to his weeping wife.

Max still stands, watching them, his breath coming in short, shallow bursts. I want to reach up and touch him, but the only thing handy is his butt and it's not the right time or place for that.

"Texas?" I ask, afraid to know the answer.

"I guess." He slumps beside me and puts his head in his hands. "Shit."

⌒⌒◦⤳

We leave not long after and our drive back to Granddad's feels silent and strained.

"What can I do?" I ask, my voice shaking, when we pull into the driveway.

"I don't know," he says, hands gripping the Cobalt's steering wheel. He hasn't turned off the car and the wipers whoosh their rhythmic beat like a heart in the rain.

I watch Max and can't imagine he'd be this upset about Kelsey. He's been so calm about it this past week, so it's something else. And he was fine, all things considered, until his dad talked with us in the hospice lobby.

I don't want to ask, but I need to know. At least I think I do. "When were you going to tell me about Texas?"

"I don't know," he says, his head drooping. He takes a deep and shuddering breath. "Dad told me a day or two ago and I hadn't decided what I was going to do. Or if it even mattered. I figured you'd be heading out before it happened."

I listen to the beat of the wipers until I can't take the silence anymore. "What's in Texas?"

"A job."

"Oh." My gut twists and my throat clenches. All this time, all these years, I'd relied on the surety of Max being here. One thing I could count on. Max is in Iowa, and he's okay. I can drive here if I need to, find him if I need to.

Even though I'd long believed I'd never see him again, I knew he was here. And that was enough.

"I've never been to Texas," falls out of me.

He sighs and turns off the car. "Me either."

We keep sitting, our breath steaming the windows, until I reach for the door. "I'm gonna make us some coffee," I say. "Think it's gonna be a long day."

He follows me in and sits at the kitchen table silently staring at nothing in particular as I get coffee going. It's weird. Kelsey died, but I feel like I'm mourning Max even though he's right here.

I set a mug in front of him, then I sit too, our knees touching. He grabs my thigh and squeezes it as if it's the only thing he has that's real.

"You're not gonna open another bar?" I ask, scooting closer.

"Can't afford one, not until the city pays me for eminent domain. And there's no telling how long that might take, or if they'll ever pay me at all." He takes a sip of coffee and sighs. "The legal fight cleaned me out. I can't afford an apartment right now. And my credit rating? It's shit. I'm lucky my beer supplier still talks to me, and they're on a cash basis."

"So once the bar's gone you're gonna be homeless, too? Jeesh. Why didn't you say something? I can help you get an apartment or whatever until you figure everything out."

He gives me a sideways glance over his coffee. "Really? You've been back for, what, a week, and I'm gonna hit you up to cover first and last month's rent so I have time to find a job? Not happening, Berk. Been adulting for quite a while now. I'll manage."

"By sleeping in your car?"

The front door opens and I hear the auction people come in. We both turn our heads that way, even though we can't see through the kitchen wall.

"Just for a night or two. The job Dad got me isn't total shit to start. Fifteen an hour plus benefits. I'll crash with my folks until I save some cash, then get my own place."

"In Texas?"

"Yeah. I guess."

"That's like half the country away from me. Two, maybe three day's drive. How am I gonna see you again?"

His voice cracks and he wipes at his eyes with his fingertips. "You're probably not."

Yeah, this hurts more than losing Kelsey. It's a punch to my gut, my throat, my everything, and I squeeze his leg too.

Sphincter-face Judy picks that moment to walk in. "What's he doing here?" she asks me, tapping her damned clipboard. "You are the *only* name on the approved list and I suggest you get him out of here immediately before I have to take additional measures."

I stand. "Excuse me?"

"There are valuables in this house and I have no guarantee, no written assurance from the home's owner, that he won't steal them."

"*I'm* the home's owner, so you have *my* guarantee. And *you* can shut your goddamn mouth."

"No, you're not. Theodore Williams signed the property over to us, for auction sale, fully effective as of yesterday." She flips a page on her clipboard and taps it with her pen. "We are contractually obligated to allow you access to personal mementos until Thursday, but if you want this house, you must purchase it from the estate at our auction."

I force my hands to remain open. I wanna kill her. Or at least beat the bitch out of her with that clipboard.

"I have a contract. Please remove personal effects and that mangy animal before we arrive Thursday morning and do not speak to me with such vile language again. Are we clear?" She purses her ugly-ass lips then stomps to the living room.

"Jesus, what a bitch," Max mutters.

I've met many control-freaks during my career, and, frankly, they're great if they're defending your side in a contract dispute, but mostly they're a pain. And it's always seemed the worst can't control their own chaotic lives so they micro-manage what little they can, even if it makes everyone around them miserable.

She's definitely making me miserable.

"I should go," Max says. He gulps down the last of his coffee then stands. "We okay?"

"Yeah, we're good," I say, accepting his tentative kiss. "I'll stop by the bar later, all right?"

"Sure." He pulls his coat on and looks at me for a long moment, as if he'll never see me again and wants to burn me into his memory. "See you around, Berk."

Then he's gone to the rain. I want to follow him, but I can't. I still have a pile of things to do before Granddad's funeral tomorrow.

I don't want to do any of it, of course, so I trot up the stairs to my bedroom and lock myself in before flumping on the bed. Then I call Lia.

We talk like we often do, and I fill her in on most everything that's happened since I left home in a rush late Saturday night.

"What are you gonna do?" she asks after I finish.

I hear Dave in the background hollering, "Where's the Desitin?"

Lia muffles the phone, but I hear her holler back, "Diaper bag!" then she's full volume again and, apparently, heading to their front porch because I hear the porch door bang closed.

"Ah, that's better," she says, and there's a faint creak of porch swing. "So. What are you gonna do?"

I sigh at the ceiling. "Take my cat and my crap to a hotel, I guess. I don't need her added pile of shi—"

"No, I mean about Max."

I sigh and roll to my side, burrowing my head into his pillow. "I don't know."

"Do you love him?"

"Did when I was a kid. I had such an insane crush on him."

The swing creaks. "I remember. He was all you talked about whenever you mentioned home. Him and his sister, but mostly him."

"Well, Kelsey was in a vegetative state and—"

"Yeah, I know. But that's how you always referred to her. *My friend in a vegetative state.* You had stories from time to time of things you did with her before it happened, but, hon, you *always* talked about Max."

"Lia, I—"

"And every time you went back home, you were all excited to maybe see him." She sighs. "And I saw how hurt you were when he always had another girl."

Leave it to my bestie to give me the bald truth. "Yeah," I sigh. "Guess so."

"And then you'd do something stupid."

Like Steve or Oliver or getting wasted and making an utter fool of myself at jazz band tryouts, I think, getting up because Bill's scratching at the door. "Yeah, I know."

"You're obviously sleeping with him," Lia says as I let Bill in and close the door again.

"Yeah." I flump back on my bed and stare at the ceiling.

"And? Is he like the others?"

"No. He's been great. We did have an argument though. Yesterday. Sort of."

"Oh?"

"Yeah. Was a misunderstanding about whether or not he's my boyfriend. All patched up now." Bill jumps on the bed looking for attention, so I pet him and he settles, purring, on my belly.

"Oh good. So you've finally seen reason?"

"Reason? The fuck you talking about? He's not my boyfriend," I mutter, wincing as I say the words. Bill just purrs.

"Oh please," she says. "Don't play your practiced denials for me. I've heard all of your secrets and held you while you bawled because he was with someone else. You've loved this guy since you were kids."

"Still," I sigh, "I'm going home in a few days and he's going to Texas. We're just having fun, then it's done."

She lets me change the subject, so we talk about the funeral for a while, and laugh at my grandfather having a harem, and other mundane stuff. Her kids and Dave driving her crazy and how it's sunny and nice outside there but still rainy-bleh here.

It's nice to talk, to relax. But she soon needs to go so she, Dave, and the kids can run an errand.

Before she hangs up, she asks me again what I'm going to do about Max, and if I love him.

The answer to both is I don't know.

I lay there for a while, petting Bill. Before I know it, it's lunchtime and I wake up curled around Max's pillow with Judy knocking on my bedroom door.

I groan my ass out of bed and open the door. "Yes?" I say with chipper annoyance.

She frowns at nap-rumpled me. "Where is the Grödnertal?"

I blink a couple of times trying to make sense of the nonsense coming from her mouth. "The groady-*what*?"

"The Grödnertal." She sighs, lips sphinctering again, and I wonder if she's like this with everyone, or if this measure of shit is special just for me. "The hundred forty-some-year-old wooden doll I'd placed on your grandfather's desk yesterday. Where is it?"

"Oh! Belinda! She was my Gram's and is in my box of stuff I want to keep. Thanks for checking." I start to close the door, but her foot's in the way.

"You can't keep that. We've listed the Grödnertal as a collectible for the auction. There are surely people coming from out-of-state to look at—"

"Too bad. I'm allowed to choose mementos, correct? Well, that doll reminds me of my Gram. It was her Gram's, who gave it to her, and she promised it'd be mine after she died. I'm keeping it. I also have her wedding rings, a box of film negatives, and, oh! My old Strat's still in the attic. I want it, too. Plus I dunno what else. I still have..." I glance over at my old alarm clock, "one day, and about eighteen hours left to decide what I want to keep. After that, I don't care what you do with the stuff."

"We have collectors coming to see the Grödnertal."

"Then they're gonna be disappointed because it's leaving with me."

She taps her damn clipboard with her damn pen. "The contract stipula—"

"Lemme see it," I say, snatching the clipboard from her while she squawks her disapproval.

"That's official paperwork! You mustn't—"

"Jeesh, it's only two pages," I say, "standard, boring..." I skim the contract, recognizing quite a lot of the legal jargon after years of reading and signing all kinds of recording rights-and-restrictions contracts.

She tries to snatch the clipboard from me, but I'm taller and keep it out of her reach.

"Here we go! Middle of page two," I say, grinning at her as I point to the particular notation my granddad wrote in the Restrictions section. *My granddaughter, Amanda Williams, can have anything from the estate she wants to keep, including the house and any contents.* And look! *Anything* and *and* are even underlined!" I tap the page with my finger. "Look. Right there. And he signed the note separate from the contract. See?"

"Yes, I see it," she mutters.

"And it's been initialed! Oooh! Looks like a *J* and a *B*. Could that stand for Judy Barret, the same person who also signed the bottom of this contract?" I gasp with feigned astonishment. "Is that *you*?"

She glares but says nothing.

"I'm keeping the damn doll," I say, thrusting the clipboard at her. "And if you keep fucking with me, I'll decide to keep the cars, the boat, the painting in the living room, all of the jewelry, and any other possibly-pricey thing I see, too. I'll leave you with nothing but clothes, kitchen crap, worn out furniture, and rusted tools, then I'll donate my trailer-load of unwanted-yet-awesome collectible shit to Planned Parenthood, tell 'em to write me a receipt for five hundred bucks, and take it as a tax deduction. Are we clear?"

She turns and walks to the stairs and down to the living room.

"I'm taking that as a yes!" I holler after her.

I turn around and Bill's sprawled on my bed, watching me. I swear he's smiling.

"Okay, buddy," I say, scritching his ears as I walk past the bed to my dresser. "I'm gonna take a quick shower and run some errands. Don't let her fuck with you, either."

He just purrs.

I hit the downtown luncheonette before heading to Tony's with a stack of meatloaf specials. MakeLoveNotWar waves when I walk in. I drop off lunches for him and his buddies. "Lunch is on me, just for being awesome," I say.

They seem happy enough with the lunches and I learn they're named Mitch, Dwight, and Henry. Dwight even gives me a high-five before digging into his meatloaf-and-mashed-potatoes like he hasn't eaten in a week.

"And for you," I say to Max as I sidle up to the bar, "a heapin' helpin' of the Daily Special from the Fayerville Luncheonette!" I slide one of the foam to-go containers toward him.

He grins and finishes filling a glass of beer before starting another. "Thanks.

I didn't think this morning's coffee was gonna hold me much longer."

"Brought some for your folks, too. They around?"

"Yeah, they're upstairs. I dunno if—" he says, but I'm already heading to the hall.

I trot right to the stairs and take a deep breath before tapping on the door.

"Come on up, honey," Deb says.

I open the door and climb up. They're sitting at the little snack table looking through some papers.

"It's me," I say before reaching the top. "Just wanted to bring you lunch, then I'll get out of your hair."

"Come on over, Berk," Deb says, waving me toward her. Rich looks at me for the first time since he got in town, and he nods. Neither are smiling, but their daughter did just pass away.

So I go into Max's apartment for the second time, only it's not his anymore. It's full of *stuff*. Boxes and bags and kitchen appliances and clothes and framed pictures and who knows what else. There's a path through to the table, the hide-a-bed, the kitchenette, and the bathroom. The rest is a random mishmash of *stuff*, piled knee-to-hip high.

They nod their thanks when I hand Deb the two lunches. "Just the meatloaf special from the luncheonette. Hope that's okay," I say, then I turn to go.

"Stay a sec, will you, Berk?" Deb says.

"Sure," I say despite the worrying twist in my gut. Rich opens his lunch and he smiles, breathing it in, but Deb looks right at me.

"You were always a good friend to Kelsey," she says. "And to Max."

"Thank you. They were always good to me."

Rich starts eating but Deb nods, pausing to take a breath then let it out again. She says, "You need to let them both go."

"What?" I ask, confused.

"We know you tried to save Kelsey, and we're thankful for that. And we're thankful you're here, now, for Max, too. But our family needs to move on. *He* needs to move on. Kelsey's really gone and we're all starting over."

"I don't—"

"Are you going to stay here, in Fayerville? Are you moving back to, what, Virginia?" Deb asks, opening her lunch.

"West Virginia. I'm heading back home in a few days. I have a gig on Wednesday. Have to be home by then."

"Um hmm," Deb says. She hasn't stopped looking at me since I walked in. "That's probably for the best. A clean break all around."

Rich scoops up another forkful of mashed potatoes and gravy. "This is really good, Berk. Thank you."

I say, "You're welcome," but keep my attention on Deb. "What's really going on?" I ask. "Something's up."

She folds her hands. "All right. You were my daughter's best friend. One of very, very few because she was, well, socially awkward and too smart for her own good. You were good for her, kept her grounded, and got her nose out of her books once in a while."

"Thank you?" I say, not sure where this was leading. "She was my best friend, too."

"My son, though," she says, "had a lot of friends. He was a regular kid, average, popular. A good boy. At least until he realized he had a crush on you. Then everything else fell aside."

I clench my teeth and say nothing.

"You leaving town nearly broke him. He barely spoke for weeks, then he dated a series of girls, all because he was trying—"

"They were all lookers, though," Rich says around a mouthful of meatloaf and green beans. "My boy's got good taste."

Deb shoots him a frown then returns to me. "Anyway, he was trying to forget you and find some other girl to put on a pedestal. Once he realized they weren't you, they'd break up and he'd go looking again, at least until one saw his softness, took advantage of it, and nearly ruined him. Don't get me wrong, you're a good girl, Berk, always have been, even though you're always trying to convince yourself you're never good enough."

That one hurt, probably because it's true. Even Lia's said so.

"But my son, my Max, needs to move on. You're his past. He deserves a future."

"You mean in Texas," I say.

Rich nods. "Yep. Got him lined up for a good job. Thirty-one thousand a year to start, plus bennies and 401k. He's a smart kid and a hard worker and'll be eligible for promotions in a year, maybe less. Might be running his own crew or even working at headquarters before he knows it."

"So you're not going to stop him," Deb says to me. "You're his past, Berk, and that's fine. Relive your childhoods and sew all the oats you kids want. Get drunk, play video games all night long, hell, I don't care what you do. Just get enough of it out of his system so he can start fresh, then let him go."

"You are on the pill, right?" Rich asks, chewing.

I give him a cool glare, then return to Deb. "Have you asked him what *he* wants?"

"Oh, I know exactly what he *wants*," Deb says. "He *wants* to run a bar and he *wants* to ball you. Both are a boy's dream, not a man's reality. His reality is taking an *adult* job with *adult* responsibilities. Both boyhood dreams are coming to an end this weekend. Are we on the same page here?"

"His life isn't up to me," I say, "and any decision he makes will be *his*, not mine."

She blinks once. Then again. "As long as you stay out of it, my son will make the correct choice."

Then she unwraps her plastic silverware and begins eating.

I, of course, am dismissed.

Max

Dwight walked up to the bar for a refill. "Your hotsy's a pretty nice gal."

Max swallowed his mouthful of beans and refilled the bourbon from the half-gallon bottle of Old Crow he kept special for Dwight. "Yeah, she is."

"How's my tab lookin'?"

Max didn't have to check. "This one brings you to fifteen, but part's from yesterday."

Dwight grinned and tipped his glass to Max. "Tell me when I hit twenty."

"Will do."

Dwight trotted back to the cribbage table and Max made another hash mark on the pad of paper beneath the bar. At a net cost of forty-four cents per ounce, charging Dwight a buck apiece for a two-ounce glass made a few cents profit, but kept him out of the cold and wet.

Berk came around the corner and Max smiled at her while putting away the bourbon. Today Dwight had more than popcorn for lunch because of her.

"Thanks for buying lunch for everyone," he said as she sat at the wall-end of the bar.

She opened her own lunch and sighed. "Just your family and the regulars."

The pair of women by the dartboard motioned for refills, so Max scooped ice into highball glasses. "How were my folks?"

Berk shrugged. "Chatty."

After he made the screwdrivers, he carried his half-eaten meal to her end of the bar. "Sprite or bottle beer today?"

"Sprite. Granddad's visitation is tonight. Afterward, though, you can definitely hook me up." She nodded toward the window. "Which one's drinking that crap you put away when I walked up?"

He brought her a Sprite. "Dwight. Little guy in flip-flops."

She chewed a mouthful of food and took a sip. "Put him on my tab, clear his balance, and upgrade him to regular wells, at least until I head home. Please. He's a nice guy."

"Yes, ma'am."

They ate in silence for a while, then Berk leaned forward and whispered, "So, Mr. Bar Man. Wanna be my date tonight?"

"To a funeral parlor? That's kinda kinky," he whispered back. "What's in it for me?"

She seemed to consider the question, a slight smirk on her face. "I dunno... Blowjob?"

"Is that all? Jeesh."

She laughed and licked mashed potatoes off her fork. "Hey, if you don't want one, you can just turn in your I'm-Burly-Man-Shit membership card right now."

"Well, since you put it that way..." He grinned and leaned close. "I'd like more than a blowjob, but I guess I'll take what I can get."

"Smart man."

He kissed her, then went to pour another customer's drink.

Berk took off after lunch but came back a few minutes before five wearing a simple burgundy dress and leggings.

Dwight whistled his approval, and she called him a flirt then settled in at the bar. "Gretchen here yet?"

"Yep," Max said. He'd showered and changed into khakis and a buttoned-up shirt. "She's cleaning the bathrooms, and no one's needing a refill. We can take off whenever you want."

"Whenever you're ready would be great. I'm supposed to get there early."

Max walked to the end of the bar. "Hey, Gretch!" he called down the hall. "We're heading out!"

"Go. I'm about done." She leaned out of the men's room and waved at Berk, who waved back.

"Can you drive?" Berk asked while Max put on his coat.

"Sure."

She tossed him her keys.

They'd barely pulled onto the highway when Berk said, "I have a question."

"Shoot."

"I'm supposed to be out of the house by Thursday morning, and, frankly, Judy..." She sighed. "We had a discussion today, and while she's no longer up in my grill, she's still pissy. Maybe it's her default setting, I dunno. Tomorrow's really going to suck, with the funeral and all of that mess, and, well, I just..."

His hands clenched the steering wheel hard enough to make his knuckles ache. "You taking off tomorrow?"

"No," she said. "Mom's coming Friday morning, and I have a meeting with Granddad's accountant that afternoon, then Kelsey's funeral's Saturday, the auction's Sunday... So Monday. I think. Maybe. Shit. I'm kind of playing this by ear."

He paused at a stoplight. "Yeah, me too."

"But, anyway, Judy and the house are really not helping my mood. And I have to be out of there by Thursday morning, as per the contract, but tomorrow's going to be a shit-fest, so..."

He turned onto fourth.

"So?"

"I got a hotel room. Already moved my stuff there, and Bill, and the little bit you'd left in my room. Do you wanna stay there with me?" She pulled a key-card from her jacket pocket. "Hotel Winneshiek, in Decorah. Here's a key. I know it's a bit of a drive, but they take pets."

Pretty sure the Highway Motel takes pets, too, for half of the price, Max thought. He paused at a stop sign and frowned at her as he pocketed the key.

"I booked Mom a room there, too, for Friday through Sunday. I can't imagine her staying longer than that. Anyway, they promised to put her on a different floor. She shouldn't bother us much. If you decide to stay."

"I'll think about it."

"Okay," Berk said, her voice soft, and she stared out the window, silent until he parked at the funeral home. "Thanks for coming with me," she said at last.

"Happy to."

She took a deep breath and opened the car door, then stepped out to drizzle. They walked together to the funeral home and Troy Haddert waiting for them in the vestibule.

After a quick round of handshakes, Max stayed close as Troy explained procedures and where to go, what to do. Berk nodded through most of it, but said little. The funeral home had already placed photos near the viewing area, mostly Ted with his plumbing crew or working on a sink or new construction, but a few were of him with his family.

"You found good pics," Max whispered in her ear.

She gave him a sad smile. "Thanks."

Then Troy led them to the casket. Max put his arm around Berk to keep her upright.

She nodded at the display but said nothing, then Max led her away, toward the coffee.

"I don't know if I can do this," she said, accepting a steaming cup from him.

He grasped her free hand. "You'll manage, because that's what you do."

The first mourners arrived a few minutes later, men who'd worked for Ted before he retired. Then a neighbor. Another plumber. A couple of old men who hung out at the coffee shop every morning. More neighbors and plumbers and friends.

Berk managed to remain in the viewing room, and Max stayed close. He fielded questions, guided people to the guest book, the flyers, or the coffee while Berk endured condolences, often seeking his gaze as if to ensure he was still there.

"Oh, God, that's the harem," she whispered, pressing against him when a cluster of old women arrived. All wore black dresses with purple corsages, except an elfin woman in a purple suit with a black orchid on the lapel.

A trim woman with a no-nonsense hairstyle pointed at Berk and Max, and the ladies moved as one mass toward them. Berk took in a harsh breath of air, and Max wrapped his arm around her, supported her.

"Berkeley," the no-nonsense woman said. "We offer our deepest condolences. He was a good man."

Max felt Berk tremble, as she wiped a tissue beneath her eyes. "Thank you."

Then she took a shaky breath, straightened her spine, and stepped from Max toward the elfin woman in purple.

The other women parted for her and a hush fell on the room as the tall, young bassist and the diminutive retiree stared at each other with tear-filled eyes.

"Dottie?" Berk asked, and the woman nodded, dropping her damp gaze.

Aw, crap, Max thought. That's the woman who called to tell us Ted had died in her bed. He took an intervening step toward Berk, but the no-nonsense woman sidestepped in front of him, shaking her head and holding up a hand to halt him.

Berk took another step toward Dottie, then another, as Dottie trembled, meek, but remained where she stood. Berk stared at her for a moment, her breath coming in short, ragged, gasps, then she bent to hug the old woman. "Thank you," she said her voice trembling as she kissed Dottie's cheek, "for helping my granddad get back to my gram."

Dottie hugged her back, and both cried, the other women encircling them in a mass group-hug while Max watched over them like their protector.

The hug disbursed, most of the harem drifting off to view the deceased or write in the book. Only the no-nonsense woman remained, and she stood beside Berk, her matter-of-fact gaze running over Max.

"Is this your young man?" she asked Berk.

Berk smiled at him. "Yeah. He kinda is." She chuckled and said, "Ellen, this is Max, my lifelong friend who helps me feel human. Max, I'd like you to meet Ellen, the only member of granddad's harem I'd had the pleasure of meeting before today."

Ellen chuckled and accepted Max's offered hand. They exchanged greetings and small-talk while a middle-aged plumber and his wife grasped Berk's arm and full attention during their fumbling attempt at condolences.

"Well, I'd best pay my respects," Ellen said, glancing at Max. "It was a pleasure to meet you."

"Likewise," he replied.

She smiled. "We all wish you both the best, and hope your relationship is as long and deep as her grandparents' was."

"Thank you."

Then she gave him a final nod and strode toward her friends.

Max watched her maneuver through the crowd with efficient simplicity and he sighed. Monday, and the pile of distractions before then, didn't leave them much time for length, depth, or anything else.

⌐○┐

After the visitation, they stopped for supper at the Chinese place on the square. Berk toyed with her Kung Pao, but didn't eat much.

She sighed and leaned back in the booth. "Are you coming to the hotel after work?"

"I don't know," Max said after chewing his broccoli beef.

He paused when she dropped her gaze and nodded. "Okay."

"Berk..." he said, reaching for her hand.

"It's all right," she said. She sighed and sat upright again to fork up a bite of chicken with her free hand. "This is just, I dunno. Confusing, maybe?" She glanced up at him. "I've never really dated anyone. I don't know how to maneuver through this awkward phase, or whatever this current thing is."

"Are we *dating?*" he asked.

"Maybe. I honestly don't know." She chewed the chicken then said, "You've dated. How's it all work? Realistically?"

"Well, most of the time the two people involved aren't permanently heading in opposite directions in a couple of days."

She sighed. "Yeah, there is that."

He took a deep breath and let it out in a huff.

"What?" she asked, searching his eyes.

He squeezed her hand. "Stay. I'll get a job; gas station, chicken plant, whatever, and, maybe, we can find a way to move forward together?"

"Do either of those things pay as well as the job in Texas?"

"No."

"I can't stay anyway. I play all over New England, Detroit, Nashville, New York... And I have contracts, gigs I've agreed to do for the next six, seven months. Here I could work out of Chicago, Milwaukee, Minneapolis, maybe St. Louis or the occasional local radio ad. Not much else. There are a *lot* of musicians up here but not enough studio opportunities to spread around the corn belt, even without adding me to the crunch. Trust me, I've looked. And I don't have any solid contacts, no drummer..."

"There's music in Texas, right? Dallas? Austin? Houston?"

"I do know a guitarist in El Paso. He might be able to hook me up with a booking agent, I guess. But his stuff's all Tejano. I dunno if it's..." She leaned back and rubbed her eyes. "Shit."

"What?"

"Where's this job you're starting next week?"

"Just outside of Houston," he said. "Why?"

"El Paso's clear across the state. Over by New Mexico. And Texas is *big*."

"Son of a bitch. Okay, how about your end? Any unskilled labor jobs or service near Charleston?"

"That pay worth a shit? Not unless you wanna work in a coal mine."

"Sure, if it means I get to see you."

"I'm not carrying around the guilt of you getting coal lung or getting crushed or any of that. I'm just *not*. I already have more than I can bear some days."

"So what are we gonna do?"

She attacked her barely-eaten supper. "I don't know."

"I don't either," Max sighed.

Berk

I leave Max at the bar then drive down to the hotel feeling really damn sorry for myself. I feed Bill then turn out the lights and crawl into a huge, poofy bed, self-medicating my misery with vending-machine chocolate and a sappy movie about a teenage girl with cancer.

I don't want to live in Fayerville, no fucking way, but twelve miles away, in Decorah? That might be okay. Or Waterloo. Mason City. Rochester. Somewhere I'm not constantly running into shitty people and the memories they bring with them.

As long as I get to see Max, even if just for a weekend booty call, I can endure the occasional shitty person screwing up my day. Right?

But he's moving to Texas and there's not anything online for studio musician jobs down there. Or up here, for that matter. We need to work. Someone needs to work. Can't live on love, after all. While I'm certainly not broke, my savings won't last forever.

"SHIT!"

Bill jumps from the bed and decides to lick his ass on the sofa instead.

So I eat another chocolate bar and dwell on whether I love him or not, whether I only love his dick or not, or if we're just getting kid-stuff-crushes out of our system like Deb says. Or not.

I don't know what time I fell asleep, but I open my eyes to see him coming into the room, backlit from the hall, and I'm thankful.

"Hey," he says before closing the door and leaving only the TV to illuminate the room. "Didn't mean to wake you."

I'm already climbing out of bed, naked except for my panties and the random chocolate smear. "I'm glad you're here."

Then he's kissing me and doing wonderful amazing things to me and pressing me onto the bed, candy wrappers and all. And I want him, I want him so damn much, so I peel off his clothes and my panties fly God knows where, and, aw shit, there's a tampon... Shit! I forgot!

"I'm on my period," I mutter, trying to press him to his back. "And I promised you a blowjob." Just doing him will be enough, I know it will. But he's bigger and stronger and resists my attempts as his fingertips tease me and make me wet.

"I don't care if you don't," he says against my lips. His kisses, God, his kisses leave me quivering as he tugs the tampon free.

Period sex? For real? I nod, how could I not? I want him so much

He leaves me for a moment to toss it away and returns with towels. Once they're beneath us his kisses and fingers return, making me slippery, making me want him, need him in me, and, this time, he lets me press him back, his dick standing at attention like a perfect soldier. I slurp him in until he cries out, then I climb on, his hands on my hips helping me find my way there.

We fall asleep after, sprawled together in the huge, downy bed, then wake to do it again before a shower and breakfast.

I wish we could stay here forever. But we can't.

We aren't late to the funeral parlor, but we certainly aren't early. Granddad's final hurrah is about how I expect, a decent amount of people in the entry and chapel but just Max and me in the family alcove. I don't want to mingle much with folks I don't know, so we wait, secluded, his hand on my knee drawing little circles around my kneecap, and mine doing the same on his thigh, only because it's probably not okay to grab your lover's junk while waiting for a funeral.

Doesn't mean I don't want to, though.

The music shifts from bland, funeral-home-hymnal-barf to the songs I supplied, starting with Clapton's *Tears in Heaven*. The chatter fades and more people filter into the chapel.

We both turn to a light rap on the door behind us. Troy peeks in. "There's, um, some people who want to see you, Berk," he says, glancing back where I can't see.

"Be right back," I tell Max, then Troy steps aside and Lia rushes in, her arms wide, Jeremy right behind her.

"Oh, Berk, honey," she says, wrapping me in her hug. "How are you holding up?"

Jeremy hugs me around my hips, then Dave's there too, baby in one arm, the other dragging Max into the tangle. I sigh, smiling. My whole family's here!

I have them sit with us at the ceremony and ride with us to the cemetery, and I do not give one flying flip about the confused stares from Granddad's friends and associates. Max and I sit alone up front under the rain awning while the minister gives the final few words of his service.

Then it's done. My granddad's buried. Everyone I love is here with me, except maybe Jen and Claude. For a moment, I think I see blue sky through a hole in the clouds.

Max takes the rest of the day off and we spend it hanging out with Dave, Lia, and the kids, or boinking while we still can.

We don't talk about Texas, or how we'll make things work, or if we have any future together at all. I don't want to look into that void, and I don't think Max does either.

Dave and Lia are staying at a hotel on the highway and it has a pool, so after sex we swim and play and generally make fools of ourselves, and it's wonderful, like a mini-vacation.

It's almost supper time and I'm half-floating in the water, my head resting on the pool's edge beside Dave, while Lia's changing Riley's swim diaper on a lounge chair and Max and Jeremy stalk each other with super-soakers. Even though it's the day of Granddad's funeral, I cannot remember ever being this happy.

"I like him," Dave says, reaching for his can of pop. "You gonna keep him?"

"He's not a puppy," I say.

"You sure?" he asks. "Have you fed him? I hear they keep coming back if you feed them."

I laugh and smack his thick shoulder. "We're just having fun. He's leaving for Texas after his bar gets demolished, and don't tell me you forgot we have a gig in Boston Wednesday."

"What? Why's his bar getting demolished?"

"Corrupt city planner bulldozing it for a housing development."

Dave sips his pop and sets it aside again. "And what the hell's in Texas?"

"Good-paying job with an oil company filling tanker trucks. His dad set it up for him."

"Aw, shit, did you tell Lia? You know she gets all upset over fossil fuel crap."

"Nope, haven't mentioned it."

"Haven't mentioned what?" Lia says, walking to the pool edge and handing Riley to Dave.

Max and Jeremy shoot each other across the pool from us. Max rolls to the concrete, wailing and feigning catastrophic injury while Jeremy closes, shooting his butt.

We all laugh, then Dave looks at his wife and says in a low whisper, "Max's bar's getting demolished Monday."

"The hell you say," Lia mutters as Max manages to get to his feet again, only to be pushed into the pool with a dramatic splash.

⌁

During dinner, Lia insists she wants to see the bar while she can, so Max drives us all back to Fayerville in my Mazda, he and Dave in the front, Lia and the kids in the back seat, and I sit in the cargo looking out to the dark and listening to them talk. My tummy's full of pasta and bread, making me drowsy, but it's nice back here. I can stretch out my legs and Lia's right there, close enough to touch.

Gretchen's surprised to see us invade, as are the guys in the window plus a handful of others I don't know watching the current NCAA game. We all squeeze into a booth after Max gives Dave and Lia the nickel tour, then he waves Gretchen over.

"Looks like a dump on the outside, sweet as hell on the inside," Lia says as Gretchen stops to take our drink orders. "Pretty awesome."

"Thanks," Max says, blushing. "Was gonna revamp the outside last fall, but decided what's the point, ya know?"

"I do," Lia says then orders a beer. Dave does too, then excuses himself to check out the jukebox.

Dave comes back and smooshes in. "You selling the juke or keeping it?"

"I don't know," Max says, as Gretchen drops off the drinks and a bowl of warm popcorn. "With everything that's been going on, I haven't really thought about much beyond what I need to get through day by day."

"*Really*," Lia says, leaning forward. "The big screen TV? The vintage light over the bar?"

Gretchen rolls her eyes. "The glasses, the booze, the damn popcorn popper..."

"No," Max says, glancing at Gretch before turning back to Lia. "I really don't have anywhere to keep them. I just figured they're gone with the rest of the building."

I sip my Sprite while Dave gives me a conspiratorial wink.

"Tell you what," Lia says, leaning forward. "What if you could sell the stuff? Like, say, a benefit auction or something? It'd maybe give you some cash to, I dunno, *put a down-payment on a new bar?*"

Gretchen nods. "Been trying to tell him to open another bar."

"That takes time, and advertising, and, really, after all the crap of these past—"

"Cut with the bullshit," Lia says. "Berk organized a benefit with only her phone and a day-and-a-half lead time *by herself.* You really think all of us can't come up with *something* profitable in four days?"

Gretchen grins, Max glances at me, but I innocently sip my Sprite and wave my bar buddies over from the window. They soon pull up chairs and we all start brainstorming while Lia paces the back hall with her phone.

Thursday passes in a flurry of amazingly messy sex, swimming, food, laughter, and probably too many trips back and forth between Tony's and Decorah.

Friday morning, though, I kiss and grope Max goodbye in the parking lot behind the hotel before he drives back to Tony's and I drive to La Crosse to pick up my mother.

She's on time for once, at least her flight is, and I wait for her by baggage claim while other people pick up their luggage. There's no mistaking her rucksack made from a ragged Cambodian tapestry that smells vaguely of what I assume is yak shit, so I snag it and wait. And wait some more. Then sit on a bench drinking a cup of coffee and playing my stupid time-waster-bubble-pop game while using her pack as a footrest.

"Mandy! Mommy's here!" my mother calls, a middle-aged red-haired woman trotting toward me in a shimmering sari with a pair of cameras dangling from her neck. The other travelers notice, confused. She's almost as tall as I am, her skin weathered by sun and wind, but she's grown too thin and I wonder if she ate much of anything in Darjeeling or Nepal.

"Sorry I'm late," she says as I heft her weighs-a-freaking-ton bag of doom. "I met the most *lovely* couple from Spain in the waiting area. They're just returning home after visiting their newest grandson. Delightful people, the Spanish," she says, lagging behind me and getting distracted by something on a gift cart.

Might be jewelry, might be a book, might be gold-plated yak shit for all

I know, but the sales clerk is mixed race—which always *fascinates* my mother, so she'll ask a gazillion questions in the hope she can convince National Geographic to send her to some remote village by goat cart and take quaint local-customs pictures—so I move to intercept her or we'll never get out of here.

"The lighting was workable, so they let me take their portraits, then we had a nice visit over coffee and Danish, and then—"

"How was your flight?" I interrupt, snagging her arm and turning her away from whatever caught her eye on the gift cart.

"Fine, fine. Too long, but that's to be expected," she says, patting my hand on her arm. "I sat beside a businessman flying here to discuss pork bellies at an agricultural conference something, something, I don't understand pigs, you know that. Why would anyone want to talk about a pig's belly, let alone listen? That sounds rather dull."

"It's bacon, Mom. Pork bellies become bacon, and bacon's good business."

I push open the exit door and we're outside, praise the rain gods.

"Really? So they actually have bacon conferences?"

"They have massive bacon *festivals*," I say, guiding her across the drop-off loop to the parking lot. "Thousands of people pay big money to eat different kinds of bacon."

"Wow. Bacon festivals. Leave the states for two years and things go crazy."

She rambles about Francis, a young man from Niger she met in O'Hare, while I'm stuffing her and her stinky-ass bag into my Mazda, and I get to hear about how he taught her native phrases so she could manage just fine if she ever landed in Niamey.

"Or I could just speak French," she says, buckling herself in. "I showed Francis your picture, and he says he'd like to meet you. We're following each other on Instagram so I can set something up, if you want."

"Not interested, thanks anyway."

She keeps talking while fiddling with every dashboard knob within reach. She always does this every time she's in the front seat of a car, maybe because she usually travels by ox and oxen don't usually have buttons to push and turn. It's useless to tell her to stop. I've tried, and it's not worth the effort or aggravation.

Mom systematically punches every screen button on my audio system, randomly cycling through channels—Jazz, Punk, financial markets, Classic Rock, talk radio... I have Sirius XM, so, annoying as it may be, it'll keep her busy while she yammers on about Great Catch Francis.

"He was very lovely to talk to, and the luminescence of light on his skin...

Incredible, but he refused my offer of portraits. He *did* say he's single, thirty-two, and in the States until the end of April. You should meet him."

"Really, Mom, thank you, but no."

"It's because Francis is foreign, isn't it? But I'm telling you, he's lovely. An engineer. Quite bright and interesting." She nudges me with her elbow before flipping from Hip-Hop to Political Commentary. "His fingers were incredibly long. Let that sink in for a moment, if you catch my drift."

I do. "The answer's still no. I'm seeing someone."

"You? Nonsense. You're twenty-eight and have never had a boyfriend. I'd be astounded if you're not still a virgin, and it's all because you can't speak French, the language of love. Didn't I tell you, speaking other languages comes in handy? At the bare minimum, you should know French, Spanish, Arabic, Swahili, Mandarin—"

"I'm seeing someone," I say again. Clearer.

Not that it matters.

"Vibrators don't count as people, Mandy." Mom rolls her eyes at me then resumes trying to fix me up with incredible Niger hunk-boi Francis the chemical engineer while clicking through a series of sports channels.

It's a fun hour-long drive back to Decorah.

Yep. Fun.

∾

We arrive at the hotel and she immediately zeroes in on a housekeeper dusting plants in the lobby while I go to the counter and get her checked in.

I explain she's my mother, I've made a reservation, and to put her room and any other charges onto my account. Just assign her as far away from me as possible.

They're happy to comply and hand me two keys. I almost return the extra, then change my mind. When she visited the summer I turned fourteen, she lost her hotel key and it became a mild pain in my gram's ass. Better to be safe than sorry.

"Okay, Mom," I say, interrupting her conversation. "We have to be at the accountant's in about 15 minutes. Let's drop off your bag and go, okay? Then we'll come back here to the hotel and I'll buy you a late lunch."

The housekeeper scoots off, mouthing *thank you!* at me while my mom's turned away from her. Before my mom can get distracted by the next shiny person or thing, I heft her stinky bag and herd her toward the elevator.

As always, she meanders, examining every detail and occasionally framing things between her hands as if setting up a shot. Her tendency to look at things with a field photographer's eye can get annoying, sure, but I do understand, at least as best I can. I do the same thing with most music. Sometimes, I'll stop whatever else I'm doing to listen and analyze and figure out how it all works together, the chords and progressions, the instrumental layers, or how it'd look written down and composed.

As I unlock her door, I wonder if Max is similar with cocktails or beers. If he sees how the sweet works with the sour, harsh against smooth, bright versus nuanced.

Considering it makes me smile and I startle when Mom touches my arm. "You okay, Mandy?" she says, her head tilting. "Been standing here with the door open and a weird look on your face."

"It's a smile, Mom. I get them sometimes."

I pick up her monster bag and lug it in. The room's just as nice as mine, but smaller and without a jet tub or a sofa.

"Fancy," Mom says, setting her cameras on the desk. "I hope it's not too expensive."

"Nope, it's fine. But we gotta go."

I manage to herd her out of the room and to my SUV without too many sidetracks. *Newbend and Associates, Investments & Estate Planning* is only two blocks away. On a nicer day—and one without my chatty, distractible mother—I'd walk, but the drive is quick and there's no one in the waiting room to chat with except the receptionist who's obviously quite busy.

We're ushered into a meeting room with a long walnut table. I've brought the entire envelope of papers Granddad left for me, along with stuff from his safety deposit box and a few other odds and ends, but Mom has nothing to occupy her. She's oddly calm and quietly thumbs through an *Iowa Life* magazine.

We don't wait long. Gray-haired Mr. Newbend enters with a slender middle-aged man he introduces as my grandparents' lawyer, Craig. Both offer their condolences before they sit across from us. They start with the will, and there's not much to it. Basically, I get all of the remaining property, investments, and financial assets. Everything. Including the house, if I want to keep it.

I'm not a millionaire by any means, but, *damn.*

Mr. Newbend indicates for me to sign below Granddad and Gram's signatures, but I hesitate. "What about my mom?" I ask, looking between her and Mr. Newbend. Both blink at me like I'm the crazy member of the conversation. "She's their daughter, I'm just—"

"We know, Amanda. I've personally handled your family's finances since Ted and Beth married, back in '61. Everything's been taken care of." He looks at the lawyer who slides another folder to my mother, then Mr. Newbend returns his gentle attention to me.

"Are all the details like I requested, Craig?" my mother asks, opening the folder.

"Yes. It took some doing, Gail, but it's all there."

She flips through, quickly, nodding as she goes. "I'm sure Bangladesh was problematic."

"A tad," Craig says with a slight smile. "But we managed."

"Ah, there it is," she says. "Looks fine. And the royalty transfer clause?"

"Page six, subparagraph G."

"Perfect!" She signs the papers then raises her gaze to the lawyer and smiles. "Thank you for doing this for me."

"How could I say no," he says, his tone gently teasing. "I did love you, back when."

They reach across the table to each other and squeeze hands, briefly, before returning to business. Mr. Newbend continues to watch me.

Mom leans over to inform me, "Craig and I dated during high school."

"Dating is a bit mild of a term," Craig replies with a chuckle. "I'll never forget the back seat of your Mustang after that Hall and Oates concert."

I say, "I don't need to know this!" but Mr. Newbend's kind, patient gaze never flickers.

"Still married?" my mom asks Craig as if I'm not even there.

"Divorced. Almost two years now."

Her voice becomes silky. "My daughter's put me up at the Winneshiek if you want to catch up later."

"No fraternizing with clients," Mr. Newbend says, his smile brightening before settling down again.

My mother stands. "Well, now that I've signed my paperwork, you assholes are fired."

Craig laughs and Mr. Newbend glances their way then back to me as if to say *Kids these days!*

"I'll show you to accounts receivable and you can close your account," Craig says, "Then we can discuss dinner once we're in the clear." He escorts my mom from the room, leaving me alone with the quiet, patient stare across the table.

"Is there something else?" I ask at last, my mind still reeling over my mom getting a date at the accountant's office.

"Other than insurance and fund transfer paperwork to finalize? Actually, yes," he says, drawing my mother's folder to him. "We need to discuss your mother's intellectual property."

Mom's chatting up the receptionist when I return to the waiting area. I stand beside her for a few moments before she notices me.

"Oh! Mandy! Are you finished?"

"Yep," I say, glowering, but she chirps a goodbye to the receptionist and floats out the door. She has to stop and look at this, or that, or talk to total strangers, but we finally get to my Mazda.

Once we're in, and she's fighting with the seatbelt like she always does, I say, "Why did you sign your royalties over to me?"

"Because after Mom passed, Dad and I decided to transfer them to you, and I told him I'd take care of it next time I was in town. So I did." Her seatbelt clicks and she turns to smile at me. "Why are you upset? Don't most people like getting unexpected income?"

"Because it's *your money*, and I don't need *your money*."

"I don't either," she says, shrugging. "So. Where were we going for lunch?"

"How can you not need money? You're always traveling and traveling's *expensive*."

She shifts in her seat to mostly face me. "Do you know what I do, Mandy?"

"Yeah, you take human interest and travel photos for magazines and stuff."

"No. I do not take *travel photos*. That's absurd. I am hired to take photographs of native and rural people living their lives in Africa and Asia. I'm very specialized. And I get paid very well."

She turns away, crossing her arms over her chest and looking out her window.

"Mom..."

"No," she says, waving me off. "Travel photography. Pfft."

We sit in strained silence for a few moments until I turn on my SUV and ask, "Why don't you want your money?"

"Because I don't need it," she says, giving me an exasperated glare. "I've been doing this job for thirty-one years. I'm a pro, and I have regular clients."

"I get that," I say, nodding, as I back out of our parking space. "I have regular clients too."

"So, what do *you* do, Mandy? Play a ukulele for tips in coffee shops?"

I hit the brakes. "What?! *No!* I sight read bass..." My voice fades out as it hits me, and I start to drive out of the lot. "Aw, shit. Same thing, different industry."

"Precisely! When I'm hired for an assignment, I'm paid, up front, for travel and regular expenses." She turns back to me again, and I see a glimmer of excitement in her eyes, the same I see when talking shop with my musician friends. "But the thing is, almost all of those travel and expense calculations are done in New York or London or wherever, by people who have—"

"No fucking clue!"

"Precisely! They just see the per diem rate for a two-week assignment. But I work with poor people, peasants, the untouchables, the folks who are mostly invisible, and I show their stories, their lives. I'm not blowing my expense account buying steak dinners in Jakarta or staying at the Ritz-Carlton in Cairo. No, I'm sleeping in a nomad's hut north of Dunburd, Mongolia or a hammock in the middle of a village in the Congo, living the same and eating the same as the people I'm photographing. I shit in holes and drink out of rivers and sometimes I eat bugs. None of those things cost a single red cent."

"I get it," I say. "And that's kinda cool."

"It is. But I have more than eighty thousand dollars sitting in an account in London, and a credit and debit card to go with it, but it just sits. Every once in a while, I'll be photographing a family or a village and there's something I can actually do to help. Most of the time, that's where the money goes. I've bought camp stoves and solar-powered lights and small water filtration units. And books. I buy a *lot* of books, especially basic readers and basic science. Because that stuff matters, and it helps people."

"Yeah," I say, feeling tears sting my eyes. Good ones for a change.

"But I have to be sneaky, because I'm technically not allowed to help. So I send it later, after I'm back at my flat in London, or hide it in my bag and leave it behind when I go to my next assignment."

She sighs, smiling. "Anyway, that's where my commissions go, and I have more than enough of that money already. The royalties, the money that comes in after someone's bought an image to use as a book cover, an ad, or a different publication than had originally hired me, that's separate."

By this time, I'm almost back to the hotel, and I look down, surprised, when she pats my leg.

"That money," she says, "has always gone to you."

"What?" I ask, waiting for traffic so I can turn. "I didn't know that."

"Your grandparents had access to it. When you needed dance shoes or whatever, they were supposed to use that account. I don't know if they really did. Everything was automated through my rights agent and I never saw any of it. Now that Dad's gone, I need to make sure it's still yours."

"Gram and Granddad never mentioned it to me, and I really don't need the money, Mom. I'm doing fine."

She delicately blows her nose. "Then find someone else to give it to. Someone who needs it. Some way it'll matter and make a difference in their life."

⊶◦⊷

We have a nice lunch at the hotel, then Mom begs off to get ready for her date. Lia and Dave aren't at their hotel, and I really don't want to talk on the phone, so I drive north, to Fayerville.

Mr. Newbend sent a file folder of papers and other info with me, including suggestions on re-investments for part of the estate stuff, a verbal reminder to let him know when I receive the check from the auction house, Mom's royalty account, and a bunch of other financial paperwork that feels more like a huge weight than a windfall. I have all this needless money while Max is scraping cash together to buy beer for his bar's last few days.

I get to Fayerville and am sitting at the stoplight roughly midway through town. Beside it, as it's been for all of my life, is a brown sign pointing downtown to the city library and city hall. I glare at it, seething. Goddamn City Hall.

It's where the Mayor—the man who's bulldozing Tony's and sending Max to Texas—works, spending his career being a shit because he's rich and powerful.

Screw that.

I turn right instead of driving on to Tony's, and head downtown, straight to City Hall. I settle myself and google a couple of things on my phone before I walk in. There's a receptionist desk behind a window, a door to the lobby area on each side, and not much else. There's definitely nowhere to sit.

Real friendly place, our City Hall.

A tidy, middle-aged woman sits on the other side of the window typing something on her computer. I probably went to school with her kids and have surely ticked her off, somehow, because that's how things seem to work around here.

She says, "May I help you?" without glancing away from the screen.

I force my hands to unclench. "I need to see the Mayor."

She continues to type. "Do you have an appointment?"

"No, but I have a land development opportunity he may be interested in."

She pauses and looks at me, squinting from behind her reading glasses, and I hold her gaze despite my thudding heart. I figure I have about a 50/50 chance of being tossed out on my ass, but I'm gonna try anyway.

She nods once then stands. "I'll see if he's available. May I have your name, please?"

"Amanda Williams," I say, pretending to be bored. "Tell him I'm looking to purchase a lot in the Murier Creek development. Immediately."

She nods and motions for me to follow her. "Right this way, Ms. Williams."

She leads me back to Mayor Duncomb who's sitting in a square room with sun-faded carpet and a scuffed oak desk, little different than any other bureaucrat's office. I hide my surprise. I'd expected something fancier, something snootier, but he is merely a city employee, after all.

Mayor Brad Duncomb looks up, smiling. He's a little grayer, a little softer in the middle, but the same greedy ass I know and loathe. I want to punch his face in, but manage to say, "Do you have a few moments to discuss a development lot sale?"

"Always," he says, motioning for me to sit. So I do.

Still want to punch his face in, though.

"Are you looking to develop residential or commercial properties?"

"Commercial," I say. "I'm interested in the immediate purchase of the property at 1726 Twelfth. Do you know the assessed value?"

He squints at his computer screen and types, then leans back to regard me. "I didn't catch your name."

That's because I didn't give it, asshole. I smile what I hope is my nicest, most-friendly smile even though it's as fake as the blue streaks in Jen's hair. "Amanda Williams."

He leans back to regard me. "And why do you want to buy Tony's Tap, Ms. Williams?"

"What's the assessed value?"

"One hundred and thirty-six thousand dollars."

I already knew that. I'd checked its assessed value on my phone before I walked through the door. "I'll pay double. Cash, check, or bank transfer, as soon as the paperwork's finalized."

"I can't sell you the bar, Ms. Williams."

"I was of the understanding that the Murier Creek development is open for lot sales. That's the lot I wish to purchase, but in its as-is state. Immediately, if possible."

"It's not for sale, Ms. Williams."

"Even at double value? That seems rather short-sighted on your part."

"It's getting bulldozed next week, then paved over. We've already hired crews."

"Then un-hire them."

He stands and gestures toward the door. "We're done, Ms. Williams."

I remain sitting. "Do you have another price in mind? I'm open to negotiation."

"Tony's is not for sale. Not to anyone, but especially not to you. I suggest you leave."

"Triple. Four hundred eight thousand. Immediate payment, purchased as is. No bulldozers."

I can cover that. Barely. Between the liquid part of Granddad's estate, my savings, and a few stocks I can quickly sell. I think. It'll leave me thin on funds, but it'll keep Max here where he belongs.

This time, the mayor sits. "You've lost your mind."

"No, but I'm about to lose my money. What do we need to do to get this finalized?"

"We don't," he says. "The lot is not for sale, even at that ridiculous price."

"That's the price of nearly eleven residential lots within the development itself. *Eleven*, Mr. Duncomb. For one small piece of real estate along the highway, and all you have to do is move the intersection a hundred feet in either direction."

"Ms. Williams, the price is immaterial and your attempts to bribe me are pathetic. That lot is not for sale. It is for bulldozing."

"Everything's for sale."

He laughs. "Your grandmother wasn't, though God knows I tried. She cost me almost a million dollars in lost income, along with that filthy, low-rent Jutland girl. Twice. And Tony Hartford? He cost closer to ten million and was a pox on my ass for far too long. And you, you Ms. Williams, maimed my son. None of this is about the money. It's about principle. I bought Murier Creek *specifically* to bulldoze that lot and pave over every goddamn dream Tony Hartford or the Jutlands ever had, and I'd happily throw you in the rebar and have my road crew entomb you in concrete along the way. Am I clear?"

I glare at the monster on the other side of that shitty desk.

He glares back. "I suggest you leave immediately, before I call the police for attempting to bribe a public official."

As I stand, he mutters, "Be thankful your grandfather decided to work with me instead of against me or you wouldn't have a pot to piss in. Now get the hell out of my office."

Intermezzo–Senior Year

Kelsey smiled at the ceiling of her 1986 Taurus, its windows steamed opaque. "Whew! That was fun!"

"Yeah, it was." Jack kissed her neck then lifted himself off her.

She reached for her jeans and undies. "It's gonna be so much better when we're off at school together. Surely a dorm bed's better than my back seat."

Jack rolled down the window and flung his condom outside, letting in a blast of chilly March rain. "About that..."

"What?" She got her jeans over her hips but struggled to get them buttoned since she couldn't stand up. "You still haven't heard from *any* of them? I have four acceptance letters. Surely one of them sent you an offer. Surely."

"I didn't want to tell you."

She sat, unbuttoned jeans and all. "Tell me what?"

"I'm not going away to any college because I don't have the money."

"What do you mean? Surely they offered scholarships, grants, student loans... Something."

He glared at his knees and shook his head.

"Jack. Hon," she said, rubbing the back of his neck while he sat bare-assed in her back seat. "What's going on?"

"My folks didn't do the FAFSA form. There's no financial aid, and I never even applied to Universities."

"*What?!*" Kelsey drew her hand away. "But we'd decided—"

"No, *you* decided. I told you that I had to take auto mechanics. And I am—"

"But you're supposed to be an engineer for NASA. It's your dream!"

"Yeah, when I was six. But reality is people like me don't go work for NASA unless they're mopping floors. If there's no money, then I can't go. That's reality."

Kelsey sat in stunned silence.

"I'm sorry," he muttered. "I didn't know how to tell you."

"Well, right after sex in my car is the perfect time. Also months after I declined the offer from Columbia, because you said they didn't accept you, is even better. Did you even *apply* to Columbia?"

He shook his head. "No. I knew there was no way I could move to New York."

"Then why didn't you *tell me?!*" she cried out. "*Why?!* I got into Columbia!! God!"

He stared at the back of the driver's seat. "I didn't apply anywhere, but I didn't want to disappoint you."

"Well, shit. Is that all?" She yanked on her shoes. "I let my number one pick college go because I wanted to go to your school, wherever it was. I lost four different grants to three different schools because I missed confirmation dates waiting for you to decide where we'd go, and now, *now*, months later, you're telling me you didn't even apply to any of them, *but* you don't want to disappoint me?!"

"You make it sound stupid."

"It *is* stupid, and it cost me opportunities I can't get back!"

She opened her door and got out, slamming it behind her, then walked around the car in the rain and yanked open the door on his side. "Right now, you need to get the hell out of my car."

"Kelsey, please, we can talk about thi—"

"Talk about what? You've had a year and a half of chances to talk about this, but instead you gave lies and excuses but did nothing while my dreams evaporated. *You should have told me*, been straight with me from the beginning, and we could have figured something out."

"I tried," he said, "but you were so excited about us leaving together I didn't—"

"Get out of my car."

"Kelsey..."

"GET OUT OF MY FUCKING CAR."

He nodded and climbed out, standing beside her in the rain.

Kelsey slammed the rear door then opened the drivers' door and got in. She hit the door-lock button and turned on the car while Jack pounded on the window.

"Kelsey! Don't be mad! Kelsey!"

She rolled the window down a crack. "Why don't you go ahead and walk home."

Then she drove out of the driveway behind the grain co-op office and through downtown, both sides of the street plastered with the same stupidly-matching *Ravens Going To STATE!* banners. She paused at the stop sign at the edge of downtown.

Left's home, but Mom's being a bitch because Dad lost another job and I've had enough of that for one day. Right's Berk's, but she's grounded for punching Lori. What the heck do I do?

The truck behind her honked and she jumped. Cory was at the wheel, sitting beside a boy she didn't know. He drove around her, rolled down his passenger window, and said, "Kelse! Meet my boyfriend, Jacob!" Jacob waved, Cory grinned, then they sped off.

She waved hello, but her cheer faded as he drove out of sight. I still don't know what to do, she thought, but I can't go home or to Berk's. "Guess we're going to town, maybe do some shopping," she mumbled aloud, then, at the light, turned toward Decorah.

Maybe a good drive and a little WalMart will clear my head, she thought. Need to pick up a phone card anyway.

She cranked up her stereo and belted along with Rihanna while heading south, but a mile or so past the edge of town her car started sputtering and coughing.

"What the heck," she mumbled. Jack had put in a new carb not two weeks ago.

Then she looked at the gas gauge. Empty.

"You've got to be kidding me!" she yelled at the dashboard. "First my stupid boyfriend keeps me out of Columbia, now my stupid brother forgets to put stupid gas in my stupid car because stupid me let him borrow it today!"

She wondered if she could limp back to town, then the engine quit and, fighting the power-steering, she barely managed to get it off the highway and onto the gravel shoulder.

She turned off the key to save her battery then sat there for a moment staring into the rain. She mentally cussed the idiot men in her life then locked the doors and flipped on her hazard lights.

She pulled her phone from her purse. "Mom's already mad at me," she mumbled, flicking on her second-hand, pay-as-you-go Nokia Berk had used in middle school. A phone with maybe three minutes left before her card ran out.

She called home, but it rang and rang until the answering machine picked up, using one of her minutes. "Mom, Dad," she said quickly, "I know you're probably mad at me for yelling and slamming the door earlier, but if you get this, I've run out of gas on the highway to Decorah, a mile or two south of town." She sighed, then added, "Yell at me when you get here." Then she hung up and reached in the backseat for the afghan Berk's gram had crocheted for her, just in case.

She wrapped herself in it and prepared to wait. They might be a while.

Berk

It's quiet at Tony's this afternoon, just the regulars and a couple of people watching basketball. My mom's prepping for a sleepover date with her accountant, and Lia and Dave have been quiet and unreachable so far today. I remind myself they wouldn't head back without saying goodbye, and remember how Lia had insisted on helping Max sell his stuff.

So who knows what they're up to or where they are. With two little kids and one hotel room, I'm willing to bet it doesn't involve a lot of nudity.

Despite the slow afternoon, Max is a bundle of nerves and Gretchen's working. Sort of. She tends bar while Max makes calls in the office and tries to buy beer, and her middle-school-aged twins are in the booth next to mine doing homework. Math and Social Sciences, such fine memories for me.

I think I got a D in both, but these two sound like they know their fractions and Dutch Renaissance painters.

At least I think Holl was Dutch.

Anyway, I hear Max, in the office, and he sounds frustrated, wanting to make a beer order, but with limited funds to do so. I want to buy everyone supper again. I want to buy this damn building. I want to buy the beer, all the beer he needs for the next couple of days, if not the next couple of years.

Blergh.

Gretchen checks on her kids then stops to ask me if I want a refill on my Sprite.

"Sure," I say, staring down the hall. She starts to go, but I call her back. "Hey, I have a question if you have a minute."

She slides into the booth across from me. "Always. What's up?"

"I kinda fell into some inheritance money, so..." I sigh and meet her patient gaze.

"How pissed would he be if I paid for his beer order?"

"Hard to say. You could just ask him."

Then one of the dudes watching the game calls her over and she zips away, leaving me to fret and stew on my own while these twelve, thirteen-year-old kids discuss Central European Architecture of the late 16th century and the beginning of the Baroque movement.

For real. Are they growing history nerds out here now?

And what the heck is a *Maderno?*

Damn kids.

I get my new Sprite and finally reach my limit of festering in my own shit, so I take my drink to Max's office and plunk my butt down in the chair by the popcorn popper.

He's still struggling to convince the uncooperative dipshit on the other end of the phone to let him buy beer partly on credit for two more days.

Two days.

Yet the dipshit with the golden key to the beer vault isn't budging.

Goddammit. I might not be able to buy the bar, but I damn well can buy every bottle of beer in this whole damn county.

I pull my debit card from my wallet and slap it on his desk. "Pay for it up front," I mutter, then slouch back in my grumpy corner.

"Hang on just a sec," he says and turns to me, his hand over the receiver. "What are you doing?"

"I'm buying beer," I say, then take a good, long sip of my Sprite. Through a straw. Because that's apparently how I roll now.

"Berk," he says, and I can't tell if it's in hope, fatigue, adoration, or exasperation.

"Just buy the beer," I say while glowering at nothing yet everything. "Hell, buy extra. Your credit's great with me."

"Berk," he says, softer this time. "I can't—"

"Yes, you can." I meet his gaze and try, but fail, to smile. "Something good has to come out of this shitty-ass week."

I sigh and take another sip of my Sprite. "Get what you need, all of it, no matter what it costs. We'll worry about it later."

He says nothing but gives me the *I can't do that!* look.

Fine.

I snag the phone from his hand.

"Hi!" I say, turning to keep the phone away from him. "Who am I talking to?"

"Uh, Jeff Glass, United Bev—"

"Hi Jeff, I'm Amanda Williams, Max's... Heck, let's call me his girlfriend. Sure, why not?" I have to stretch and shift around to keep Max from the phone. "And I'm going to pay off whatever balance he has, plus pay for his beer order. In full. Right now. You take VISA, right?"

"Berk! Give me that phone!"

"No." I stick out my tongue at Max then return my attention to my new buddy Jeff who's just confirmed they do indeed take VISA. "How much beer's he ordered for this weekend?"

Jeff rattles off some quantities and labels, all mainstream-domestic-boring-cheap shit, and I 'uh huh' in the appropriate places while Max scowls at me with his arms crossed over his chest.

"Got any Calypso Street in stock?" I ask, sticking out my tongue at Max again. Jeff confirms they do indeed, so I order four twelve-packs. Plus two each of five different Sam Adams' blends, some Dog and his Smuttynose buddies Baltic and Rhye, a decent hard cider, and at the end, well after Max has slumped onto his boss' chair with his head in his hands, I ask about their selection of good stuff from small breweries.

Jeff floats some ideas my way, so I ask for two twelve-packs of each then I pluck my credit card off of Max's desk and read Jeff the numbers.

Max looks up. "Aren't you even going to ask the total?"

"Nope," I say, waiting for Jeff to confirm the charge.

He thanks me profusely, and promises to include the receipt when it's delivered later today.

And we're done. I hang up and toss Max the phone.

He stares at it, sighs, then looks up at me. "I don't have that kind of money laying around, Berk. Probably never will."

I sit by the popcorn popper again and reach for his hand. "Today has been a mess for me, and I need to do *something* to help someone. It's less than a grand, and even if it isn't, I don't care about the money."

"Well I do," he says, standing. He shakes his head at me then walks out of the office.

"Well I don't!" I follow him down the hall. "I don't need money, but between Mom and Granddad I've suddenly found myself with a fucking investment portfolio and more cash than any one person has a right to have, *and* since there aren't any cutesy Caribbean Islands to buy right now, I decided to help the guy I love. Well, I couldn't save his bar, but I damn sure can send it to its last hurrah with some decent beer."

Everyone's staring at me and I turn to Gretchen first. "What's college running these days?"

She babbles, her eyes wide.

"Write down your mailing address and I'll send you a check. Start a college fund. Even with inflation, I'll cover the first two years. Your kids are too damn smart to not get to college."

Then I turn to Dwight, who's gawking. "As for you, I'll cover first, last, and six more month's rent at any decent residence in this town. Get yourself a roommate if you want, but for God's sake, lemme buy you a coat and some damn shoes."

"Are you okay, Berk?" Max asks, but I ignore him.

"You want a new truck?" I ask Make-Love-Not-War. "Bet I can even get you a Bernie sticker to put on it. One of my buds back home worked for him last election. Probably get you a t-shirt or two, too. I'll pay cash and you can drive it right off the lot. Just go pick one."

"How about you, Henry? What do you need?" I ask the quiet guy I've barely spoken to.

"Nothing, Ma'am," he says, holding my gaze. "I'm retired with a pension, we own our home free and clear, and we're doing just fine. Thank you, though."

"Berk?" Max tries again, grasping my hand, but I shrug him off as I stomp to the two strangers watching the game.

"How about you fellas? Need a little extra cash?" I say as I pull my wallet out of my pocket. "Don't know you, but here are a hundred bucks apiece. Do what you want to with it." I throw the cash on the table then I walk right out the door.

⤙⌂⤚

Still no pick-up from Lia, so I drive to my hotel and wallow where my aggravation won't be contagious. Max calls five or six times, but I don't see a reason to answer just so he can yell at me.

I know it's weird to be so aggravated over free money, but I've worked for everything I have, literally practiced my craft until my fingers bled, dragged myself and a bass guitar to gigs almost everywhere east of the Mississippi. I arrive early, leave late, and get better and more respected for my craft with every job.

It's money I *earned*. This stuff today… It belongs to Granddad and Mom, not me, and it just feels heavy, tainted by Granddad's death and Mom abandoning me as a kid, maybe, I dunno. And what good does it do? Can't bring Kelsey back or save Max's bar, but I still can help people with it, right?

I end up ordering room service and watching HBO until I get tired enough to sleep. It's after one and I feel like I've just drifted off when I hear a keycard in the door. Max comes in—I see his silhouette from the light in the hall. He's quiet, surely trying not to wake me, but he strips and slides into bed.

I snuggle up to him and bury my face against his skin.

"Sorry I got mad," he says. "Guess I'm not used to anyone trying to rescue me."

I smile and kiss his shoulder. "I didn't mean to get mad, either. They made me take Granddad's money and I just wanted to do something *good* with it, ya know? I want to *help.*"

"I know," he says, and we kiss and make up, but it's pretty clear we're both exhausted.

So I hold him and he holds me and, somehow, we go to sleep.

Kelsey's memorial service is in the library, which I guess kinda makes sense, considering how smart she was. I'm there, of course, with Max, and his folks are there. Jack the Super Nurse is not—Deb said he probably had to work—and two of the people reading nearby sort of pay attention.

Basically, though, it's just us.

Ten years in a vegetative state is a long time, and she wasn't exactly popular in school.

Kelsey's in a stoneware crock on one of the smaller tables along with a few framed pictures, including the one my gram took. I never did find the negative and I'm kind of relieved I didn't. In a silver-plated frame with a mat, it's already the largest picture on the table, other than her senior portrait, which is a 5x7 that sat on a shelf in their kitchen.

My senior pic was 11x14, printed on canvas and framed, and it hung in the living room. I got to choose from dozens of proofs. Kelsey, if I remember right, had three to pick from.

When you're a kid, you don't always recognize how poor some of your friends are. It's normal to eat bulk-bag fish sticks with them or watch VHS tapes that skip a little or that the only pet they ever have is a fish.

My granddad was a plumber, even owned his own company with several trucks and a crew. My gram stayed home, championed warm-and-fuzzy causes, and had creative explosions. We had a nice house, decent stuff, and always had a stocked fridge. Kelsey's folks worked low-paying jobs and managed to scrape by. They didn't have time for warm and fuzzy. As an adult, I see it, plain as day right there among the photos on the little table. As a kid, it was normal. Invisible. The way things were, like the yarn holding my gram's afghans together, just part of the fabric of Kelsey and Max's life.

I realize now why my Gram invited them over for supper so often. And, maybe, why they accepted and took home the leftover steak, chicken, or bratwurst.

Rich talks first, and he's angry about losing her because she was going to be somebody. Maybe a doctor, we all know that's what she wanted to do, and she'd worked her ass off to get the grades. He's almost done when my phone chirps with a text message. I mutter, "Sorry," and turn it off. Was my mom. I'll call her back.

Deb asks me to come up next, so I do, even though I don't know what to say.

I start with, "She was my best friend, and I loved her," which then segued into the trip we all took to the lake the summer before our Senior Year and catching minnows with her in the shallows and how she'd cup them swimming in her hands, smile at them, then set them free again. And that's what I remember first when I think of how kind she was.

I wipe at my eyes and am about to return to my place beside the magazine rack when I meet Max's gaze. He's looking at me the same as he did that evening at the lake. I wish I could go back there, to that day, and kiss him right in front of everyone then make sure Kelsey always had a full tank of gas every single day until she finished med school, so maybe, *maybe*, it all would have turned out differently for all of us.

But I can't, and it won't, so I walk to stand beside him. He takes my hand and I take his and, for just a moment, I wish I could stay in this shitty ass town.

⌁

After we've all said goodbye to Kelse, I follow Max and his folks to the door, then realize I have to pee.

"I'll be right back," I tell him. "Meet you at the car," then I head deeper into the library, to the ladies' room, turning on my phone as I walk.

Mom's text says she's going to spend the weekend in Minneapolis with Craig and he'll get her to the airport so I won't have to. Love you, Mandy, buh bye.

And that's that. I don't know whether to feel relieved or disappointed, but I text back, telling her to have fun.

I finish my business in the bathroom and walk out to see a man standing beside the table where we'd held the memorial service. His back's to me, but he's too tall and slender to be Jack, brown hair, skinny jeans, and, as he rubs his eyes, I realize it's Cory fucking Hildebrandt.

I am there, next to him as if I flew, and it takes every last ounce of control I have to not knock him on his ass right there beside the encyclopedias.

"What the hell do you think you're doing here?" I say and he turns, startled, his eyes wide and weepy.

But he doesn't cower like he's caught sneaking or fluff up like he's gonna fight me. He's bawling, his face blotchy and red, and, before I can move, he hugs me. Goddamn Cory fucking Hildebrandt *hugs me.*

"I still miss her, Berk," he wails against my shoulder. "She was my friend, sometimes my only one. Why'd anyone want to kill her?"

My hands are in fists and my breath's coming in short, desperate gasps. I can't kick his ass in the public library, but he's bawling like his heart's broken and I don't know what to do.

"What the fuck are you doing?" I snap in my best whisper. "Get your filthy hands off of me!"

"Sorry," he says, letting me go, and I jerk back a step or so. Right then, at that sharp moment, I wish I would've kept some of Granddad's tools. Big, heavy ones.

Not that I'd bring one into the library for a memorial service. That would be weird.

"I should've killed you," I scream in a whisper. "Beat you until you died."

He crumples to his knees in front of me. "I know you think that, and I understand. I do. But I *never* hurt her, I swear Berk. I got there right before you did. I swear on my life. She was like that when I got there."

People have turned their heads to watch us, but I don't care. "You lie," I snarl, my voice still low-ish. "I saw you, your hands on her, her blood on you. I *saw* it!"

"No. I'm telling you the truth. I was with Jacob. And we'd..." He stands again, nearly a full head taller than me. "We'd just finished making love when I got Kelse's text."

"What? She *avoided* you. How'd she get your number?"

"I don't know! But she got it somehow, said she was at the athletic shed, wanted to talk, and it was important. Come right away. So I did, because she'd kept my secret and I owed her."

"What secret?" I snap, wondering if I could bludgeon him to death in the library, maybe with an encyclopedia. Then I think of that kid's game, Clue, and realize my life has turned surreal.

"That I'm gay. Jesus, Berk, I confessed to Kelse in middle school and, as far as I can tell, she never told a soul. Did she tell *you*?"

I shake my head, my resolve to hate him cracking. Troy had mentioned Cory'd had gay porn in his room, he married some French-chicken loving asshole, and I know he never dated anyone in school, although a lot of girls tried. The only girl he ever seemed interested in was Kelsey.

The only girl who knew he was gay. The only girl who could be his beard. Could I have been so utterly wrong all these years?

His eyes search mine, pleading. "I'm gay, Berk, always have been. I've never had sex with a girl and absolutely *did not* hurt or rape Kelsey. She was my friend, too. I swear. And I came to help her because of a text, same as you."

"My dad made me. He hated I was gay, even destroyed my phone because it was filled with texts and pics from Jacob, so I had no way to prove Kelsey'd texted me. I've always wondered if Kelsey was killed because I'm gay, or because someone wanted to get back at me over some stupid teenage shit."

He wipes his eyes again and takes a shaky breath before walking past me. "So maybe it is my fault, even though I didn't do it."

$$\sim$$

"You okay?" Max asks when I finally get to the car.

"I dunno," I say, buckling in. "Cory was there, where we had the memorial."

"What?" he says, turning to gawk at me.

"Yeah." I tell him what Cory said, how he was crying, and how maybe I believed him. Maybe.

Max sits there, staring out the windshield for a long time.

"I dunno," he finally says, starting the car. "I know when he got married a lot of people were talking about whether a gay guy'd really rape and beat Kelse or not. So it's possible. I'll give him that. But if he didn't do it, who did?"

"I have no idea," I mutter. I can't fathom anyone hating Kelsey enough to beat her that badly.

We drive to the luncheonette downtown for brunch and Max's folks are already there, waiting for us with Kelsey's ash-filled crock on the table so she can join us, in spirit or something. We sit and start looking over the menus when Rich insists he's paying and Max and I are *not* allowed to argue about it.

Then Deb asks what took us so long to drive the two blocks to the luncheonette.

Max explains what happened with Cory and me in the library, and his parents stare at us like we're insane.

"Sweetie," Deb says, grasping his hand. "This insanity isn't *you*. We love Berkeley but she's always been prone to exaggeration and you're obviously a bit fuddled from your romantic affection." Then she gives him a chipper smile and returns to her menu while I merely blink.

Yo, Deb. I didn't bring someone's ashes to lunch.

Anyway, I keep my yap shut and read the menu. Had enough drama for one day, thanks anyway.

"It kinda makes sense," Max says, gripping my thigh beneath the table. "He did marry that guy right after—"

"You were suspended for defending your sister after he tried to kiss her," Rich says. "Punched him good, I heard."

Max slouches back in his chair. "Yeah, well, I never told you Kelsey got really mad at me. Said she was handling it and I shouldn't have punched him. Plus he was a big-shot jock, but never dated anyone. Ever. Half the girls in school wanted him, but the only girl he even acted like he wanted to date was Kelsey." He leans forward again. "Just *Kelsey*."

Deb looks at me as if to say, What madness are you feeding my son?

"Oh! Eggs Benedict sounds good!" I say, pointing at my menu.

Then the waitress is there to take our orders and we don't talk about Cory anymore.

Intermezzo—Senior Year

Lori, Brittany, and Julia drove north on W34, drinking Dr. Pepper and a sharing a bag of Cool Ranch Doritos, just like they shared their brand-new, matching, blue-heart tattoos.

"We are so gonna kick ass at State!" Lori hollered. She tossed the bag to her wing-girl Julia, and dared to touch her swollen lip—still hurt like a sunuvabitch—before returning her hand to the steering wheel. Dad's Hummer or not, the rain had shifted to sleet and she needed both hands to drive.

Brittany whooped in the back seat. "Think of the shopping we can do in Des Moines!"

Julia said, "Think of the city boys!"

"You have a boyfriend," Brittany teased, leaning forward to nudge Julia. "What's Troy gonna say about you chasing other boys?"

"Nuthin'," Julia said. "He does whatever I say."

"Just because you blow him," Lori said. "A boy'll do about anything if you blow him. Heck, I got Bucky to buy me my iPhone after a blowjob." She squinted into the sleet. "Hey, some loser's broke down up ahead."

Julia leaned forward to squint into the dark. "Where? I don't see nuthin'."

Brittany slid over to the driver's side backseat window. "On my side, heading south." They passed the car with blinking hazards and she scooched back to her regular spot. "Looked like Jutlands' car."

Despite the sleet, Lori glanced back at her. "You've gotta be fucking kidding me!"

"Nope. Dented Taurus, no hubcaps. It's their car."

"Wonder if it's Kelsey or Maxie," Julia said, licking her lips. "He's kinda cute. I'd do 'im, and maybe make Troy watch."

"Eew. He's a dork loser, like his sister," Lori said. She turned onto a gravel road and managed to wrestle the massive vehicle around to face the highway again.

"Sorry, Jules, but I think he'd turn you down. He's got a thing for Berk," Brittany said.

"Just because she's a dyke." Lori waited for a car to drive past, then she pulled onto the highway, heading south toward the broken-down car. "Guys always want what they can't have."

"Thought you said they wanted blowjobs," Brittany teased.

"That too. But if she wasn't a dyke, she'd be totally out of his league." Lori touched her lip again. "Bitch sure punches like a guy."

They pulled off the highway close behind Kelsey's Taurus, the Hummer's headlights shining into the car. "Too short for Dork, must be Brainiac," Lori said, putting the Hummer in park. "Let's go."

"We gonna help her out?" Brittany asked.

Lori opened her door and hopped out. "Nope. I need payback for my lip."

⁂

Kelsey looked up when headlights pulled up behind her. A truck, its high-beams on. She sighed, relieved. "The cavalry has arrived," she said aloud and opened her car door.

"Glad you're here," she said as she climbed out of the car, her Hello Kitty flats skittery on slick gravel. The truck's headlights blinded her, leaving her blinking in icy rain, and she heard little beyond the rumble of the truck's engine. "I ran out of gas—"

A shadow split the light. "Hey, Brainiac. Having car trouble?"

Crap. It's not Dad.

Kelsey took a step back. "Yeah, but I'm fine. Waiting for my folks." She turned to her open car door, but Lori grabbed her by the shoulder and yanked her back around.

"Pretty sure you were waiting for me," Lori said, then punched Kelsey in the mouth, just like Berk had done to her the day before.

"Ow! What'd you do that fo—" Kelsey gasped, falling backward, her feet pedaling to stay beneath her but unable to find good purchase.

The back of her head hit the thin edge of her car door with a hard *thwack*, and she slid down to land on her butt, legs splayed in front of her. Her vision evaporated and the back of her neck felt hot, maybe wet.

"I... I can't..." One hand lifted toward her face, then fell limp to her lap, but the other merely twitched in the gravel no matter how hard she tried to move it. "See," she said, both hands twitching. "Can't see."

"What'd you do?!" she heard Brittany Miller scream in the hazy, sleety white while Julia Gifford bayed her creaking laugh.

"She cost my dad his job so I hit the fucking bitch," Lori said. "Just like her dyke bitch hit me."

Max

After brunch, Max and Berk helped his parents load the U-Haul trailer just outside the back door, starting with the hide-a-bed and other furniture. Berk remained in the trailer, stuffing and stacking boxes and bags wherever they fit.

Max carried a box of dishes down the stairs and paused, watching Berk. She stood with one foot on the easy chair, other foot outstretched as a counterbalance, ass toward him, and stretched to shove a bag of clothes into to an open hole behind the waist-level stack of packed-in boxes.

God, I love yoga, he thought, lost in the symmetry of her ass.

"Damn," his dad muttered from the step behind.

The bag didn't quite fit, so she stretched forward, shoving it in, counterbalance foot pressing against the arm of the chair and tightening her ass even more.

His dad let out his breath.

"She does yoga," Max whispered back.

"No shit?"

"No shit. She's bendy." He took a step down then turned his head to wink at his dad. "*Really* bendy."

He took another step down and heard his dad follow.

"Damn. Wonder if I could get your mom to do yoga."

Lia poked her head around the corner and grinned at them. "Hey, boys! Enjoying the view?"

"Every chance I get," Max said, reaching the bottom.

His dad blustered but said nothing as he dropped off his box and trudged up the stairs again.

Berk had apparently managed to get the bag to compact enough because she turned, grinning, to Lia and Max. "Where the hell have you been?" She jumped down from the trailer and accepted a hug.

"Rochester."

Berk leaned back, brows furrowed. "What's in Rochester?"

"Staples," Lia said. "Po-dunk Iowa doesn't have crap for quick printers and office supplies. Got the stuff, if you wanna come see."

"Yes!" then Berk hurried into the bar, Lia following.

Max sighed and shoved his box into the trailer. He turned around to see his dad watching him. "Where'd Berk go?"

"Into the bar to look at posters and stuff. We're selling the decor tomorrow." He jumped down and grabbed his dad's box to pack it into the trailer. "Maybe make a little money before I say goodbye to everything."

"Max, wait."

Max turned back, box in hand. "Yeah?"

His dad looked him in the eye. "I've made a lot of mistakes. I know that. But you're not me, and I forget that sometimes. So do whatever you gotta do with Berk, or with your bar. The job will be waiting whenever you decide to come get it. Just... Just don't let your life be a failure like mine."

Then he patted Max on the shoulder and walked back to the stairs.

♪〜♪

Despite the drizzle, Max and Dave hung a vinyl GOING OUT OF BUSINESS AUCTION ◆ SUNDAY 2 P.M. ◆ LIVE BAND ◆ EVERYTHING MUST GO! banner across the front of Tony's upper floor while the girls prepared to drive around town asking other businesses if they could hang posters.

"What do I owe you for all this?" Max asked, settling his end of the banner onto a hook. The same hook that had held the south end of his *Grand Opening* banner three years before.

Dave grunted, stretching to reach his hook. "You'll have to ask Lia."

"Don't you be doing this shit too," Max said. "Everyone's hiding prices from me lately, prices for stuff I ought to be paying for, or they just outright buy it whether I agree or not. Like the posters. I offered to pay, and your wife agreed, but now you're backing out? I might be tight, but I'm not fucking destitute."

"Dude, I get it. I honestly do," Dave said, snapping the banner over the hook. "But I don't know the bill, man. I really don't. I stayed in the car with the kids while she dealt with the retail. She didn't mention the cost and I didn't see the receipts."

"Great," Max mumbled. And Berk was in there probably paying for it all, anyway.

Half an hour later, everyone except two people who didn't want to leave the NCAA game and Mitch who'd volunteered to hold the fort, stood out in the parking lot to admire the four signs. The big banner sprawled across the top floor, one on each far side hung about chest level high, and another vertical sign covered the front door, all promoting the Live-Band Benefit Auction to sell his furniture, barware, lighting, electronics, and fixtures.

"Everything must go," Max muttered, stewing in a mix of excitement and loss. Beside him, Berk squeezed his hand.

"At least you'll make a little back," his dad said, patting him on the shoulder. "Hey, we're gonna head out. Maybe make it to Missouri before it gets too late."

Max hugged his folks and sighed, watching them go, before turning his attention back to the signs. "They look great," he said to Lia. "Thank you."

She beamed. "I'm delighted to help. Still have to drop off payment to the last radio station and get signs up all over town. Wanna come along, Berk?"

"Sure!" she said, while Max struggled to comprehend the scope of Lia's marketing slam.

"Radio? You bought *radio* spots?"

"With four days notice on the sale? Damn right I did. Three broadcasters plus the community college, so nine stations total," she said. "And there'll be a big ad in nearby papers tomorrow. I'd have done more but there aren't a lot of avenues to mine up here. Plus I lost a day driving to Rochester to get materials designed and printed. Hit another radio station on the way back, though, so it all worked out."

Max felt the bottom of his gut fall out. Radio. Newspaper. God knows what else. Oh, shit. Oh, shit.

"Didja get a band?" Berk asked, still giddy.

"Yep!"

Dave gave him a *Sorry, dude* shrug but said nothing while the women squealed their excitement and decided to head out right away to hang posters around town.

Berk gave him a quick kiss then scampered to Dave and Lia's SUV while Lia spoke quietly with Dave. Max sighed and watched Berk go, then Gretchen stood in front of him and said, "Hey, mind if I tag along with them? I know more about this town than—"

"Go," he said, shooing her toward Berk. "Have fun."

She grinned and hurried to Berk, hollering," I can go! I can go!"

Berk resumed squealing with delight and it wouldn't have surprised him if all three danced around the parking lot like teenagers before they left.

Berk

We put up posters almost everywhere in town. Other bars. Gas stations. The grocery store, retail shops, restaurants, the auto repair place on third, even the post office. Any bulletin board we can find gets a poster, and any open business without one, we asked first. Big posters, medium, and little, we have one for any size space, and only three places say no.

Jen calls when she and Claude pass through Decorah, and I give her directions to Tony's while push-pinning a letter-sized poster to the Casey's bulletin board next to one advertising my granddad's auction. Gretchen's taping a pair of tabloid-sized posters, front and back, on the door and Lia talks-up the clerk and buys us all fresh coffee, like we're part of a well-rehearsed gig. Then we're off to the next place, then the next, and, by then, we're pretty much out of posters.

The posters have a rockin' feel like *live-band this weekend!* announcements, not the boring, text-heavy look of a regular auction poster. I hope folks'll see them and come. Max needs some good news.

A guitarist I barely know named Stan is at Tony's when we return. He and Dave stand in the middle of the place working out where to set stuff up in the morning while Max tends bar.

It's a busy Saturday night with the regulars and eleven people watching tonight's game. Nearly all of them are drinking bottle beer. I smile. With luck, tomorrow will rock.

We get to bed really late and we both want to sleep in, but there's simply too much to do.

Gretchen beats us to the bar, and the three of us have barely started moving tables when Lia and Dave arrive with Jen and Claude. Need to make room for the band to set up, for people to maybe dance a little, and for folks to look around at what's for sale while drinking, because it never hurts to move some booze while coaxing people to spend money. It gets kinda snug. Have to stack a couple of tables, move the juke to the hall and pinball machine to Max's office, but we make it work.

Early lookers start showing up before ten and I use them as an excuse to sneak out for a bit to check Granddad's auction and pick up any extra papers or cash Judy's found.

There's a lot of stuff up for bids, most of it spread out in tents to protect it—and the auction goers—from sputtering rain. Farmers are checking out Granddad's Mustang, three middle-aged men look over the boat, and a young couple with a baby keep eying the pickup.

I wander around the house, which looks weird with none of our stuff in it, then scope out the tents. My grandparents' things are laid out and sorted into similar groups like tools, collectibles, housewares, crafty stuff, books, et cetera. There's three tents worth. For a few moments I feel guilty about not taking more, but I don't need it. Someone else can get good use out of anything here, even the moose-head cheese knife I've just looked at and set aside.

A small, diapered child with sticky hands and no coat grabs my leg for balance before scooting off again. He's dragging and chewing one of my gram's half-finished stuffed rabbits so I look around for the kid's mother. Everyone else in this tent is either elderly, middle-aged/middle-class, or—wouldn't you know it?—Lori and her slimy hubby, their backs to me while they dig through my gram's kitchen stuff.

"Lori? Walt?" a man my mom's age says as the kid scampers past Lori and drags the bunny in the mud. "You wanna watch your kid? He's getting into stuff and gumming up the merchandise."

"Oh please," Lori snaps without looking at her kid or the guy, and Bucky doesn't seem to even notice the initial comment. "Who's gonna wanna buy a ratty rabbit doll?"

"Me," I say, and everyone in the tent turns to look my way. "My gram made it. So maybe I'll buy it."

Lori turns. "Well fuck you," she starts, "for bein—" She blanches and blinks. "Berk?"

"Yep. She taught me how to sew, so maybe I'll finish it and give it to a kid who actually wants it," I say, staring at her. "Hell, maybe I'll buy her sewing machine too. Would that be better for you? Would that make you watch your damned kids? If I bought my dead gram's sewing machine and sewed up that rabbit? Would it? After all, we all know the world revolves around you."

She looks side to side for help, but Bucky's already snagged the kid and scooted out of the tent, rabbit and all.

She licks that damn skinny scar I gave her a decade ago and doing so seems to give her strength. "Why can't you leave me the hell alone?" she snaps, her voice rising. "All you've done is destroy my life, and here you are, pissing on yet another day of it, when we finally get our tax refund and wanna buy a few decent things for our apartment and kids."

The other folks watch or politely leave the tent. Doesn't matter, really, because I'm sure nearly everyone in the yard can hear us.

"What are you talking about? I haven't done anything to your life!"

"I was pretty until you hit me!" she says, knuckle dragging across the corner of her eye.

"I punched you once, in high school," I say, "because you were bullying Kelsey. And, what, a week later, you and your shit-bag friends jump me and put me in the hospital? I think you've more than paid me back for your stupid split lip." I return to looking through the assortment of life-stuff on the table and pick up a glass cracker dish that shimmers like a carnival.

"Don't you turn away from me," Lori snarls from right beside me and I almost drop the dish. "You know damn well you deserved every bit of that ass kicking for fucking up my face. Don't start your shit up again. This time I'll do more than kick, just like I did to your brainiac friend. *Namaste* my ass, bitch."

"That's enough!" some other woman says from across the tent. "How many lives do you have to ruin?"

I keep Lori in front of me while glancing to my right. It's Brittany Miller and, for a moment, a piece of me wants to roll up and cover my aching eyes, but Britt's glaring at Lori, not me.

"I've lived most of my life terrified of my own shadow," Brittany says, taking a step toward us, "scared some cop's gonna kick my door in because you forced me to help you. Nothing I ever do can atone."

Lori gives me a sideways glance and backs away. "Shut up, Brittany."

"No. She died, Lori. *Died.* Because you wouldn't let me help her after *you* hurt her. I became a goddamn ER nurse. I *save* people and it's bad enough you've forced me to carry around a decade of guilt, but I will *not* be an accessory to murder."

"You ain't got shit on me!" Lori screeches, taking a step back.

Then Brittany reaches into her purse, a big sprawling thing, and pulls out a metal relay baton in a zipped plastic bag. It's Fayerville Ravens blue and covered with brown smears and fingerprints.

Lori backs away, out of the tent, calling Brittany a bitch the whole while.

I watch her go, along with everyone else still in the tent and we all look back and forth at each other and the smeared blue baton in Brittany's hand. Over in the corner of the tent, a skinny young guy's on his phone talking with the cops.

Intermezzo-Senior Year

"The back of her head's dented in and there's blood everywhere! We have to take her to the hospital!" Brittany screamed from the back seat but Lori kept driving, her goal just ahead.

"No. We're gonna dump her."

Brittany held her bloody hand beside Lori's face. "Look at this! She's alive and *bleeding* and we can't dump her! We have to take her to the hospital!" Then she pulled her hand back and muttered, "Screw you. I'm calling 911."

"No, you're fucking not." Lori slammed on the brakes and unhooked her seatbelt. She lurched around and yanked the phone out of Brittany's bloody hand, then threw it out her own window. "We're all stuck with this. Together. You hear me. If we don't do this, we'll *all* go to jail."

She put the Hummer into gear again and continued down the highway to the side-road leading to the high school. "I know a place we can stash her. The lock's busted."

"At the school?" Julia asked. "Are you crazy?"

"Nope. I know just what to do."

While the other two girls fretted, she drove past the football field to the athletic shed and stopped, leaving the Hummer running. "Let's go," she said, jumping out of the driver's seat and yanking open the backseat door to see Kelsey and Brittany covered in blood. "You too, Jules!" she barked and Julie opened her door just like any good pet.

At first Brittany refused, begged Julie to call an ambulance, but her resistance didn't last long and the three of them managed to carry Kelsey to the athletic shed. Lori jiggled the latch to open the door.

"Bucky showed me how to pop the lock a few weeks ago," Lori said, taking one of Kelsey's arms. Julie had the other and Brittany held both feet, the heavy load, because she was being a little bitch. "Lots of kids come here to fuck."

"I have," Julia giggled, then they dropped Kelsey onto a sprawl of baseball bases and used condoms.

"Let's go," Lori said.

"We can't just leave her here to bleed to death!" Brittany said, grabbing Lori's jacket with her bloody hands. "Everyone's going to Des Moines on Monday, so it'll be Tuesday, at the earliest before anyone finds her, and she'll be *dead*. This is bad, but if she dies, we'll have *committed murder!*"

"Yeah." Lori paced in front of the door. "They'll lock us up. Crap. Okay. Okay. Does she have a phone?"

"Oh thank God, you've finally seen some sense," Brittany said, kneeling and rifling through Kelsey's pockets. She pulled out an ancient, scuffed-to-shit Nokia. "Yeah, she has a phone. I'll call—"

"The hell you will." Lori snatched the phone from her. Julia just nodded.

"What are you doing?!" Brittany screeched.

Lori shoved the phone into her bra where Brittany couldn't grab it right back, and she put on her winter gloves before pulling a baseball bat from the bin. "We're making sure someone else gets blamed." Then she lifted the bat and, ignoring Brittany's screams, slammed it down, hard, onto Kelsey's head. Julia, too, reached for a bat.

They hit her a few times, leaving bruises and maybe breaking a couple of bones. Brittany tried once to run, but Lori grabbed her and flung her onto Kelsey. "Who's covered in her blood?" she snarled, standing over Brittany with her ball bat. "Not me, not Jules."

"You wouldn't!"

"Oh, yes I would," Lori assured her. "You wanna join her or go to prison?"

"No, no, I want to live."

"Good, then pull her pants down. All the way off. Or I'll bash your fucking head in too."

She stepped back and watched while Brittany complied, her hands shaking.

Lori pulled out Kelsey's crappy phone. Just needed a little luck. "Do you have Cory's new number?" she asked Julia.

"Nah, but Troy does."

"Get it."

Brittany looked up. "Cory? Why are you calling Cory? He's the center for—"

"Because he spent the last three, four years chasing this little bitch. Everyone will believe he's snapped."

"Got it!" Jules said and showed Lori her text screen.

Lori keyed in the number and texted a quick message to Cory. *it's kelse need 2 talk 2 u asap vital meetup @ athletic shed NOW.*

Then, as soon as Brittany got Kelsey's pants off, she hit send. "Stick something in her snatch."

"What?" Brittany asked, apparently still not quite with the program.

"Find some goddamn thing and make it look like a rape or I'll bust your fucking head in."

Julia, always the eager assistant, handed Lori a relay baton, and she handed it to Brittany. Brittany dropped it twice, then managed to hold it.

"Put one of those nasty condoms on it, so the docs won't see it wasn't a dick. Do it!"

Brittany cried, but did as she was told.

"Now run home. Go. Before I change my mind."

Brittany bolted into the rain, taking the condom-wearing baton with her.

"What now, Boss?" Julia asked.

"Hang on." Lori sent a new text, this one to Berk.

I'm @ the athletic shed. Cory's raped me, beat me, oh shit, he's coming ba

She hit SEND again then wiped the phone with her shirt, still clean from beneath her coat. Once wiped, she pressed Kelsey's bloody fingertips on the keys and tossed it aside to land who-knew-where in the mess of athletic equipment, blood, and used rubbers.

Jules and I are mostly clean, she thought as they hurried to the Hummer. *Brittany'll have to keep her mouth shut or go to jail too, so it all comes down to Cory and Berk.*

Berk

I sit on the steps with the handful of other witnesses, then we're separated and taken to Granddad's office to talk. The deputies take my statement about Lori commenting on her ancient split lip and all she and Brittany'd said before Brittany pulled the baton from her purse.

They take good notes, I'll give them that. And with that, I'm free to go. Brittany, though, was put in the back of a police cruiser and taken away. I hope she's telling the truth, and that someone will pay for what happened to Kelsey.

Judy's standing in a nearby doorway watching me talk to the deputy, her mouth smooshed into her usual sphincter pucker. I want to flip her the bird, but I just don't care right now. Let her be pissy. I have other things to deal with.

"Amanda!" she barks at me as I'm heading for the door, so I turn, sighing, to receive whatever sphincter-monkey-shit she wants to fling upon me.

"You have a few more papers and a spot of cash," she says, thrusting an envelope at me. "Were you planning on staying for the auction, or have you already caused enough drama?"

"Nope, I'm done," I say. "Mail me the check when it's all finished."

I flip her my unicorn hand on the way out the door.

By the time I get to the bar, the benefit is ramping up with live music, plenty of beer, and a lot of people looking to buy. It's gonna be a helluva party!

Gretchen's mom and sister have volunteered to watch the kids upstairs, so it's mostly a grownups-only affair. Lia's at a fold-up table by the front door to take donation and sale money, Max and Gretchen tend the bar, and I don't have a lot to actually do, so I mostly sit with Lia and listen to the band, or with Lia and Jen and just *be*. I only get a few minutes to really talk with Max, to let him know about Brittany and the auction at Granddad's, but he's soon called away to handle yet another question.

As I sit with Lia, I realize it's weird not playing. Dave's up there hitting the bassline with Joe, who he didn't want to work with the entire time I've been down here. They mesh well. Maybe he'll be okay if I break up our partnership and move to Houston, I think, watching Max mix a Tequila Sunrise in a plastic glass like the pro he is.

All the real glassware's in boxes, ready to go to the highest bidder.

"What's wrong?" Lia asks. "I'd think you'd be happy to help him make some money."

"I am," I say, sipping my Sprite. "I just don't know if I wanna move to Texas."

"Texas? Why would you move to Texas?" she asks, grimacing. "Your life is East coasty and upper Midwesty."

"Cause he's moving to Houston for an oil job," I say, nodding my head toward Max. "They have music down there, right?"

"Yeah. I hear the Austin music scene's pretty rockin'. Don't know much about Houston, though." She pauses to watch me, then Max, for a few moments. "You really love this guy, don't you?"

"I dunno." I shrug. "Maybe."

"I'll take that as a yes," she says, laughing.

"You gonna try to talk me out of this?"

"Nope. All that's between you and him."

We start selling stuff at three and, by then, half the people there are pretty pickled and ready to buy. The vocalist, a pretty, plump gal named Lynnette, handles the first round of items, unoccupied tables and chairs, mostly, along with some barware, and brings in almost five hundred bucks before starting another music set.

A lot of people have been checking out the pinball machine, juke, and vintage lights and signs, so they'll probably go late.

Max comes to us with a couple of pops and sits beside me for a minute. "This is really great, Lia. I forgot to thank you before."

"Pfft. You're family now, buddy. Stuff like this comes with the achievement badge."

We all laugh, but I know it's true. He did get an achievement badge, and so did I. I hold his thigh and kiss him and decide that, somehow, we'll figure this out, even if I have to take stock in Southwest Airlines to make it work.

We dance together every now and then, when the beat's right and he's not swamped at the bar, and it's nice.

"Maybe this is like the prom we didn't have," he says before kissing me. We're swaying, my arms around his neck and his hands on my butt. "But I doubt I'd be determined to make love to you tonight."

I nuzzle his neck and it smells like him, like home. "I did finish my period."

He pulls back enough to grin at me, then we're smashed together again and swaying and I'd rip his clothes off right here and drag him behind the bar if we didn't have an audience.

But it's all winding down, only the last cool items left, and the band takes a break after our slow dance song. Furniture's gone. Glassware's gone. Taps, fridge, and beer signs are gone. Popcorn popper's gone—Dave bought it—and even the Christmas lights around the front window are gone. Only the bar itself, the *gorgeous* vintage stained-glass light above it, the pinball machine, and the juke are left.

Well, and the booze. What hasn't already been demolished, that is.

It's not quite five and much of the crowd has left too, leaving nine people besides us. Lynnette the vocalist stands beside the pinball machine and starts taking bids while the band packs up. It's been friendly bidding so far today, but three people want it. The price rises quickly, finally settling out at just over forty-two hundred dollars.

Then it's the juke, a gorgeous full-sized bubbler filled with a crap-ton of my favorite music. Dave and Joe wheel it out of the hallway. A couple of guys want it, but I do too, so I hold back, waiting, until it's down to one bidder and the price is a little over three grand. Lynnette makes her last call for bids and I say, "Thirty-five hundred."

Max looks at me like I've lost my mind, but I don't care.

My opponent and I go back and forth, fifty, twenty, a hundred bucks at a time, until it finally settles in at forty-three-fifty. Then it's mine.

And it'll fit in my Mazda. I measured it yesterday.

I'm all excited and skip over to Lia to pay while Max just shakes his head. The crowd moves on to the bar light, which quickly sells for eleven hundred, then the bar set itself, along with all the liquor on it, from cheap wells to the *really* good stuff on the top shelf in back.

They're still dickering over the bar when Max and Dave help me carry my supremely awesome jukebox to my car. Go me!

Ten, fifteen minutes later, when it's done, when everyone's paid and the band and regulars who aren't too drunk have left to wait for us at the barbeque joint in Downtown Decorah, it's just me and Max.

He stands in the middle of Tony's, not much left beyond the bare shell and a couple cardboard carriers of bottled beer, and he sighs. "I loved this place," he says as I wrap my arms around him. "And I love you."

"Think I love you too," I say, and he turns, kissing me, and for one bright moment, all is happy in my world.

Back at the hotel after supper, we make love, both of us this time, and I don't want to leave him and I don't want him to go. He made about thirty grand selling the stuff in the bar, but after paying the band, with travel and all, plus Lia's printing costs, it knocked him down to about twenty-five thousand dollars, which isn't enough for a down payment on any turn-key bar listed for sale in Iowa or West Virginia. Plus there's his job in Texas and I have to be in Boston on Wednesday and, shit.

SHIT.

So we make love again and sleep till morning, then one last time because I need to get on the road. But I don't want to go. And he doesn't either.

His car's still in Fayerville, but his clothes and Bill's travel pen are in my Mazda when we sit in the hardware store parking lot across the street from Tony's at seven-thirty in the morning, watching the demolition crew get set up. We each sip one of the last bottles of beer. I'm drinking Calypso Street Lager and Max a Sam Adams Pilsner.

I don't think we know how to say goodbye.

A pair of Sheriff cars drive past, lights on but no sirens, and they pull into the Kwik Shop next door. Three deputies and the Sheriff himself get out and walk in. They come right back out with Lori while her coworker and customers stand in a clump and stare. She's not in cuffs, but they aren't taking her shit either.

Then they're gone, heading downtown. I hope they find the truth, whatever it is.

The demo crew fires up the big machinery and neither of us speaks as the bulldozer knocks in Tony's front wall. I do, however, finish my beer.

"You know," I say as I stuff the bottle back into the cardboard carrier and stick a finger into the cage to scratch Bill's cheek, "with all this inheritance money, I can help make the down payment on a decent bar in West Virginia, or anywhere you want. You can call it a no-interest loan and we can even get paperwork drawn up if it'll make you feel better. Just a loan. Until the eminent domain money comes."

Max smiles a little and glances at me. He stares at Tony's for a couple of moments more, then puts on his seatbelt.

Guess that settles it.

His hand on my thigh, I start up my Mazda and we head home.

The End

Also by Tambo Jones

SPORE
MORGAN'S RUN

Dubric Byerly Mysteries
GHOSTS IN THE SNOW
THREADS OF MALICE
VALLEY OF THE SOUL
FIRE: A LARS HARGROVE STORY

Short Stories
ENDORPHINS
SID